West of Alva

Dave Eagleston Sr.

DAVE EAGLESTON

ACKNOWLEDGMENTS

This book is dedicated to the farmers of the United States who spend their lives working the land day after day, year after year. These *ordinary* people make it possible for us to have food on our table, but have little influence on government import and export policies. These same men, women, and children could care less about the latest fashion trends, but love our country, respect the environment, and fear God. They *are* the heart of our military and the soul of country music. And from time to time they've even been known to indulge city people like me.

1 THE ATTIC

T he fresh spring wheat blew like a sea of golden waves outside my bus window. A light brown hawk drifted motionless high above the wide yellow field and then landed on a nearby fence post as I rode past. It was the beginning of the spring of 1961. I was on my way to work on a farm located "just west of Alva, Oklahoma," according to my father. "About fifteen miles west," he had said.

He always says things like that even when he knows I don't understand the whole east-west thing yet. As the big bus rolled past farms and wheat fields, I tried to figure out why my parents would send me off to work for someone they didn't even know. I sure couldn't understand it. But all my efforts to talk them out of it had failed; I finally had to give up.

The farms we passed looked a lot alike, and as they merged together in a blur, I stopped seeing any of it. But I could feel the moisture on my face as a tear trickled down my cheek. I scrunched down in the seat, repressing the sick feeling in the pit of my stomach. Late in the afternoon, the half-empty bus pulled off the main highway into a dusty lot. We were stopping at a run-down filling station. The place didn't look large enough to be a regular stop, but we were pulling in anyway.

The huge Greyhound bus groaned to a stop beside the gas pumps as dust blew past us, signaling our arrival. At the front of the bus, the driver looked into his rearview mirror and called out in a strong accent, "Hey, young fella, this is Bronson's Corner." He hopped out to retrieve my suitcase from the luggage compartment. I forgot about the driver and looked out the window. I'd never seen anything like Bronson's Corner before, and I wasn't sure which felt worse, my disappointment or the nervousness lurking deep within me.

Shoulders slumping under it all, I followed the driver down the steps, thanked him for the ride, and watched him climb back into his black leather seat. The muscular, serious-faced driver slammed the door, gunned the noisy engine, and steered the long bus onto the highway. He left me there without another glance, standing alone in the dirt and clutching my suitcase.

The strong smell of diesel slightly faded as I glanced around. It took me about a second to quickly scan the landscape. There were two small gas pumps, an old house with a general store in the front, a wooden garage off to one side littered with greasy car parts, and an old Ford pickup with a cracked front windshield parked beside one of the gas pumps. The grimy filling station might have looked a little better if someone, anyone, had been there to meet me. But no one was. I stood there for a moment, wondering what to expect inside the store. The taste of fear, as thick as the diesel I'd just smelled, rose in my throat.

After working up my courage, I opened the front door of the general store and walked into a dark, cluttered room. The store consisted of several long wooden shelves loaded with dry goods, canned goods, cereal, and other food products. One aisle contained huge burlap bags of animal food along with rope, nails, and other hardware products. The musty smell of rope and dirt hung in the air like an invisible free sample of the products for sale.

In the next aisle, two men stood near each other. As one man removed tin cans from a cardboard box, he handed them to the other person, who stacked them on a shelf and lined them up neatly. The taller of the two wore a dirty white apron. He carefully slid the green-labeled cans to the left, then placed the new yellow-labeled cans on the right. The older man wore dirty coveralls, a dark green shirt, and a well-oiled cowboy hat. At first, they didn't see me, so I hesitated, not wanting to interrupt them. They were talking about someone named Perry.

"Well, I'll tell you," the man with the apron said, "if Perry doesn't shovel out his barn pretty soon, the cows will have to crawl in on their knees just to get milked." He added another yellow can on the shelf and continued. "There's enough cow manure under that roof to fertilize half of Oklahoma." The older man laughed and started to answer. Then all of a sudden, he seemed to notice me standing by the door.

He glanced down at my suitcase and slowly dragged out his question, "Can I help you, son?"

"Sir, is this Bronson's Corner?" I said, shyly.

The older guy hesitated. The man with the blue apron, who seemed to be the store owner or manager, smiled and spoke before his friend had a chance to reply. "It sure is," he said. He had a friendly face, and his pleasant expression was just enough to help me relax a bit. "Are you looking for someone in particular?" he asked.

"Yes, sir," I answered. I took a deep breath, then clutched my suitcase a bit tighter. "I'm hoping to find a farmer by the name of Pierce."

The older man dropped the can he was holding. The yellow tin missed his left foot by a few inches, banged onto the wood-planked floor, then rolled slowly toward me. The two men looked at each other as if I had asked about a ghost or something. I stooped down and picked up the escaping product, which I recognized as creamed corn. The store owner took the missing can from me, then stepped back while he rubbed it clean with his apron. He glanced over at his friend.

"Go ahead," he said. "Tell him."

"What?" The older man asked.

"Tell him."

"OK, OK, I'll tell him."

"I'm Henry Pierce. Who are you, son?"

"My name is Matt, sir," I replied. "Matt Turner. I just got off the bus from Tulsa."

4

The two men stood silently for a moment. Neither said a word. That queasy feeling in my stomach made its way into my throat again. I wiped my sweaty palms on my jeans.

"My father told me he stopped in here for gas this winter and talked to you. I think he spoke to you about whether you needed a hand to work on your farm."

The tall, lean farmer, who was looking more surprised by the moment, shook his head and took off his weather-beaten hat. His head was multicolored, deeply tanned across his face up to his forehead, then pure white the next few inches up to his hairline, where his hat had cheated the sun. Right on top of all that, a mat of stringy gray hair sprang up in all directions as it escaped the confines of the cowboy hat. His eyes were dark brown, set deep into his face. Around them, small thin lines revealed the years of hard work in the sun and wind. Below his nose, there was a mustache, shaggy and gray like his hair, in need of a good trimming.

Still not cracking a smile of any kind, Mr. Pierce extended his right hand. I gave him mine. It was the first time I'd ever shaken hands with a farmer. Even a blind man would have known Mr. Pierce wasn't from the city—his skin was rough and callused, his grip firm but friendly. Mr. Pierce may have been old, but he was solid and sure.

"Sir, my father did talk to you, didn't he?" I asked.

"Son," he sighed. "I kind of remember talking to a city salesman come in here one day. Told me about his son all right. I guess I might have said something about needing a hand. But I didn't take it real serious-like. I never gave it a second thought. Your dad kind of acted like he was just talking."

He scratched the back of his head, then continued, "Now, son," he said, "your dad never wrote or called me up. I guess I forgot the whole thing."

The store owner smiled and asked politely, "Matt, how old *are* you?"

"Fifteen. I'll be sixteen in the fall."

The two men huddled together and spoke under their breath. Mr. Pierce shook his head once again. As I waited for him to tell me to go back home, I wondered how long it would be before that bus would be returning to Bronson's Corner. It looked like I might be getting right back on it.

"Well, I don't know about all this," Mr. Pierce said, taking a deep breath. Then his wrinkled face changed expressions for a moment. Right then, he reminded me of old Mr. Tucker, our junior high school principal, who I had spent a fair amount of time with during the semester.

"Son, do you know what a Poppin' Johnny is?" Mr. Pierce asked.

"Uh, no," I replied shyly. "Is it some form of toilet?"

"No. No, it isn't," he said, holding back a slight grin.

"Well, did you ever drive a pickup?"

"No, sir. I never drove one, but I'd sure like to learn."

Mr. Pierce looked over at the store manager, who looked down at the can in his hand. Mr. Pierce, looking exasperated, faced me again.

"Well, have you ever even been on a farm?" he asked.

"I'm sorry." I apologized, grabbing my suitcase, ready to give up. "Maybe I better just go back to Tulsa."

"No, son," Mr. Pierce offered. "It's just that, well, you're just about the biggest surprise I've had since they bombed Pearl Harbor."

I put my bag down and felt the heat rise in my face. It was even worse than that time in junior high when I tried to kiss Jane Ellen in the library. She just laughed out loud, and everyone turned around and saw what had happened. Now, more than ever, I wished I'd stayed at home. Mr. Pierce studied me for a long moment, put his crumpled hat back on, and stepped a little closer.

"Son, can you wash dishes?" he asked with a tone of authority in his voice.

"Yes, sir," I said.

"Well then," he said. "Now we're getting somewhere. Last week I was telling Dale here I might get me a little help this year. Wasn't I, Dale?"

His friend Dale, the store owner, stood with look of surprise and exchanged a kind of knowing look with the farmer.

6

"Right," Dale said. "That's right, Henry. You were just saying it the other day, and by golly, I guess your help just rode in from Tulsa."

"Guess he did at that," the farmer agreed.

I guess I just did.

Without another word, Mr. Pierce picked up my suitcase and started toward the door. Dale and I followed him outside to the old green pickup parked beside the gas pumps. He tossed my case in the back, took a deep breath, and turned to Dale.

"Dale, we're going on up to my place," he announced more formally than seemed necessary.

"Okay," Dale grunted. "Don't get lost."

I got into the old pickup and watched through the back window as Dale sorted through the trash in the truck's cluttered bed. He grunted as he lifted a well-worn black tire out of the trash.

"Hey, you're in luck," Dale said. "It's only flat on one side! I'll have it fixed next time you come in."

With a chuckle, Mr. Pierce started the pickup truck. The engine sputtered, the cab shook gently, and the gears ground angrily as the old farmer shifted into first, then slowly drove away from the gas pumps onto the highway. As we gained speed, I looked out the window and alternately glanced at my new boss, hoping he would say something. He didn't. I had so many questions I wanted to ask, but he didn't seem in the mood to talk. I wondered what kind of man he was and what kind of farm I would be living in. But who knows, Mr. Pierce might even have a pretty daughter just like those farmers on the television.

I put my questions aside for a while as I rode along and viewed the Oklahoma Panhandle with its red clay dirt, golden wheat fields, and occasional farmhouses. While I watched the rapidly moving scenes pass my window, a gentle trace of my mother's perfume rose from my shirt collar. The sweet feminine fragrance pulled me back to that morning when I'd left her to start on this summer's journey.

#

Mom stood near the stove, cooking my favorite breakfast: eggs, bacon, and leftover cornbread. She wore a green corduroy housecoat, and her long black hair was done up in those pink plastic rollers. She was a darn good cook, and leftovers were never thrown away in her kitchen. While I ate, she stayed near the stove longer than usual. I had the feeling she didn't want me to see her face.

"You know," Mom said, "working on a farm will do you a lot more good than hanging around here this summer."

"I know, Mom. That's the third time you've said that this morning."

"Sorry," she apologized, wiping her long, thin hands on her pretty everyday apron. "I want you to know I'll miss you. But I do think all this is a good thing. Farm people work hard, but they always seem to care more about their families than city people do."

"Yes, ma'am," I said. I finished my breakfast in near silence, thinking about what I would miss in the city. I had just finished the eighth grade, and all I could think of was spending the summer with my friends. Most of the guys were on Little League baseball teams, and I was on one too. A couple of my buddies even had paper routes. The few times I had gotten up early to help throw the morning paper, we drank coffee and ate stolen doughnuts which we carefully removed from large boxes delivered to stores in the early morning. When we found them, we were careful only to steal a few from each box so that the boxes appeared full. Warm, sweet, and oozing with that creamy vanilla filling, those stolen treasures were worth the risk of getting caught. That was one of several reasons to stay home instead of leaving for somewhere entirely unknown for the entire summer.

But my father had other plans, and I could not argue with my father. He came into the kitchen while Mom and I were talking.

"Well, son," he said, "you couldn't find a job around here, so you might as well take that farm job I found for you. It's better than watching TV all day."

I stared at the remainder of the two eggs in my plate, lost in concentration.

"Are you listening to me, boy?"

8

"Matt," Mom said, "your father is talking to you, son."

"Yes, sir," I said. I glanced at my father, who had his hand right behind my head, ready to slap me. "I'm listening, Dad."

Mom went back to her cooking, and Dad stuck his chest out and continued, "I went to a lot of trouble finding a job for you. It'll be good training for football next fall. The hard work, good food, and fresh country air will make a man out of you, boy."

That was his favorite phrase. Everything would "make a man out of you." During the past few weeks, I had tried desperately to talk him out of making me work on the farm, but it was so hopeless that I gave up.

After breakfast, Dad stayed at home, expecting a business call, while Mom drove me to the bus station. We stood on the sidewalk near the bus I was about to board. I looked into Mom's blue eyes and wanted to say something sweet. But I just stood there. I don't know why, but I didn't tell her the things I should have, the things I felt. I wasn't angry at Mom, but for some reason, I acted like I was. Maybe I was just stubborn, but I never told her how much I would miss her. Just before I climbed up the steep steps of the Greyhound bus, Mom kissed me on the cheek. I guess that's when her perfume got on my shirt collar.

"Matt, I'll miss you," she said.

I walked past the other passengers and found an empty seat. The bus drove away a few minutes later, while I looked out the window at my mother standing on the sidewalk. She smiled as if it didn't bother her, but I knew it did. It bothered me too. It was the first time I'd ever been away from home by myself.

As I sat in the old Ford pickup with the wind blowing on my face, I could still picture Mom waving to me. Any other time, the sweet scent of rose on my collar would have embarrassed me to death. But not now. It was a tender taste of home. With no idea how long the image of Mom would stay with me and no idea what lay ahead, I bounced along the bumpy Oklahoma highway. A hundred questions ran through my mind as a thousand stalks of wheat passed outside my window. I'd never have predicted it or chosen it for myself. But there I sat, riding in a beat-up truck with a quiet, elderly farmer I'd never met before. I was about to spend the summer away from home, my family, and my friends. Mr. Pierce said nothing and continued to drive, each mile putting me farther and farther from home.

The lingering silence lay thicker than dust on the dashboard, and it stayed with us all the way to his farm.

#

On television, all the wheat farms I'd seen seemed to be beautiful places with comfortable little houses, large, well-fed families, and at least one pretty girl. But this sure wasn't television; this was rural Oklahoma in all its stark reality. As we drove up the muddy drive, I could see that his farm wasn't anything like I had imagined. The small, dilapidated house needed at least 100 gallons of paint. Hiding behind it was a flimsy gray barn, a structure that looked like one of Oklahoma's strong winds could tear it apart in one steady gust. Rusty farm machinery sat motionless, abandoned in a sea of waist-high grass. Rotten fence posts spread listlessly like limp spaghetti every which way. I wondered how the animals managed to stay in the fields at all.

I followed Mr. Pierce into the house, eager to meet his family. But the moment we were inside, I realized there would be no large family to greet me. There was no family at all. Henry Pierce, farmer and boss of the place, was a bachelor. I was stunned by the fact that he had no wife or family. I immediately began to worry about the stark, filthy surroundings. *Good Lord, will I have to stay in this pigpen all summer?*

The cluttered interior of the house looked like a rural version of my sister's room after one of her famous slumber parties. No, on second thought, this was far worse than Suzie's bedroom. Old magazines and newspapers lay scattered about everywhere. Dirty coffee cups and glasses sat on every inch of counter space throughout the kitchen, and a two-week collection of dirty dishes was stacked precariously in the sink. On the dingy kitchen floor, a group of well-fed cockroaches strolled slowly from the middle of the room toward their territory under the fridge. I wondered how many friends they had under there. It took me no time at all to realize Mr. Pierce didn't need a farmhand as much as he needed a good maid.

While I stood looking at the mess and wondering if the roaches were coming back, Mr. Pierce spoke for the first time since we left the gas station.

His question caught me off guard. "Son, can you cook?"

"No, sir," I said, wondering how I could have ever wound up in a place like this.

"Well, I guess you're going to learn to cook then," Mr. Pierce grunted.

"Yes, sir," I agreed sheepishly.

I was beginning to think that my dad must hate me. It's one thing having a father send you away all summer to "make a man out of you," but this was a place a father would send you as punishment.

"Son, are you hungry?"

I glanced around the kitchen again, hungry, but not sure I could eat anything in this mess. I muttered, "A little, I guess."

"You go on outside then and take a look around the farm while I fix us something."

"OK," I mumbled. I didn't look forward to eating there, but I suppose I was too hungry to refuse.

"Oh, and be careful of June," he warned. "She can be an ornery old girl."

"Who's June?"

"She's just an ole worn-out piece of horseflesh that runs around with the cattle on the east section. 'Bout this time of day she generally wanders down around the barn."

"I'll look out for her."

"All right then," he said. Then, without warning, Mr. Pierce shoved a large stack of old magazines off the cluttered table and onto the floor. The magazines crashed to the floor, shooting a small cloud of dust into the air, and sending a stray cockroach running for his life. An inch or two closer and the filthy insect would have had the dubious distinction of meeting death by *LIFE* Magazine.

I left Mr. Pierce in the kitchen, went out behind the house, and had my first real look around. The sun was almost down for the day. Walking along the fence toward the barn, another surge of homesickness seemed to crush me. Nothing about this place seemed worth spending a summer away from my friends—or my mother. I missed her now more than ever. Even on this stinky farm, the fantastic scent of her perfume refused to go away. The foreign surroundings and the increasing loneliness threatened to overwhelm me, but I told myself I was NOT going to give in to crying.

A lonely cow wailed somewhere in the pasture, its cry increasing my feelings of abandonment. I said that I wouldn't cry, but I began to think that I might.

As I walked toward the barn, I was barely able to hold back the tears. The musty scent of stale wheat greeted me as I opened the barn door. Among the rubble, I made out the shadows of two large machines that I barely recognized. As my eyes adjusted to the semi-darkness, I could see an old green and yellow tractor along with a strange-looking harvesting machine. I stood alone in the dark, cluttered barn and knew that staying on this farm was going to be the hardest thing I'd ever done. I thought about running away, maybe going to Bronson's Corner. It wasn't too far to walk, but the road was muddy and the sky looked like it might rain anytime. I had to forget about running away.

I wasn't sure I could stay, but something in my heart didn't want to give up so early. At the very least, these rusty old machines would need someone to drive them. I figured if I was going to have to live in this mess, at least I could drive a truck or a tractor.

I hurried out the back door of the barn and found a chicken coop with a couple of dozen chickens wandering around aimlessly in the shade. Beyond the high, wooden fence of the corral was a winding trail leading off into an endless pasture.

The sun was going down, and a beautiful orange tint spread across the lime-colored grass in the open field. It was a pretty sight that gave me a moment of peace in spite of the glum surroundings of this poor man's farm. Walking back toward the house, I noticed the large wooden windmill spinning in the breeze. Below it was a huge water trough with a fence across the center. Half of the water was accessible from the pasture while the other half lay on my side of the fence.

It was at that moment I saw June for the very first time. Tall, gray, a little bit skinny for her size, an old horse slurping water out of the trough from the other side of the fence, her two giant eyes were watching me carefully. I sauntered up to the fence, dipped both of my hands into the fresh water, and held out my hands to her, offering her a drink. I made a clicking sound with my tongue, trying to attract her.

"Will you be my friend?" I said.

The large, graceful horse looked up at me for a second, then turned and trotted off into the field. I had been ignored in school several times when I had tried to make friends with some of the pretty girls. But a farm animal had never rejected me. I headed back to the house with a heavy heart.

#

When supper was ready, Mr. Pierce and I sat at the kitchen table facing each other. He barely said a word. The constant silence was louder than any family argument I had ever experienced. Above our head, a tiny light bulb showered the room with light. Without a light fixture of any kind, the exposed bulb added a harsh cast to the silent room's sense of loneliness. After eating a meager supper of lima beans and stale cornbread, Mr. Pierce and I cleaned up the dishes. Though he said nothing, I could tell he was watching me work. Back home, I always dodged any form of kitchen work. But somehow in this farmer's home, I wanted to get the dishes clean because we would be eating on them the next meal. On the kitchen table, Mr. Pierce stored leftover food instead of putting it in the fridge. That didn't seem right, but I said nothing.

"We're getting up early tomorrow," Mr. Pierce said. "So, I'll show you the room where you'll be sleeping."

"Yes, sir," I said as I grabbed my suitcase and followed him. A narrow wooden stairway rose above the hall and into the loft. The wood creaked as we climbed the stairs. The loft was a small rectangular-shaped room littered with old clothing, books, and a few pieces of discarded furniture. We stood in the center of the room for a moment.

"I have one bedroom downstairs," Mr. Pierce said. "But it's small and too hot in the summertime. We'll sleep up here."

"Both of us?" I said, disappointed and a bit frightened.

"That's right, son. But of course, we have to clean it first."

He pointed to the two windows that faced each other from opposite walls.

"Sometimes we get a pretty good cross breeze from those windows. That's going to be our air conditioner."

"Yes, sir," I agreed. On the floor, a mouse scampered out from behind a stack of books, then disappeared behind the dusty bookshelf. Mr. Pierce must have noticed me flinch.

"Ah, don't let that little fella bother you," he chuckled. "They don't eat much. Let's clear this place out, and he'll have to find him another home."

We swept out the attic, took the garbage behind the house and crammed it into a large barrel used for burning trash. When the attic floor was acceptably clean, we placed a small mattress on either side of the room, just below the windows. There were no box springs or headboards, no pillowcase or fancy sheets, only a striped mattress and pillow for each person.

In the middle of the room, another bare light bulb shone from the ceiling with a long string attached. As I settled into my bed, Mr. Pierce pulled the line, and the room went black. After several minutes my eyes adjusted to the darkness. In the dark, I felt shaky and nervous about being in a strange house with a grown man, a stranger to me. I didn't like it at all!

I lay there with one arm propping my head up so I could see out the window. From time to time, I glanced over at Mr. Pierce, having no idea what to expect. When I looked out the window, I watched a star-filled sky and felt its soothing effect on me. It was a spectacle of bright, twinkling lights—millions of miles from the two of us.

"That's the other good thing about being up here," Mr. Pierce said, "watching the sky."

We had been together most of the evening, and he had talked so little. It surprised me when he offered the beginnings of casual conversation. I didn't say anything for a moment.

"Are the stars always this bright?" I asked.

"Not always," he said quietly.

As I looked out the attic window, discovering the starlit heavens, I thought again of my mother.

"Mr. Pierce, have you ever been married?"

"No!"

"Didn't you ever want to?"

He didn't answer for what seemed like a long time. Then I heard him take a deep breath.

"Goodnight, Matt," he said.

"Goodnight, sir."

The room remained silent as worry, darkness, and sleep took over.

2   CAMP ALVA

During the next few days, I learned a lot about Mr. Pierce's farm and his farm equipment as we worked long, hard days in preparation for the upcoming wheat harvest. The machinery was rusty and out of date, but somehow the old farmer managed to keep it all running. My new boss was a patient man. He taught me how to grease the tractor, fix tires on the combine, and repair the wooden siding along the top of the big red truck.

"We're going to need all of these pretty soon," he said. "Got to get everything greased up and ready to run after it's been sitting here all winter."

After a week, I understood the basic plan of how the harvest would work. When the wheat was ripe enough, we would harvest it by pulling the combine with the John Deere tractor. The combine would roll across the wheat, with its giant wooden blades spinning, cutting the tips and grain off the wheat. When the combine's bin was loaded down with freshly cut grain, the wheat would then get transferred into the big red storage truck. After we dumped several loads into the truck, Mr. Pierce would drive it into town, where it would be weighed and sold at the granary. That was the plan.

Of course, the plan depended on all the rusty equipment working correctly in spite of challenges like hail, insect infestation, or flood. To do the work, the old farmer had all sizes and shapes of machines, and all of them had one thing in common: they all soaked up grease. So, my first job on the farm was to lubricate everything that didn't have legs. I found out that it was work I could do. But after greasing all the farm equipment and getting more familiar with them, I considered the old green pickup my favorite. It was a 1943 Ford pickup with long, black running boards, a four-speed transmission, and a tall rodlike gearshift lever located on the floor of the cab, right in the center. There was a flathead V-8 engine under the hood, which was the most popular engine used in hot rods back home in Tulsa.

Every day I made up some excuse to drive the old pickup for a few minutes. In the driver's seat, I could reach the pedals without much effort, but the problem was shifting gears. It took a while, but slowly I progressed from those first gear-grinding efforts to a smooth, gentle rhythm. Soon, I began to think of myself as a real pro, but Mr. Pierce kept a close watch on me.

And it wasn't long before I started enjoying the animals on Mr. Pierce's little farm. In addition to old June, Mr. Pierce had about twenty cows, ten or twelve pigs, and a few dozen chickens.

June loved attention and managed to get her own way. So, when I took her for a ride into the pasture, it was a battle of our wills. The first few times I rode her, Mr. Pierce demonstrated the best way to put on a saddle and bridle. Then he held the spirited animal as I attempted to mount her.

"She can be stubborn," Mr. Pierce said. "She puts me in mind of a stubborn woman I once knew."

I wasn't sure what he meant by that comparison, but I nodded.

"Walk her out into that pasture there," he said. "When you get past the fence, just let her have her head, letting her go where she wants. She'll get used to your weight. Pretty soon, you can do the leading."

"Yes, sir," I said without confidence. Mr. Pierce slapped her on the hip, and off we went at a fast trot. When we passed through the corral gate, I released the tension from the reins, but I held onto them. June flexed her long neck, feeling the freedom, and went across the wide pasture, which sloped downward toward the creek. After a few minutes, we were far enough from the house that I couldn't hear the familiar humming sound of the windmill turning. The only sounds were her giant hooves clopping in the dirt and the creaking of the old leather saddle I sat in.

Mr. Pierce had been right. June quickly adjusted to her new rider, so I decided to try my hand at taking control. I gave her a little poke with my heels, and she broke into a gentle gallop. Before I knew it, June was doing fine. But I wasn't so sure what I should do next. I'd only been on her a few times and had no idea how to slow things down.

Near the creek, a line of blackjack trees grew along the edge of the water. June trotted across the creek bed as water splashed against my legs and tree limbs passed within inches of my head. I hugged the leather reins and shouted, "WHOA, June. Whoa!" On she went and went and went.

Snorting a bit now, June trotted up the side of a small hill where I darn near fell off. I leaned forward, clutching the saddle horn with both hands. For some reason, she stopped on the crest of the hill.

I took a deep breath and felt the relief coming back into my queasy stomach. Reaching down, I stroked June's long, bluish mane and felt the moisture of the gathering sweat. Suddenly, I noticed a red blur out of the corner of my eye. It was coming right at us.

I raised my feet to kick June into high gear, but the horse moved before I touched her. She had a mind of her own all right. She took off down the hill so quickly that I struggled to stay in the saddle.

"Hold it, June!" I shouted. "Wait a minute, girl!" I thought the first part of the ride had been fast. Well, it was nothing compared with this blinding speed. We were down the hill in no more than a split second and crossed the creek so crazy, I don't think we ever touched the water. As she flew between the limbs of the blackjack trees, I dodged left and right, trying my best not to get clotheslined. I still didn't know what was chasing us.

"Slow down, June. Slow down!"

Once we were in the pasture, I held on tight and spun around in the saddle. I finally got a glimpse of what was chasing me. "Run, June! Let's get going!" I yelled.

Right on our tail was the meanest-looking animal I had ever seen in my life—a giant red bull with long, sharp, menacing horns. It was so close I moved forward in the saddle, trying not to get harpooned by those sword-like horns. I wanted to climb up on June's neck to escape what seemed a certain stabbing death. "Hurry, June! Move it!" I yelled, louder this time.

Now we were flying across the open pasture headed for the corral. June racing as fast as her strong legs would take us, me bouncing up and down on her back like a pogo stick, and the angriest bull in Oklahoma a few steps behind us, trying to put a large hole in me.

All of a sudden June slowed down to a trot. "What are you doing?" I shouted. "Don't stop now!" I looked behind me, and to my surprise, our angry friend was stopped quite a distance behind us. He stayed back there for some reason, and somehow he didn't look quite as menacing. He seemed almost proud, as if he was the winner of some great battle.

"Good job, girl," I said, stroking June and trying to catch my breath.

June ambled along. It felt good to slow down and stop bouncing. A few minutes later she stepped back in the corral. I climbed down out of the saddle. My legs felt like jelly. My rump was so sore from the saddle I could hardly walk.

"I see you met Pluto."

I turned and saw Mr. Pierce standing on the other side of the fence from the corral. I forgot my soreness for a moment as I began to worry about what he might think of me running June so hard. Then he smiled. Even with his stained, crooked teeth, this aging farmer looked ten years younger.

"Yes, sir," I explained. "We were on the other side of the creek, and June lit out before I knew what was happening. I just tried to hold on."

We both walked closer to the horse. I began to brush the animal with the thick brush Mr. Pierce kept in the barn. "Well, Matt," he said, "you go in on the porch. Right there by the big sack of potatoes you'll find some carrots. Bring her a batch."

When I brought the bright orange carrots back, he had already taken her saddle, blanket, and bridle off, and stored them in the little tack room in the barn. With an air of joy and respect on his wrinkled face, Mr. Pierce worked carefully around June. Surely he didn't mean what he had said that first night when he'd called her an old piece of horseflesh.

"Here's the carrots, Mr. Pierce."

"Good. You give her some, Matt. I want you two to become friends. She worked hard for you today. Show her you care."

"Yes, sir."

While he brushed her from the other side, I stood near her head, holding the clump of carrots with one hand and stroking her mane with the other. "Here, girl."

She sniffed the fresh carrots and bit half of them in one quick chomp. I jerked my hand back and wondered what would be left of my hand if she had wanted a whole mouthful. Not taking any chances, I waved the remaining carrots under her nose and threw them on the ground. June leaned down with her huge teeth chomping loudly. She gulped the last of her reward.

Mr. Pierce came around and handed me the brush. He was still grinning. I guess he must have seen the first bite she snatched, which almost took a couple of my fingers with it.

"Brush her down, son. She'll need water too. Then leave her in the corral for the night."

"Mr. Pierce," I said. "Why is that bull so mean? We didn't do anything to scare him."

He took a crumpled Lucky Strike package out of his shirt pocket, removed a cigarette, and lit it. The smoke hung in between us, its smell mixing quickly with the dust from the corral.

"Pluto never bothers anyone unless they come into that circle of trees above the creek."

"Doesn't June know that?" I asked.

Mr. Pierce took his hat off and wiped beads of sweat from his brow. "Sure she does," he said. "Guess she took you there just to have a little fun."

I looked at the horse, trying to figure if she was that smart. "Is that your idea of fun?" I asked the silent animal. "It wasn't all that fun for me."

Mr. Pierce laughed as a good-natured smile crossed his weathered face. As I brushed June down, Mr. Pierce stood on the other side of the large horse, stroking her neck affectionately.

He looked across at me and said, "You asked me a question the other night."

"Yes, sir," I said, searching my memory. Seems like I had asked a hundred questions. I clenched my teeth, a blank stare on my face.

Mr. Pierce's eyes shone with that knowing look grown-ups often have. "You asked if I had ever had a girlfriend."

"That's right!" I said, remembering the conversation. "Did you have one?"

He stood for a moment, leaning gently on his horse. I stood a bit closer to the animal, not wanting to miss a word.

"Well, I'll admit I was in love once," Mr. Pierce said, his voice steady, but gentle.

"What happened?" I asked.

"She was the most beautiful girl in Woods County. We went to dances on Saturday nights, and we went to church when I could get off. We made such a handsome couple that the whole town stopped to look at us when we passed by. That was back . . . Well . . . It was a long, long time ago."

June moved nervously between us. Mr. Pierce's large callused hands stroked her evenly, and the big horse settled. As he soothed the animal, Mr. Pierce's voice dropped to a weaker, less confident tone.

"I met that girl," he said. "while I was in the Army during the war. I was stationed right here in Camp Alva."

"Camp Alva?" I said. "I didn't know there was an Army camp in Alva."

"Most people don't know about it," he said. "On account of it being a prisoner of war camp. There were German soldiers and officers, some of the worst leaders of the Nazi Party. I was an MP. It was my job to keep them in there."

"What's an MP?" I asked.

"Military Police," he said. "There were several hundred MPs stationed at Camp Alva and almost 5,000 German prisoners. We called them POWs."

"Wow," I said, thinking of the films I'd seen on TV: various movies and old newsreels were showing American prisoners in German POW camps. The conditions were always horrible, and I couldn't imagine having a POW camp in the United States. I wanted to ask him more about the POW camp. I glanced at Mr. Pierce and waited. His eyes were fixed on something off in the distance—either something in the sky or something in his past.

"What did being in the Army have to do with your girlfriend?" I asked.

"She was a telephone operator," he said. He patted June softly. "And the most beautiful girl you ever saw. We took long walks by the river. Sometimes she would bring a picnic lunch. Most Saturdays we went to a dance. Those were wonderful years, son."

"It all sounds great," I said. "But heck, why didn't you just get married?"

"Something happened," he said. He looked down at his hands and stopped stroking June. "After that, I could never hold my head up in Alva again."

"What happened?" I asked.

When he answered, his voice was almost painful, "She wound up getting married to someone else. She married into one of the best families in these parts. They own a lot of land and cattle, and a couple of years ago her husband struck oil on their farm. I guess he can give her anything she wants."

"But what happened before that, Mr. Pierce? Why did you break up?"

"It was really bad," he said. "Real bad."

I looked at his sad, melancholy eyes and remembered what my grandmother always said. "Don't push too hard when people are hurting." So, I didn't ask any more about the "really bad" thing. Not right then, anyway.

But I did try another angle, "If she meant that much to you, she must have been pretty."

"I didn't say she was pretty. I said she was beautiful. Dark hair and skin so soft I can still remember how good it felt—and ride! She could sit a horse better than most men. But what I remember most of all was when we'd sit on the porch swing and talk. Just talking and holding hands."

"What was her name?"

"Jewel," he said with pride. "Jewel Krisswell. That's just what she was, an Alva Jewel." Mr. Pierce patted June one last time, then turned and walked away, ending our conversation about Jewel.

That night, after we turned the light off in the attic, I gazed out the window at the stars. I tried to imagine what Mr. Pierce and his girlfriend, Jewel Krisswell, would have looked like when they were younger. They must have been a handsome couple and probably cared a lot for each other. I didn't know what had happened. But I figured if two people loved each other that much, it must have taken something evil to split them up.

#

The old farmer's cooking tasted the same those first few weeks. Every night we sat under the same naked light bulb at dinnertime. After I got over my homesickness, I began to tolerate the food and tried to find ways to improve our surroundings. There were rags, soap, and water. With a little effort, I managed to clean some of the old pots and pans we were using. Little by little, it started looking better. After supper, when it was time to clean up the kitchen, Mr. Pierce would lean back in his old wooden chair.

"Well, it was a long day," he yawned. "Want me to do the dishes tonight, son?" I knew he didn't mean it. But his asking and my refusing had become our ritual.

"No," I said. "I'll get this done in no time." He grinned and moved out of the way as I picked up the remaining forks and knives. The few times that he did help, his heart wasn't in it. Things got put away dirty—if they were put away at all. So, I had concluded that I could do it better without his help.

"Come on outside when you're finished," he said, reaching for another cigarette as he went out the screen door. "We're both starting to smell like the barn," he called back over his shoulder. That meant it was time for a bath.

I finished wiping the rinse water off the glass pitcher with a wet tea towel. Stripped to the waist, I sauntered out the back door barefoot. It was dark out behind the house, and a single light bulb down by the barn barely pierced the darkness. Because the farm had no shower or indoor tub, we took our baths in the aluminum water trough under the windmill. It wasn't my first bath in the water trough, but I still felt a little shy about it. But like everything on that farm, you try hard enough and you can see the good in it. And that's what I did. The outdoor bath had just enough light so you could see what you needed to see, but it was dark enough to hide what you didn't want to be seen.

Mr. Pierce sat waist-deep in water; the orange glow of a hand-rolled cigarette framed his wrinkled face. A blue cloud of smoke hovered near him, then got whisked away by a soft breeze. Off in the distance, a lonely cow cried in the night.

"Son," Mr. Pierce said. "Get in careful now. This is the last of my tobacco."

"Yes, sir."

Wearing only my undershorts, I stepped gently into the cool, dark water and found a good place to squat as far from Mr. Pierce as I could get. In observance of an unspoken rule between us, Mr. Pierce remained on the opposite side of the horse trough. I felt around on the bottom of the tank for the right spot. Finding one, I relaxed and sat down. The fresh well water was soothing to my weary legs and my sore behind. Across the water, Mr. Pierce waited for me to settle in, his expression a bit impatient. Having another person around was something new for Mr. Pierce.

"Tomorrow's Saturday," he said. "Need to go into town. You want to go?"

"I don't know," I said, unsure of how they might treat a stranger.

"Well, keep this in mind," he said, "during harvest time we won't be able to go too often. We'll be too busy. So, you might want to go in while you can."

I didn't have to be told twice.

"Yes, sir," I said. "I'd like to go with you."

I thought about the little town of Alva and tried to imagine what it might look like on a Saturday. *Maybe there will be some cute girls.* While I sat in the water trough washing my face, my mind drifted toward the Army camp in Alva.

"Mr. Pierce," I said. "What was it like working in that prisoner's camp?"

He tossed the tiny shreds of his cigarette away and sighed heavily. He finally said, "It was a tough assignment. We needed a lot more men. That was the main problem."

"Why didn't they give you more men?"

"There was a war going on, and the Army didn't have enough MPs."

"Well, how did you wind up working there? I mean, how did you get a job like that?"

"I signed the papers to join the Army the day after they bombed Pearl Harbor," he said. "Just like everyone else. After boot camp, they sent me to the Military Police training base in Fort Gordon, Georgia, and I went from one assignment to the other until they sent me to Alva as part of the 401st MP Company. I'll never forget the day our unit arrived in Alva; it was the first time I saw a real German, and the first time I saw an angel. You see, in those days the best way to get around was by train. The United States government controlled all trains. So that's how we got to Alva—by troop train."

I sat still in the water trough. It was quiet for a moment or two. I thought he might not continue at all, then finally he said,

"Guess I better tell you how it all started . . ." And we headed off into the memories Mr. Pierce had safely preserved of Camp Alva.

Camp Alva

On a cold January evening, while snow fell along the foothills, a troop train came skidding to a stop in the little town of Alva, Oklahoma. Two hundred and fifty soldiers, including one MP by the name of Henry Pierce, were being transferred to Camp Alva from Camp McCain, Mississippi. When the train stopped at the railway station, the soldiers climbed down the steps and stretched their weary legs. Henry and the other soldiers knew the pitfalls of their assignment and had talked openly about it all the way from Mississippi. They were being assigned to Camp Alva to guard German prisoners, mostly Nazi officers, and hard-core SS troops; super Nazis—or as they were formally known: the Schutzstaffel. These men were the most dangerous enemy soldiers who had been captured in Europe and Africa and had recently arrived in the United States. Some of the MPs had seen German POWs in other camps, but they were learning that Camp Alva was the "dumping ground" for the worst of the worst when it came to Nazi troublemakers.

It was the winter of 1944, three years into World War II. Most of the folks around Alva were legitimately worried over the frightening possibility of German prisoners escaping. They had talked often about their fears. Many had discussed the possibility of moving, but no one did. The POWs were housed in a newly constructed camp, built much closer to their town than anyone had ever imagined. Sure, the folks in Alva were just as patriotic as everyone else in America, but they were shocked at having several thousand Germans only a stone's throw away.

But that night, the talk around town focused on some good news; help was on the way. The moment the troop train arrived, the folks of Alva felt a lot more comfortable.

The weather had been unusually cold that winter, and by late afternoon, a thick layer of gray clouds finally gave up its soft, wet snow. Soon the streets were painted over with the untouched whiteness. When the soldiers stood still for a split second, their jackets turned white along the shoulders and their breath condensed in small vapor puffs rising above them. One of the more experienced soldiers standing near Private Pierce remarked that the little train station at Alva looked almost European in the falling snow. Henry Pierce took it all in, excited about his first real assignment as an MP, and said, "It's a beautiful evening."

A few of the younger MPs kicked snow at each other playfully but fell into line when a rugged-looking sergeant appeared. The sky grew dark, and the lights from town twinkled. Duffel bags were retrieved, cigarette butts were stamped out, and the arriving soldiers quickly assembled next to the depot for a head count. All horseplay was over as they faced their sergeant.

Staff Sergeant Swim stood five-feet-eleven, with massive arms, a thin waist, and a left jab as fast and powerful as a Golden Gloves boxer. He was all business when it came to the Army and would tell anyone that it was his duty to God and Country to teach every young man in his outfit how to be a "damn good soldier." He drank openly and met girls secretly. Consequently, he understood that men needed to blow off a bit of steam once in a while. It was common knowledge that as long as his MPs returned to base on time after a weekend pass and reported for duty sober, the good sergeant would leave them alone. He had a deep, megaphone-like voice that commanded respect. However, he had proven worthy of respect over and over again. His strength wasn't in his loudness, rather it was in his ability to stand up to men twice his size with no hesitation.

"Watch your step around the 'Swimmer,'" a corporal on the train had told Private Pierce. That was their nickname for the sergeant. "He's a hard man," the corporal had said. "I know a guy that got drunk with the Swimmer once. The sergeant told someone about the time he had found the bodies of American soldiers. Guys who had been captured and mutilated by the Japs. That's right, and it's common knowledge that the Swimmer earned his first Purple Heart in the Pacific. He got his second Purple Heart *and* a Bronze Star in France."

Private Pierce had also overheard other people talking about Sergeant Swim. They had said that for the past year he had run the toughest, most efficient POW outfit in Camp McCain, Mississippi. The prisoners feared him, and sometimes he was loathed by many of his soldiers. He took no insolence from a prisoner and no cowardice from an MP.

As Henry Pierce tried to get a better look at the Swimmer, he remembered all the things people had said about the man. He felt the familiar pangs of fear in his stomach. A shy, somewhat introverted young man, Henry Pierce was taller than many of the other MPs but preferred to let other people do most of the talking. What he lacked in his communication skills, he more than made up for with his mechanical skills. Private Henry Pierce could disassemble, clean, and reassemble a weapon faster than anyone in his platoon, not to mention he was an expert shot.

"Fall in!" Sergeant Swim shouted, his booming baritone heard above the muffled sounds of the departing train.

The men stood at attention and watched as their captain walked up and stood beside Sergeant Swim. Some of the men in the front rows heard the captain give the order for head count, but *everyone* heard the sergeant echo the order—no mistaking the power of that voice. As the head count continued and everyone was reported as "present and accounted for," the captain stepped forward and faced the men. He was a tall man with wide shoulders and a young, handsome face. Traces of blond hair jutted out from his khaki-colored officer's crush cap, blending in with the feather-like snow particles.

"Men," the captain shouted. "We are here to do a job, and by God, we are going to do it. Some of you have seen firsthand what the Nazis are capable of, and some of you have never seen an enemy soldier. But you all have two things in common; you are Americans, and you will work together to get this job done. When it comes to our prisoners, remember it is your responsibility to either keep them in line or punish them—to either guard them, or if necessary, shoot them."

"Sergeant Swim," the captain said.

"Yes, sir," Sergeant Swim shouted.

"Let's move out."

With the captain's speech ringing in their ears and the wet snow gently brushing their face, the anxious MPs marched along the edge of town, past restaurants, bars, homes, and hotels, to the infamous Camp Alva.

The POW camp was well organized and resembled a standard Army camp. There were four compounds with 32 single-story wooden barracks capable of holding 50 prisoners each. The compounds were surrounded by a number of eight-foot-tall barbed-wire fences. Large, flat, open spaces, 20 yards long, separated the tall fences. Open spaces designed to provide the tower guards enough time and visibility to see escaping prisoners before they reached the last fence. Thirteen ever-present, hovering guard towers were manned 24 hours a day by heavily armed American soldiers. A top-of-the-line infirmary located on the north end of the camp was staffed by the US Medical Corps to administer care to the POWs and MPs alike.

As the main gates swung open, Sergeant Swim marched his MPs into the POW camp, where a handful of happy American soldiers stood by to greet the arriving troops. Private Pierce, on the outside column, got his first look at Camp Alva. Even though the snow fell thicker now, obscuring visibility, several POW barracks were visible as well as several administrative buildings. Private Pierce scanned the snowy landscape further until his eyes came to a rest. Standing only a few feet away from him, behind a barbed-wire fence, were three grim-faced German officers in their famed black SS uniforms. Private Pierce was stunned. He had not been overseas, so these were the first German soldiers he had ever seen face to face. Sure, he had seen enemy soldiers in the newspapers, on posters, and in the movies, but he had never looked into the eyes of a real German soldier. The unexpected sight of them, as foreign and as gruesome as he had imagined, shook him to the bone. To make matters worse, he and the other arriving MPs had not been briefed on the policy of German POWs being allowed to wear their own uniforms. Since he expected them to be wearing prison garb, the image of three German officers, arrayed in full Nazi uniform, complete with the famous tall leather boots and SS insignia, was enough to make an American soldier's blood boil, including Pierce, who stumbled right into the soldier in front of him.

The column of MPs turned the corner and marched toward a large building in the middle of the camp. In the dimly lit area, Private Pierce was able to make out a few local people who were headed in the opposite direction toward the camp gate. Most likely, these were civilian workers going home for the night. Through the falling snow, he saw two civilian men dressed in brown suits and overcoats. Behind them was a young lady who wore a long black winter coat with a white wool scarf and a pair of ankle-high work boots.

The pretty girl walked a few steps behind the two men in front of her. When Private Pierce stumbled, she glanced at him and smiled good-naturedly. He wasn't sure if she grinned because he looked like such a fool or because she liked him. It didn't matter, though. She smiled, and that was something.

The thrill was gone, however, when a tough-looking bull of a man rushed toward Private Pierce, yelling obscenities about staying in step. Sergeant Swim's shouting was embarrassing, but not enough to block out those tender thoughts of the pretty girl walking in the snow. Private Pierce would remember that shy look on her adorable face and the very second their eyes met.

For a long, long time, he would consider that embarrassing yet poignant moment his welcome to Alva. But for now, the picture of her in his mind's eye would have to do until he could find out who she was and why she wore men's boots.

3   NEW IN TOWN

As I listened to Mr. Pierce and pictured the POW camp in my mind, my thoughts were suddenly interrupted by the sounds of a car coming up the road. I couldn't see what kind of car it was until it squealed right up the driveway toward us with its blinding headlights aimed directly at the water trough.

"Who in the world is that?" Mr. Pierce asked.

I froze for a moment, trying to think of what to do. Should I stay in the water or risk being seen in my underwear? Before I could decide, Mr. Pierce stepped out onto the grass and slipped on his overalls. Almost as an afterthought, he tossed a towel at me.

With Mr. Pierce shielding the car's bright lights, I stepped out of the water, put the towel around my waist, and tried to see who was paying the surprise visit. The car skidded to a stop several feet from the water trough as it kicked up a nice, dirty dust cloud. Now the dust hung heavily in the air, obscuring the car's headlights and giving Mr. Pierce and I a good coat of dirt on our wet bodies. The driver left the motor running and kept on the lights. He stepped out and walked toward us in a kind of swaggering, prideful step. I couldn't see his face, but Mr. Pierce must have recognized him. The old farmer's shoulders slumped like he'd had the air sucked right out of him. It was someone he didn't care for. I could see that much.

The night air felt cool against my wet body as I struggled to pull on my jeans and button up the fly. I cocked my head to one side to try and get a better look at the stranger without drawing attention to myself. He was a tall, squarely built man, about the same age as Mr. Pierce, but well dressed in pleated slacks, starched shirt and a vest. From what I could see, the stranger looked nothing like any of the farmers around Alva.

Noticing me, he moved past Mr. Pierce and leaned down, staring into my face. I gripped the towel and stepped back, almost stumbling. I had seen a few rough-looking people before, but this man—he wasn't just rough, he looked evil. His eyes were two black dots suspended in deep sockets without a trace of emotion. His forehead was large, thick, like a cliff above a cave. For a moment, he stood there looking down at me, a sober, somewhat sinister look on his face.

Beads of bathwater trickled off the back of my head, down along my spine, and goose bumps formed along my wet, dusty skin.

When he finally spoke, his voice was guttural and his expressions were creepy.

"Well, well, Henry," he said. "I heard you got a boy working for you. But this one looks too young and too scrawny to be much help around here."

Mr. Pierce tried to answer, but the stranger cut him off.

"Hell, son," he said. "You look like a wet rat that just crawled up from the creek." Then he grinned and leaned even closer to me, "Why don't you get back up to the house while I have a little chat with this ole man here?"

His voice had a deep, harsh tone, and he spoke with some unknown authority. I glanced at Mr. Pierce. His face had a frightened, embarrassed expression. My knees started shaking, but I didn't want to leave a helpless old farmer alone with the stranger.

"No, sir," I said. Then a bit sheepishly, "I didn't finish my bath yet. I'll just wait here."

The stranger stopped smiling. His face grew mean and threatening, and his breath smelled as foul as a can of dead worms.

"Look, kid, I don't know who you are, and it doesn't matter anyway. You best take your towel, your soap, and your rubber ducky and get into that house before I kick your butt so hard you won't be able to wipe it till New Year's."

Mr. Pierce, who had been staring down at the ground, looked up at me and spoke softly, "Matt, go on ahead. I'll be along in a few minutes." His eyes were moist, and his expression betrayed the hurt that he didn't want me to see.

"Yes, sir," I said.

I went inside, but watched from a dark corner of the kitchen window, puzzled at the situation going on outside. The two men stood in front of the truck with only the harsh light beaming from the headlights, illuminating their silhouettes. The tall stranger did most of the talking while pointing his finger accusingly at Mr. Pierce. Mr. Pierce stood there looking at the ground, saying little or nothing to the man. After a few minutes, the stranger got back into his car, spinning it around in the dirt driveway, as he sped back into the night.

Mr. Pierce walked back into the house, head down, shoulders slumped. When he was inside, I turned toward him.

"What was that all about?" I asked. "Who was that jerk?"

"Wish I had a cigarette," he said. He ignored my question and walked through the house toward the stairs.

"Who was that jerk?" I repeated.

"Always run out when I need one the most," the farmer said, still acting as if he hadn't heard my questions.

"Come on, Mr. Pierce. Who was he?"

I followed him up to the attic, where he fell on the mattress without even taking off his clothes. "I owe him some money," he said. "Don't worry about it, son. Turn the lights off. I'm bushed."

I went back downstairs, locked the doors, and turned out all the lights. Returning to the attic, I pulled the cord on the dusty overhead bulb. The little room grew dark and quiet. So quiet I could hear Mr. Pierce breathe. I waited there on my mattress across the room; waited for him to say something, something that might explain what had happened. Instead, he just lay in the dark and kept to himself.

Mr. Pierce never said another word that night. Out of respect, I lay quietly without asking, all the questions haunting my mind. His breathing was heavy for a long time; then it eventually slowed to normal. I closed my eyes. Even with my eyes closed, I could still see those two black dots watching me and that cold empty stare. A chill went along my back and made the hairs on the back of my neck stand on end. I strained to think of something less frightening, but I just couldn't. I opened my eyes and gazed out the window at the stars, but they too were alive with mystery. A cluster of stars that resembled the face of a ghastly, evil man looked down at me. I turned face down on the lumpy mattress. I took in the familiar, musty odor of the old mattress and tried my best to sleep.

#

The next morning was Saturday, a day for a change of scenery and a chance to see Alva. I hurriedly pulled on my jeans, ran a comb through my hair, and headed downstairs. A pleasant, familiar smell greeted me before I reached the kitchen. What in the world was going on?

In the warm, cluttered country kitchen, Mr. Pierce sat at the table drinking coffee from his favorite white mug. I stood near the stove, feeling its heat, recognizing the heavenly aroma of biscuits baking in the oven.

"What's going on?" I asked. "Did you win the $64,000 question and hire a cook?"

"No," he said.

"Well, who's cooking the biscuits?"

"I am."

"Well, they sure smell great. I didn't know you could cook biscuits. Why didn't you tell me before now?"

"I don't know," he said. He stood up and walked over to the oven. "Guess I thought we needed something extra this morning." I stood in front of the oven, taking in the amazing smell of good food.

"Watch out!" Mr. Pierce said. He pulled the oven door open, which created a warm gust of escaping air.

"These look done to me," he said. "Hand me that towel over there."

We both sat down at the table and ate the biscuits with a little butter and homemade blackberry jam his niece had given him. I drank a cup of stout coffee after putting four spoons of sugar into it. It wasn't that I liked the taste so much, but drinking coffee made me feel more mature.

I sipped the strong, black liquid while glancing over the rim of my cup. Mr. Pierce sat with one arm across the back of his wooden chair, his body twisted sideways as he gazed out the kitchen window. The gentle morning light filtered through the dusty window, casting its soothing rays over the thoughtful farmer. Again I held my tongue. I wanted to question him about the stranger. I figured he didn't want to talk about it. The truth was, as my grandmother would say, it wasn't any of my business. I continued munching on the best breakfast I'd had since being on the farm. Mr. Pierce got up and walked toward the door, closely guarding his mysterious secret.

#

To most people, the thought of driving into a little town like Alva, Oklahoma, might not seem too exciting. But if they had been working on Mr. Pierce's farm with no TV and little or no conversation, they may have seen things a bit differently. I know I did.

We approached the town from the south side. A two-lane highway ran past the town, and off to one side sat a small college, Northwestern State College. Mr. Pierce drove past the college and turned off the highway at Alva's one lonely stoplight. From there, he drove a bit north toward the center of the city as I gazed out the truck's window at the bustling little community.

A narrow, two-lane street cut the town of Alva in half from east to west. On both sides of the road were small buildings and shops, adorning the center of town. To me, it looked just like any other small town in western Oklahoma. There were cafés, a hardware store, and a five-and-dime. At the end of Main Street, where the street crossed the railroad tracks, was a ten-story concrete wheat silo. Mr. Pierce pointed to the silo.

"That's where we will be taking wheat come harvest time."

"It's sure big," I said.

"Yep," he said. "Let's drive back into town now."

After two weeks, I was thoroughly enjoying the change of scenery from the dilapidated old farm. The sidewalks and streets were full of activity. Half of the people dressed like farmers and the others looked as though they were town folks.

Mr. Pierce parked in the shade of one of the large oak trees lining the street along the city square. We got out of the truck slowly and faced each other across the pickup's cluttered bed. I felt slightly excited, hoping he would let me prowl around a little on my own.

Mr. Pierce took a brown handkerchief out of his pocket and wiped the sweat from his forehead. He put his cap back on his head, carefully adjusting the brim. Then he glanced over at his reflection in the barbershop window. Maybe I wasn't the only one with a little prowling on my mind. "Well, Matt," he said. "Think you can stay out of trouble?"

"Yes, sir!" I answered with a bit more enthusiasm than was necessary.

"Got any pocket money?" he asked.

"No, sir," I admitted.

"Here, take this with you in case you see something in the five-and-dime." He handed me a fifty-cent piece and a quarter. I accepted it, gladly.

"Thank you, sir."

He started to walk away, then turned back. "By the way," he said. "That thing last night?"

"Yes, sir."

"This is a small town, son. So let's just keep all that to ourselves."

"Okay," I agreed. I didn't know anyone in town anyway.

I watched him walk toward the bank. After he was inside, I had the funniest feeling I was being watched. I turned around. Two teenage girls sat on the fender of a shiny black Chevy. One of the girls whispered something, and they both giggled loudly. An older lady walked past the girls. They said something about her, then laughed out loud. The woman shook her head and walked on.

The two girls were about my age but dressed like girls much older and much wilder. Tight jeans, blouses with the top button undone, and collars pulled up like a rock-and-roll singer. Their clothes and their rebellious attitude made them appear out of place compared with the other people I had seen in town. The shorter girl wore a pair of skintight jeans and a boy's white shirt, oversized for her thin body. I felt a little uneasy as I noticed it was unbuttoned just far enough to reveal part of her white bra. My eyes lingered for a second or two. Then I consciously turned my eyes in another direction.

I looked, instead, at her friend: brown hair, teased and plastered with enough hair spray to coat the bottom of a battleship. Pink, sleeveless blouse with the collar turned up, and the shirttails tied neatly in a knot above her tiny waist. Her jeans were so tight they looked like someone had painted them on her.

Without a doubt, the second girl was the prettier of the two. And she knew it. She also knew I was looking her over. I had seen girls like these two before. They were the type of fast girls who usually hung around boys who liked to smoke, drink, and fight. Boys we called "greasers." I looked closer at the car they were sitting on and figured their boyfriends couldn't be far away. I knew it was time for me to move along.

"Hey!" One of the girls called out. "You're not from Alva, are you?"

I stopped on the sidewalk and turned back toward them. The pretty one had asked the question. She poked her friend, and they giggled again.

"No, I'm not."

"Well . . ." she demanded, dragging the word out.

"Well, what?"

"Well, where are you from, Mars?" Both girls laughed out loud.

"I'm from Tulsa," I answered.

"Big deal," she challenged with a smirk.

"I didn't say it was a big deal."

"Sure you did. Everything about you says you're a city boy. And you think it's a big deal, too."

"Okay," I said. "So where are you girls from?"

"Well, we're not from this dump!"

"That's right," her friend agreed, trying to outdo her. "We're not from this dump. We're from Enid."

"So what are you doing here?" I asked as the pretty one slid off the fender of the Chevy. She walked toward me with her thumbs tucked into the back pockets of her jeans. She had round full lips, and pretty brown eyes. For a split second, she looked sort of innocent. Changing her mind about her move toward me, she cocked her pretty head to one side, spun on her heels, and walked back toward her friend.

"We're spending the summer here with our uncle," she said.

"That's good," I said, trying to be friendly. "What's your name?"

"I'm Linda, and this is my sister, Betty. Hey, you got family here?" she demanded again in her know-it-all tone.

"No, I'm working on a farm west of town."

"Whose farm?" Betty asked.

"Henry Pierce."

Both girls laughed uproariously at my admission. "That's not a farm, and he sure ain't no farmer," Betty said.

I had stayed pretty cool so far, but that remark upset me. "Your sister's got a big mouth, Linda. Is that how people act in Enid?" I turned and tried to walk away.

Two steps into the street I heard Linda call out, "Hey, Tulsa, where you going?"

This time I walked on without answering, wishing I had ignored them the first time.

"Don't be such a snob!" Linda hollered. "Come here and take back what you said about my sister! You better come back and apologize! I mean it!"

Her shrill, whiny voice rang out a half block away. Rounding the corner, I walked quickly, not knowing or caring where I was going. Along the sidewalk, farmers in clean coveralls and women in soft summer dresses walked in the same direction that I was headed. Ahead of us was a park that looked like an inviting green oasis in the summer heat.

The afternoon heat bore down as I strolled along that blistering sidewalk. Starting to feel myself sweat a little, I glanced over my shoulder from time to time, expecting to see that Chevy screeching down the street loaded with Betty and Linda's muscle-bound boyfriends.

On the edge of the park, a group of boys was in the midst of a baseball game. Parked nearby were a couple of dozen pickups. People were arriving at the park carrying picnic baskets and holding the hands of their overeager children, who could barely contain their excitement about the fun ahead of them.

Past the baseball field, there was a lovely, tree-lined section of the park. Several families escaped the scorching sun by spreading their blankets along the grass, in the shade of a long string of birch trees. Preparations for the picnic were taking place. By the enormous size of the gathering, it appeared as if the whole county might be involved. Ten to fifteen card tables and several picnic tables were crammed with enough food to feed half the town. Behind the tables, women stood talking to each other and chasing children away from the mountains of homemade apple pies, decorated white cakes, and chocolate chip cookies. I strolled past the food, savoring the rich aroma of fried chicken and potato salad, wishing I knew one of the families. *One way or the other*, I thought, *I'm going to get some of this delicious food.*

Right at the edge of the trees, a group of elderly farmers squatted down and watched the baseball game from a distance while they caught up on the news of each other's life. One of the older men carved on a tree limb with what looked like a well-sharpened buck knife. He mentioned one name, and it was obvious they were discussing politics.

"And how about that Kennedy?" he asked. "Who in the world ever heard of a Catholic president anyway?"

The other farmers chuckled, so he continued while stroking the wood with his blade.

"And another thing," he said. "He even admitted he sent our troops into Cuba."

I perked up when I heard the discussion about Cuba, since it was Mr. Pierce's habit to listen to the news on the radio while we ate supper. It had caused me to become more interested in current events. I'm sure my teachers would have had a hard time believing it. But it was true.

When the farmer mentioned Cuba, I knew that they were talking about the recent news: President Kennedy taking responsibility for the Cuban invasion. The news had also reported the president of Cuba, Fidel Castro, had offered to give us back soldiers which he had been holding prisoner. Castro said that he would give us our soldiers if the United States would give him some new tractors. Mr. Pierce had laughed the day we heard that report. Back home, I had seen pictures of Fidel Castro on TV. I thought he looked kind of scary in his army uniform, scruffy-looking black beard, and a big Cuban cigar. I knew that Cuba was a small country, but Castro didn't seem a bit afraid of President Kennedy.

One of the other farmers pulled a clump of grass from the ground and rubbed it in his hands like he was testing it in some way. Then he smelled it. With his deep, serious voice, he spoke to the "park politicians."

"Tell you something 'bout Kennedy," he said. "Other night, my son, Kevin, came home from school and said everyone was talking about the president. Said they have a new song up there. Goes something like this; 'Since Kennedy is the leader of us, the Baptists all sit at the back of the bus.'"

The men laughed and glanced down at the ground as if embarrassed by the sound of their own laughter. At that point, someone noticed me standing there.

"Matt," he said. "What are you doing in town?" It was Dale, the general store owner.

"Hi, Dale," I said. "Mr. Pierce and I just drove over for the afternoon."

"Well, come on over and have something to eat," Dale said. He turned to one of the men squatting in the grass near him. "This is the Tulsa boy I was telling you about that's working for Henry this summer."

Dale introduced me to the group one at a time. They were friendly enough, but each one looked me over carefully. Though I felt a bit out of place, it didn't bother me too much. All I was thinking of at that point was the fried chicken and potato salad.

"You're from Tulsa, huh?" One of the men asked. He was a short, fat farmer who leaned against a tree with his arms folded across his chest. "Worked on a farm before?" he asked. A cocky smirk crossed his chubby face like a shark sizing up a tuna.

"Hey," Dale interrupted. "Give this boy a rest, will you, Perry?"

So this was Perry. He looked like a farmer who wouldn't shovel out his barn. I remembered the remark Dale had made that first day in the general store and it made me grin.

"What's so funny, son?" Perry asked. I glanced around and shuffled my feet as the other men waited for me to answer. "Oh, I was just thinking about all that food over there," I lied.

"You mean you don't like Henry Pierce's cooking?" Dale quipped. The farmers smiled and looked at each other as if they understood, and Perry let it pass.

"Don't worry, Matt," Dale said. "You're mighty welcome here." He scratched his head as he continued, "Hey, come with me a minute. I want you to meet my son before we eat."

Dale led me across the park to the baseball field, chattering away as I tried to keep up with his long-legged pace. I wanted to ask him about the stranger who visited us on the farm, figuring he might know what was going on. When we were right behind the backstop, Dale paused. Noise from the excited onlookers grew louder. A runner sprinted to home plate. The crowd went wild and the catcher, a boy as big as Paul Bunyan, stood his ground and tagged the sliding runner. Dirt and dust filled the air, making it almost impossible to see players or the umpire. As the crowd screamed their cheers and protested, the ump yelled, "Out."

I wasn't interested in the baseball game; I had other things on my mind. With dust settling down I turned to Dale and blurted out, "Dale, did you ever know a mean-looking guy about six-feet-four who drives a big car?"

Dale never heard my question, because the out at home plate ended the game. Most of the people were not happy. Several people yelled and complained about the tag at home, but then the crowd broke up. Everyone was walking around us in every direction. Dale headed across the ball field, and I followed him. He spoke to a few people, then pushed his way through the little crowd. He turned around and motioned for me to catch up.

"Come on. I think my boy's over here." I did my best to follow him through the disorganized shuffle of bodies and then bumped right into the oversized catcher who was still wearing his chest padding and face mask.

The catcher put his hands on his sides. His dark eyes stared at me angrily through the frame of his mask. "Watch where you're going there, stupid," he said.

"Sorry, man," I said. His bulky size and the look on his sweaty face were intimidating.

Paul Bunyan pushed his face mask up over the top of his head. Sweat dripped from his forehead down across his face. The aroma from the dirt and sweat on his uniform caught me off guard. I stepped back, giving him plenty of space. Without another word, he turned toward his teammates, then ran to catch up with them. As he ran, he glanced back at me.

I turned back in the direction I had been walking and looked through the crowd for Dale. The crowd was thick, making it impossible to see him. I hurried forward, trying to spot him, and as I did, I bumped into someone else, someone much softer and someone who smelled much better than the sweaty oversized catcher. The collision almost knocked me to the ground. As I regained my balance, I looked into the face of another stranger. Long brown hair, beautiful blue eyes, and a slightly tanned face. This stranger looked at me with a shy but cute grin on her face. People were crowded all around us, but I couldn't see them. I could only see blue eyes.

"Uh . . . um, excuse me," I stuttered. She smiled and started to answer, but before she had a chance to speak, Dale was there beside us.

"Matt," Dale interrupted, "I can't find Jerry anywhere." Dale seemed to notice me staring at the girl. "Well now, it looks like you met someone else though."

"Sort of. But we haven't introduced ourselves," I said. *That sounded stupid*, I thought.

"This young lady is Carol Rudy," Dale said. "Carol, this is Matt Turner."

We said hi to each other, and I waited for Dale to say something else. Better yet, he could leave. I was in luck because Dale did both.

"Carol," Dale said. "I'm going to look around for Jerry. Will you take Matt over to the picnic tables? I've invited him to eat with us. I'll find Jerry and catch up with you."

"Okay," Carol said, smiling nervously. I liked the way she talked. Dale resumed his search as Carol and I stood just looking at each other. I liked the quiet, relaxed way she stood. Neither of us moved. So I decided to break our little sound barrier.

"Are you hungry?" I asked. Carol didn't answer, but nodded her head. I was even impressed by the cute way she nodded her head.

"Well," I said. "I'm so hungry if they let me loose near one of those tables, I might try to eat some of the silverware."

Carol giggled as we walked toward the picnic area now surrounded by people. Our route wasn't very straight, but more of a half circle that took us quite a way from the picnic and allowed me more time to try and get to know her. She was bashful and hard to read, but seemed to be enjoying herself and didn't appear to be in a hurry to join the others.

At the edge of the park, we came to a children's swing set. Luckily for us, most of the children were in line to eat, so we were able to find a couple of empty swings suspended from a tall wooden frame. I felt comfortable with Carol the minute we met. Yet, I felt tongue-tied-unsure what to talk about. But it didn't seem to matter to her. For the first time I could remember, I was with a girl who didn't need a constant flow of conversation.

Always before, it seemed like the girls at school talked every single minute. Yak, yak, yak. They talked about everything from Elvis Presley to the school's new shop teacher. Sometimes, when I stood in the hall between classes, I was glad when the bell rang so that I could say good-bye to the girl I was pretending to listen to at the time.

It seemed different with Carol. We could talk or not talk; it didn't seem that important. So we just swung for a while and stole quick glances at each other. And then, Carol started our first real conversation.

"Did your parents buy a farm near Alva?" she asked.

"No," I said.

"Do you have relatives in town?"

"Nope," I said.

Carol glanced at me. Her eyes narrowed suspiciously.

"Are you from Enid?"

"No," I said, now grinning. "I'm spending the summer working on a farm west of town."

"Oh, really. Whose farm?"

"Henry Pierce's farm," I said hesitantly, waiting for her reaction. And she didn't let me down either. Her cute little face grew serious, almost grave. You'd have thought I mentioned the name of a Cuban spy.

"Did you say Henry Pierce?"

But before I could answer, a car skidded around the corner with its unmuffled exhaust pipes blasting the neighborhood like a hollow machine gun.

As people in all sections of the busy park turned toward the loud, speeding vehicle, the noise vibrated throughout the park. I glanced at the ruckus. A taste of surging fear rose in my stomach like bile burning into my throat. There they were, the wild sisters from Enid, as loud and rebellious as the convertible they rode in. Two older boys sat in the front seat of the Chevy convertible. The car slowed a little, then slid up to the curb, one tire jumping onto the grass. The other three passengers looked at Betty and seemed to be asking her a question. Betty glanced around the park, then looked in the general direction of Carol and me. Betty's expression changed from a scowl to a sinister grin as her hand came up. She pointed directly at me. Now everyone in that car and most everyone in the park, including Carol, was looking toward me.

4 FISTFIGHT

The unwelcome car filled with giggling teenagers was parked about 30 yards from Carol and me. They looked more out of place in Alva than I did. The car doors flew open, and faster than I could say "I don't know these people," four obnoxious-looking kids jumped out of the Chevy and stomped right up to us.

Betty and her sister strolled toward us behind a couple of tall, husky boys with thick, greasy hair, long sideburns, and openly rebellious attitudes. The two boys swaggered across the grass, wearing black short-sleeved muscle shirts, rolled up tightly on their bulging biceps. They completed their James Dean look with beltless Levis, white socks, and black penny loafers. Sunlight glinted off the shiny two-inch taps on the toes of the taller boy's shoes. I knew the metal taps weren't there for dancing; they were for fighting. I had seen mean guys like these two in Tulsa. Guys who would fight with their hands, their knives, and their feet. And if they ever got their opponent on the ground, the poor guy would suffer from the relentless kicking made more ruthless by those metal taps. Once I watched as a poor high school student got kicked like that and wound up in the hospital for several weeks. Now, more than ever, I wished I had never turned around to speak to either of those Enid girls.

Carol watched them nervously as they walked toward us. I wanted to say something to her, but there was no time for an explanation. I tried to keep cool, but anyone could see I was afraid.

Now the two greasers were right in front of us, making a show of being right in my face. A cigarette dangled from the mouth of the taller, tougher boy. Linda stood behind the tall boy with her ever-present smirk.

"John," Linda whined. "That's the guy who called Betty a scumbag and said she has a big mouth."

"Is that right?" John asked. He flexed his bulky biceps and took a long drag from his cigarette.

I didn't want any trouble right in front of Carol. And besides that, these guys were at least two years older and thirty pounds heavier than me. Things weren't looking so good. Ten minutes ago, I had met the most beautiful girl in Alva, and now I was about to rumble with two boys that looked like they had just broken out of San Quentin. A fight was inevitable. So I tried to think of how I could get in the first punch. It was something my brother had taught me a long time ago. Someone was about to score the first punch, that was for sure.

"Hey, buddy," I said, trying to smooth things over. "I don't have a problem with these girls or you either, for that matter."

"Hey, punk," he snorted. "I didn't ask you if you had a problem." His face was sweaty and threatening, his expression as cool as a glass of iced tea. His green, revolting eyes peered deep into my tortured soul, sensing my palpable fear.

Taking another step closer to me, he said, "Listen. This is all I want to know. Did you call my girlfriend a scumbag or not?"

I swallowed. "Your girlfriend?"

"That's right, punk," he said. Before I knew it, his large hands shoved me backward, catching me off balance. Wavering slightly, I caught myself and stayed upright.

"Nobody calls Betty anything. Now, you apologize to her, you hear?"

I didn't want to apologize for something I didn't say, but it was starting to seem like a good idea. Maybe it was a way to avoid getting my teeth kicked in. I glanced at Carol, who had stepped back several feet, looking pretty frightened. The other greaser, shorter but no less threatening, stood close to Carol. An evil, depraved grin crossed his pockmarked face. Somehow, I had to come up with a way out of this.

"All right," I said. "I'm sorry."

The second greaser raised his fist in the air in celebration. "Can you dig it?" he said. "I told you he won't rumble. Let's watch him crumble."

The two Enid girls laughed and were looking pretty smug about that time, but I didn't care. I just wanted them to go away. Even John looked as though he might be ready to leave, allowing me to breathe a little easier. It was a pleasant feeling.

Without saying a word, John slowly took his cigarette out of his mouth, held it near my face, and flipped it into the air, high above my head. I looked up, unconsciously watching the glowing inch of white paper rising into the sky. I never saw what happened next.

He may have hit me with his right hand, his left, or both; I have no clue. And what difference does it make? The sudden blow caught me by complete surprise and hurled me backward onto the grass.

One second, I was looking up at his cigarette, and the next instant, I was plowing grass with my nose. My head was spinning like a windmill as I tried desperately to get up. Dazed, I looked up at John's ugly face, daring me to do so.

"Get up, punk!" he shouted. "Get up."

The two Enid girls and his ugly pal were close by, screaming wildly. "Do it again, man! Hit him again!"

Slowly I stood up, only to see him coming at me for another attack. Quickly, I darted across the grass, avoiding his fist, but too slow to avoid getting kicked in the side. The large steel taps on his right shoe dug into my skin like a claw hammer.

I got up on one leg, only to get kicked again. This time, he kicked me so hard I crashed back to the ground. Now the big guy hung out closer to the girls, savoring his power.

Maybe it was my turn.

Struggling, I stood up, dazed, and suffering from his brutal attacks. He turned toward me as I clenched my fist and watched the evil smile on his face. It was my turn. His hands were down, so I pulled back to swing, ready to hit him with everything I had.

"Hey! You boys break this up!" someone behind me yelled. This guy was a native Oklahoman and a deputy sheriff. He grabbed both of us and looked strong enough to whip both of us at one time.

"Wait a minute," I pleaded. "I didn't do anything."

Without answering, the deputy led us to his car parked at an angle in front of the black Chevy. An angry crowd from the picnic had gathered. They seemed shocked that such a thing could happen in their little town. I stood there, hoping someone would come forward to stand up for me. Couldn't everyone see I hadn't thrown a single punch?

I turned to look toward Carol. She was right behind me with a frightened look on her face. I felt the officer yank my shirt. But, before I got into his car, I noticed an elderly lady near Carol. The woman had her arm around Carol and seemed to be leading her away from the crowd. Carol went with her but looked back at me several times.

As the police car pulled forward, I sat in the back seat while John sat in the front. Glancing through the window, I searched the crowd again for Carol, but I couldn't see her. All I could see were the enraged faces of the country people who had come to town to enjoy a Saturday picnic and were shocked at how fast their peaceful little park had turned into a violent free-for-all.

The deputy drove across town while the Enid sisters and greaser number two stayed right behind us in the Chevy convertible. We stopped halfway down a residential street. The deputy opened the car door and let John out. What was going on? He didn't give the boy a warning or anything. He just opened the door and let him out. John looked back at me with a half grin on his face.

"What about me?" I asked as John stood beside his car, combing his long, greasy hair. From the Chevy, I heard someone yell, but I couldn't understand them. The deputy ignored my question and the barrage of insults from the teenagers. He drove to the police station without another word.

Inside the police station, the large deputy sheriff had me sit on an uncomfortable wooden bench in the hallway. I sat there for what seemed like two or three hours. The police station was quiet. Perhaps there were no prisoners that day, or maybe it was because the deputy ran a tough jail. I don't know. However, it was quiet and had the lingering smell of Pine-Sol.

While I waited, I thought about Carol Rudy. How disappointed she had looked as they drove me away. And what a fool I was for falling for that greaser's stupid trick.

"Come in here," the deputy yelled.

I got off the hard wooden bench, my muscles aching and sore from the fight. Depressed and worried, I sauntered into the deputy's little office where he sat behind a small, cluttered desk. Leaning back in his chair, the enormous Indian cop laced his fingers together behind his head. His face was rugged, with a strong square jaw, but his eyes were bright and kind.

"Ever been in trouble before?"

"You mean like in school and stuff?"

"No, no, the police," he said. "Ever been in trouble with the police?"

"No, sir."

The deputy looked at me as if he were trying to figure out if I was lying or not.

"I guess you're telling the truth," he said. "What are you doing in Alva?"

"I'm working on a farm. We just came into town to spend the afternoon."

"Whose farm you work on?" This time his voice had a bit more of an interested tone instead of the probing police sound of it.

"Henry Pierce," I said. I waited for him to laugh.

"Good man, old Henry," he said, surprising the heck out of me.

"You know Mr. Pierce?"

"Sure. Henry and my pa were friends years ago. When I was a kid, we spent a lot of time hunting on Henry's old farm property."

"You mean that section of wheat about five miles west of his house?"

"That's right," he grinned. "Through the years, I bet I shot two hundred rabbits and at least ten deer on that section."

I was surprised and happy that he had good things to say about Mr. Pierce. But I was still sore that he let that greaser off so easy.

"That's great," I said. Then more selfishly, "Think I can go now?"

"Oh sure, kid," he said, sitting up in his chair and putting his hands on the desk. His face transformed from a smile back to a more serious police officer look.

"Now you seem like a pretty nice kid, so I'm going to warn you about something. Don't start any more trouble around Alva. Make sure you don't have any more run-ins with either of Thurman Spencer's darling little nieces. You understand?"

"No, sir, I don't understand. I don't know Thurman Spencer or his nieces."

The deputy scratched his head and grinned. "Well, you know them all right. His two nieces were the innocent little things trying to get your head kicked in."

"Those two girls? Sir, I just met them today, and they did most of the talking. Who's their uncle anyway, the mayor of Alva?"

"Their uncle's not the mayor, but he owns the mayor. Thurman Spencer is a big shot in this town, so I think it's best you stay away from those girls. I got you out of that park and brought you down here for your own good. If Thurman Spencer would have seen that fight and had thought his nieces were being bothered, he would have told me to find some way to put you in jail. Son, he has a lot of power around here. He's wealthy and politically strong; he's large and he's mean. So stay away from him. Whatever you do, stay away from Thurman Spencer."

The way the deputy described him made me wonder if he could be the guy who'd bullied Mr. Pierce out by the windmill. I wanted to know more, but the deputy stood up and walked me to the front door. I looked out into the street. It was already dark, and

I didn't know where to go next. Once again, the deputy seemed to know what I was thinking.

"You trying to figure out where to find ole Henry?"

I nodded my head.

"Try the pool hall, two blocks over."

"Thanks," I said.

Stepping out into the night, I sighed. I had learned more about the little town that afternoon than I wanted to know. But there were still a lot of questions to be answered.

I quickly followed the deputy's directions to the pool hall, and once inside, I could see that the smoky bar had lots of cowboys, city folks, and farmers. Several of them wore large western hats, blue jeans, and drank beer like it was water.

A strong, thick mixture of cigarette smoke and stale beer filled the dimly lit room as I edged my way carefully through the local crowd. I could barely make out the customers' faces at first, but after a moment, my eyes adjusted to the darkness.

From the back room a loud jukebox blared the chorus of Elvis Presley's "Don't Be Cruel." The tables were crowded together and the aisle was overpopulated with legs, feet, and a variety of boots. Inching my way forward, I carefully navigated the obscure, cumbersome lounge, squinting in the dark like an older man who had just lost his spectacles. Unable to find Mr. Pierce in the bar, I continued my search in the back room. A large, immovable pool table was the first thing that greeted me in the pool room, and its bulk, which I collided with, caused me to walk even slower and gave a few of the pool players a nice laugh. Two other pool tables adorned the room with bright, circular lights suspended above them. Players, some standing, some seated, and most holding beer cans, stared as I walked past them, careful not to interrupt a game or bump into anything else.

People stared at me as they had at the park and in the streets of Alva, but it didn't bother me as much. I guess I was starting to get used to it. Ignoring the curious customers, I focused on finding Mr. Pierce, getting the heck out of there, and maybe finding something to eat. I had missed out on that great-looking picnic at the park. Just past the third table, I walked around the last group of players. A half-empty rack of pool cues hung against the wall, and below it, there was a small wooden table with a couple of chairs. It was empty except for the gray-haired man slumped across it, snoring loudly. Standing beside him, having mixed feelings of relief and concern, I tugged at the back of his coveralls. "Mr. Pierce, it's time to go home."

"Hey, Henry!" someone yelled. "It's your shot." A few people laughed, but Mr. Pierce only moaned softly and moved his head to one side in slow motion.

"I said I wanted a drink," Mr. Pierce mumbled. He lifted his head slightly,

"Give me a . . . drink."

Clunk! The old farmer's head hit the table solidly, but without fazing him. Laughter filled that section of the room as the players enjoyed someone else's humiliation.

I shook my head, disappointed and depressed. The old man looked helpless, and he looked all too familiar. Just like my father when my father drank too much. But I didn't have time to think about that, since it was up to me to drive home. Sure, I knew how to handle the pickup, but would I be able to avoid the police?

A few minutes later, I sat in the driver's seat after one of the bartenders helped me load Mr. Pierce's listless bulk into the truck. I started the pickup, backed into the street, and then drove slowly and cautiously out of town. Reaching the dark, empty highway, on the south edge of Alva, I eased onto the two-lane highway to complete our long trek toward the farm. As soon as we were well out of town, I sat back in the seat a bit and eased my white-knuckled grip on the steering wheel. Cool fresh air streamed through the open windows of the old pickup, providing a welcome relief to what had been a long, hot, eventful day.

Even though a night breeze blew through the truck, my hands felt clammy on the steering wheel, as white lines along the pavement flew by in a blur. In spite of the dangerous situation, it was a struggle to stay awake. Mr. Pierce leaned against the passenger door with his head tilted back and eyes closed. But he wasn't the only one that needed rest. At that moment, sleep was an unwelcome third occupant inside that truck, and its attractive powers threated to pull me in.

The dim white light from the dashboard painted Mr. Pierce's wrinkled face. It was important for me to stay awake, so I started to think about what I had to do. First, I had to drive to the farm, then I would have to get Mr. Pierce into the house. How was I going to do that?

"Don't ride the clutch," Mr. Pierce mumbled.

I glanced over at him, and in the dim light, I could see him looking at me with one eye wide open and the other eye trying its best to stay somewhat open.

"Yes, sir," I said. "I didn't think you were awake."

"I'm doing okay," he said, his other eye now starting to appear. "Thanks for looking after me at the pool hall."

"You're welcome," I said, not sure of what to say after that. I didn't want to embarrass him.

There wasn't much talk between us during the drive. We were tired, and I guess we both had our disappointments on how our "big day" in Alva had turned out. After we got back to the farm, I parked the truck and let Mr. Pierce go on up to the attic while I scarfed down the last two leftover biscuits from breakfast. The biscuits weren't as good as the fried chicken, potato salad, and apple pie I'd missed during my hours at the jail. They were stale, hard, and flavorless, but I savored every morsel, wishing there were a few more.

The wooden stairs creaked as I crept up to the attic, half hoping that Mr. Pierce was already asleep. Lights out and tucked into my window-side mattress, I was eager for the quiet of the night to think about my day. It was silent in the room, but I thought I should say good night. But Mr. Pierce broke the silence.

"Son," he said. "You may not know it, but I was in the Army a long time before I ever drank. All my buddies drank, but I didn't much at first."

It wasn't something I would have ever asked a grown person, but he sounded like he wanted to talk about it. So I nudged him a little, "Well, why *did* you start?"

"Don't know for sure," he said. "But it seems like it all started around Thanksgiving."

"You mean at Camp Alva?" I asked. "I bet I know what happened," I said.

"Oh, you do."

"Bet you had a date with Jewel right before Thanksgiving."

"No," he said. "That wasn't it, son. Oh, sure, we were dating by then, but what happened was something a lot more serious."

"Well, what did happen?"

"Well," he started, "the MPs always called it the Thanksgiving escape."

"Escape? Really!?! Did some of the Germans escape?"

The little attic was quiet, and the only sounds heard were those of an old farmer breathing softly in the dark. It had become easy to discern the difference between his normal breathing and his sleep-breathing. He wasn't sleeping yet, that was for sure.

"Well, Matt, some did, and some didn't," he said with a kind of strange tone to his voice.

"I'd like to hear about it, if you feel like talking, that is." It was quiet for another moment or two, so quiet you could hear the creaking of the windmill turning on a late-night breeze. Then the lonely bellow of a hungry cow somewhere out in the east pasture. I could feel its pain, but was glad once again for those two biscuits. Somehow those familiar country sounds seemed to make Mr. Pierce's dilemma much less frightening to me, and I wondered if it had the same effect on him. It may have, because I heard his breathing change to longer, heavier inhales and exhales, and I knew I wouldn't find out about the escape—at least not that night.

Even on good days, Mr. Pierce had very little to say, but over the next five days or so, he kept to himself and hardly uttered a word. It made me think of how it was back home when my mother was upset about something and she gave Dad the silent treatment. I figured she did it as a kind of punishment. However, Mr. Pierce was much better at it than my mother, because he didn't want to talk. I did my best not to push him, because I figured between the incident with the big stranger and his passing out at the pool hall, the poor man had just about lost any remnant of confidence he'd ever had.

But enough is enough. After a week of the hardest work I'd ever done and Mr. Pierce barely speaking to me, I was ready to explode. We sat at the table one night without a word exchanged between us, and I had had enough of the way things were.

"Okay, I give," I said.

Mr. Pierce looked up from his plate of brown beans.

"Whaddya mean?"

"I give up. I mean, whatever I did, I'm sorry."

He pushed a piece of greasy pork across the plate and put his fork down on the table.

"You didn't do anything, son. Just forget it."

"Then why haven't you said a word since last Saturday?"

"I've had a lot on my mind," he said.

I knew that, but he did make up half of the human population on the farm, and I couldn't go on talking to myself forever.

"Mr. Pierce, how can I forget it? I don't know what to forget. Tell me what's going on."

"What's the use."

"Maybe I can help."

He walked over to the counter and put his plate and fork in a gray tin pan filled with water. He leaned against the porcelain sink, gazing out the window.

"I don't know if it's going to work out, Matt."

"If what's going to work out?"

"You staying on a broken-down farm with a drunkard."

"Sir, what are you talking about? I think we're getting along great," I lied.

He continued to stare out the window and said, "No, son."

"Mr. Pierce, I'm here for the summer, and you can't get rid of me that easily. Please, tell me what's going on so I can help."

The discouraged old farmer turned to look at me. I smiled, hoping to get him to relax. "Matt, tomorrow morning I'm going down to Dale's place to call your dad. It's probably better if you go on back, son. I'm sorry, but I think it's best."

Slowly, my smile wilted as his words sunk in. I wouldn't mind going home. I would enjoy it—just not this way. Not without knowing what was wrong and why that mean guy by the horse trough that night was bothering a nice old guy like Henry Pierce.

"I'm starting to get the hang of it around here," I pleaded. "My father is going to think *I* did something wrong, no matter what you say. He won't be happy, and I will be the one to bear the brunt of it. This isn't fair, Mr. Pierce. I . . . I . . . don't understand any of it."

The old farmer shuffled toward the front room, hesitated, turned around and came back. Back and forth across the noisy linoleum floor he paced, his boots plopping with each step, his right hand stroking his chin in deep concentration.

"Is this about Saturday night? Is that it?" I asked.

"Partly, but it doesn't matter," he said.

"The heck it doesn't. You're about to send me home, and everyone's going to think I couldn't hack it. Sure, I'll try to tell them I did a good job, but they'll laugh at me. Listen, Mr. Pierce, I don't know what's going on, but I think maybe Thurman Spencer has something to do with it."

Instantly, Mr. Pierce turned toward me, his face showing his surprise. The question had struck a deep nerve. As he sat down at the table, his wrinkled eyes squinted under thick, bushy brows. It looked as though my guess was right on the money.

"How did you find out his name?"

"Good guess," I admitted.

"What?"

"Well," I said. "Saturday I met Thurman Spencer's 'sweet' little nieces. We didn't get along very well, so I went to the park where I met a nice girl named Carol Rudy. While we were talking, the nieces came along with a couple of thugs who started a rumble."

"Started what?"

"A fight," I said, and I went on to explain the rest of it. Mr. Pierce didn't seem at all surprised by any of the story. Except for one thing, that is. "Did you say Carol Rudy?"

"Yes, sir," I said. "Do you know her?"

"I suppose I should," he said. "Remember that woman I told you about? The one I almost married?"

"Sure. You sat on the front porch and made out with her 30 years ago."

"Made what?"

"Made out. You know, hugging, kissing, and stuff like that. Kids call it 'making out' these days.

"Oh," he said, looking a bit surprised and squinting suspiciously.

"But what's that got to do with Carol?" I asked.

"A lot," he said. "The woman I . . . 'made out' with is Carol's aunt."

It was my turn to sit down. I knew Alva was a small town, but now I could see just how little it was becoming. I looked across the table at him. He smiled for the first time in several days.

"Did you happen to meet Carol's aunt?" he asked.

"No, but I think I saw her. An older woman led Carol away from the fight."

"That was her, all right. Wasn't she beautiful?"

"I don't know, sir. I didn't get a good look."

"Well, take my word for it. She's still a beautiful woman, and her niece reminds me of how she looked when she was younger."

"She must have been a knockout then."

"She sure was," he said, looking off somewhere.

"Mr. Pierce," I said, wanting to focus on his problems. "Let's get back to that guy. Thurman Spencer? Why was he up here the other night anyway?"

"He's a two-legged snake in the grass, that Thurman."

"But what's he got to do with you? Why do you let him push you around?"

Mr. Pierce looked offended, and for a second, I thought he was going to deny it. Then he took a deep breath and gave in.

"Well," he started, "Thurman and I were in the same unit in the MPs out at Camp Alva."

"Really," I said. "Was he one of your buddies?"

"I guess he was. Sort of, that is."

"What do you mean 'sort of'?"

"I mean the Germans outnumbered us by about 20 to 1. With those odds, every American soldier is your buddy. Thurman and I didn't know each other all that well, but we were both on duty that Thanksgiving. After the war, we both stayed in Alva, and he never let me forget that night. After the war, every Saturday night, when I went to the pool hall, I would find him there, drinking, just like me."

"What's wrong with that?"

"Nothing, I guess, but last year we had the best crop of wheat in Oklahoma history. I made over twenty-two bushels an acre. Then one night, just after harvest was over, I was down at the pool hall celebrating. After drinking a while with Thurman and listening to the jukebox till the place closed, I got in my truck and headed home.

"It was a rainy night, and someone in the bar said the main highway was closed off. So I decided to drive out along the old dirt road. I had just passed the cemetery when I crashed into something. My head hit the steering wheel, and it knocked me out cold. When I came to, it was pouring rain. I was lying on the ground looking up at Thurman Spencer.

"We were both soaked. Thurman leaned down and called me an old drunk. He said I'd done a darn fool thing this time. He pointed over his shoulder and told me I'd rammed the back end of a car. There was a man severely injured in the front seat.

"I tried to get up and see, but Thurman held me down and told me there was nothing anyone could do for that guy. He said I'd better get on back home, and then he asked me if I could drive. I told him, 'Yes, I can drive.'

"Before I went to my truck, I went around to the front of that wrecked car and looked in the window. Sure enough, there was a man slumped across the front seat with blood all over him. I stood in the rain and tried to open the door to see who he was, but Thurman grabbed me and pushed me back to my truck.

"'We gotta go get the police,' I said. But Thurman said he would take care of it because I was so drunk. He said otherwise they'd throw me in prison. So I did like he said. I guess he took care of it all right. The next morning he came out here and told me the man in the car had sure enough died. I was shocked."

"Didn't the police want to talk to you about it?"

"No, Thurman said the chief of police owed him a big favor. He told me to keep quiet. I didn't know what to do. I was so frightened. About a week later Thurman came back, but this time he was starting to act funny—not like an old Army buddy at all. He told me the chief of police wanted money or he was going to make big trouble. I asked him why we didn't just go and see the chief. Thurman told me he had to give the chief $4,000, so now I owed that much to Thurman."

Mr. Pierce took off his hat and scratched the top of his head. He replaced his hat and looked at me with those sad, penetrating eyes of his.

"Son," he said. "The only way I can pay him back is to give him half of the harvest money when we bring the wheat in."

I looked closely at Mr. Pierce. No wonder he had let Thurman Spencer bully him around the other night. It was like he owed his soul to the devil. I felt frightened for him and wondered if there was any way I could help. It was a lot worse than I had imagined. We had to do something, but I had no idea what.

"Maybe we should go and talk to the police, Mr. Pierce. I met one of the deputies the other day, and he said he knew you. He said you were friends with his father." Mr. Pierce looked at me, and for a moment, his humble expression gave me hope. Then he frowned again.

"No," he said. "We can't do that, Matt. I was drunk that night, and they'll call it leaving the scene of an accident. Thurman Spencer told me what the law says about that, and it's too late now. I should have just stayed right there until the police came."

"All right," I said. "But at least let me stay and try to help you with the harvest," I pleaded. "I'll keep your secret."

He shook his head, and his shoulders slumped as if he were carrying the weight of the world on them. In a way, I guess he was.

After a long pause, he finally gave me my answer. "Okay, Matt. Let's see how it goes."

"Thank you, sir."

I was glad to be able to stay, but I was wondering how in the world I could ever help him out of this terrible situation.

Later that night after we had gone to bed, I stared out the attic window. The sky was black, without the slightest trace of light. A gentle breeze drifted into the attic window with its smell fresh and moist. Even a city boy knows the clean scent of rain when it's on the way. I could feel it coming.

Soon, a bolt of light sliced the sky to the southwest. From time to time another orange shaft illuminated the wheat fields for a few seconds here and there, then darkness fell again.

The air grew cooler as the first drops of rain fell against the tin roof of the barn, hitting it like tiny pebbles. At first, the rain struck in short, slow intervals, then the drops increased, and soon it was a soft, steady beat—an evening shower. I relaxed, closed my eyes, and thought about Mr. Pierce's problem. At last, I knew what kind of trouble Thurman Spencer held over him like an anvil. Somehow I figured there might be more to it all. Maybe more to it than Thurman Spencer was telling. I didn't see him as the kind of guy who would do anyone a favor.

At least I'd found the first piece of the puzzle. But knowing this much only made me hungry to find out more. With the steady beat of rain on the roof, I pulled an old quilt across my waist, closed my eyes, and tried to picture the accident Mr. Pierce had described. Slowly my imagination went from a faint glimpse of Mr. Pierce looking into a crashed car to the fistfight at the picnic, and on to the snow falling on three Germans at the POW camp. Soon I lost the battle of wills, as the fresh, cool, rain-soaked air filled the attic and sleep won the imaginary war inside my mind.

5   GOLDEN WHEAT

After my third week on the farm, the wheat became golden and brittle, and to my inexperienced eyes, it looked like it was ready to be harvested. Over the past few days, I had watched as Mr. Pierce had walked waist-high into the fields. Each morning he snatched several heads of wheat in different rows, examining them carefully. He rubbed his callused hands together in a circular motion, crumbling the wheat, separating the chaff from the grain. It was his midmorning ritual.

But one morning he watched the chaff fly away and studied the grain in one palm. He walked back to the truck with a strange look on his face. It was an expression I had never seen on his face before—determination. He got into the truck and glanced across at me.

"Matt," he said. "I guess we better hook up the combine and pull it over to that old homestead. It's time to bring this crop in."

"Wow," I said. I wasn't sure what else to say, but I felt excited that it was finally time to start. It was almost enough to make me forget the other things causing all the heartache recently. Right then, I was just thrilled I would be able to work on a harvest and do something meaningful. Mr. Pierce had taught me to drive everything on the farm, and I think he was getting tired of practicing. Now it was time to work.

"Want me to drive the tractor or the truck?" I asked.

"Well," he said. "Since we have to go on the highway for a few miles, I better drive the tractor, and you follow me close behind in the pickup truck. Keep her tucked in close now."

"Yes, sir," I said.

After packing a lunch and a Mason jar of iced tea, we started off toward the section of land he called "the old homestead." It was the original section he had purchased from an old farm family after the war. To get to it, we had to take the highway for a few miles, turn off onto a winding dirt road and follow it another three miles. It was only five or six miles from his farmhouse, but it was different there. The fields at the old homestead were nice and flat, surrounded by oak trees and blackjack trees. And the soil was different too, darker, more fertile somehow. And there were large rocks stacked evenly near the road.

We left the farm, and Mr. Pierce drove ahead on the tractor, pulling the old combine. I crept along behind him in the red storage truck doing about twenty miles per hour. It seemed like the slowest I had ever driven, and I wanted desperately to go around him. But I knew better. It felt like it took forever to get there, and the closer we got, the more my excitement grew.

As we drew up almost even with the wheat field, we passed the foundation of the old family farmhouse. It lay there in a crumpled heap—a stark, yet silent reminder of those struggling pioneer days. Beyond it stretched a vast, healthy wheat field, about a mile long and a half-mile wide, guarded by its trees and boulders along the perimeter. A barbed-wire fence ran along the front of the property with a wide gate on one end.

We pulled up close to the gate, and I jumped down from the truck to remove a loop of wire from the top of a wooden post. I opened the gate to let Mr. Pierce drive through, then I drove the truck in, leaving the gate wide open according to Mr. Pierce's instructions. By the time I caught up with him, Mr. Pierce had driven along the inside of the fence and parked. All alongside us as far as my eyes could see, the tall stalks of wheat grew thick and golden. It was a beautiful sight, and I was thrilled and kind of scared all at the same time.

With the John Deere tractor idling slowly, Mr. Pierce climbed down and explained again how we would work the equipment, "I'm going to take the first round or two," he said. "Why don't you stand up on the combine and watch what I do. Pay close attention now to how close I put the left tire to the outside edge of wheat. That's how I aim the combine. It's pretty simple, but if you miss some wheat, you'll have to turn around. And this thing isn't easy to turn. But when you do have to turn, slow the tractor down first, then turn. That's about all there is to do. Just watch, and in a while, I'll let you try it."

It was almost noon when we started. Mr. Pierce drove the tractor and pulled the combine right into the uncut wheat. As he went forward, the combine's giant wooden wheels, called reapers, chopped the wheat and scooped it into its mainframe. Long stalks of golden grain tumbled into the belly of the mainframe and there they were cut and threshed and tossed about. A few seconds later, they flew out separate places; the precious grain flowing into the large holding tank and the discarded stalks feeding overboard. Behind the combine, rows of short stubs remained in the ground like freshly cut grass, as the useless, straw-like stalks were carried away by the south wind. As the combine crossed the massive wheat field, it left a beautiful pattern, row after generous row.

Around and around the field we went as dust, dirt, and straw whooshed continuously behind the tractor and combine. It was a bumpy ride at times, but thoroughly enjoyable, and from time to time Mr. Pierce looked back, his wide grin showing his excitement. As Mr. Pierce maneuvered into a turn, he allowed for the distance it took to bring the combine around behind him. It was a skill he had perfected and one that I was itching to try. I hadn't felt so excited since I made the football team in junior high. But through the excitement, I intently studied everything he did so I would be ready when it was my turn. Chugging along, the combine's massive wooden blades swished through the stalks of wheat, slashing them to the ground, and row after row we began to harvest wheat.

From time to time, I surveyed the large holding tank where the precious grain accumulated. Slowly, it covered the bottom, then gradually rose higher and higher. When it was almost to the top, I reached in, grabbing a handful. I held it, studied it, and popped it in my mouth. The first time I'd eaten fresh-cut wheat since Mr. Pierce had told me about chewing it. The grain had a strangely familiar taste. Not sweet, but fresh and wholesome. After a while I chewed it like gum.

When we had completed two trips around the large field, the holding bin was just about full. "It's up to the top," I yelled. Mr. Pierce nodded and drove us over to the big red truck. He pulled up beside it while I prepared to transfer the wheat to the truck. At that moment, I secretly felt important, but still a bit scared. After all, this part of the operation depended on me.

The wheat transfer was straightforward; the grain was fed from the grain bin in the combine through a long metal spout where it spewed into the large rectangular open bed of the empty truck. As soon as I had positioned the spout above the truck bed and switched a small lever, the old combine was pumping a steady flow of beautiful grain into the red truck.

This golden wheat quickly filled the bottom of the truck and made a large mound on one side. After half of the wheat was transferred, I carefully moved the spout toward the front of the bed to even out the load. A fine mist of metallic-like wheat dust rose from the growing heap into the hot afternoon air. It only took ten minutes to unload what had taken more than one hour to cut.

We had our first load of wheat safely in the truck, and I stood there beaming with pride, my face covered with the dusty powder. I looked down at Mr. Pierce in the cab of the truck drinking tea out of our Mason jar.

"How many loads will it take before we go into town?" I asked. Mr. Pierce finished his drink, held it up, and offered me some. I took the jar and gulped the sweet liquid.

"The wheat gets a bit thicker as we move thataway," he said, pointing to the next area of tall, uncut wheat. "I figure maybe four loads, five at the most."

"Well . . . uh . . . ," I stuttered, unsure of my words.

"Yes," he grinned. "You can drive the tractor now, Matt. But why don't you eat a sandwich first?"

"No thanks, sir. I'm not that hungry yet."

I guess he could see the excitement written across my face. He got out and stood by the tractor while I climbed into the seat. I was bustin' a gut from wanting to pull that combine, but I didn't want to mess anything up either. I knew if I didn't do a good job, I would be delegated to sitting in the red truck for the rest of the afternoon.

"All right, Matt. Just take her out nice and slow like I told you. It should take about two and a half times around this field to fill up the hopper, and then we'll stop and transfer your load."

"*My* load!" I repeated, liking the sound of it.

"Only one thing, son," he said. "When you're full of wheat, don't leave the field. Just stop, and I'll drive out to you—saves time and saves gas. So, if you're ready, go to it, son."

I reached for the throttle on the John Deere tractor, but Mr. Pierce put his hand over mine before I could shove it out of idle. I looked at him, "What's wrong?"

"Nothing," he said. "You're just missing something, that's all."

"I am?" I asked, looking around, trying to figure out what I had missed.

"Sure," he said. "Just reach under the seat there." Mr. Pierce's face had a unique expression. It was hard to read. I bent down and reached under the seat, then glanced up at him, trying to figure out what he was doing.

"That's right," he prompted. "Reach right back there."

With my right hand, I felt the usual greasy tools and rags, and then I touched something different—soft leather. I pulled out a pair of brand-new, dark brown leather work gloves. The stitching was perfect, the leather smooth, clean, and soft. I gently guided the fingers of each hand into their new home. And even in the dusty farm field, the fresh smell of unspoiled leather filled my nostrils.

"Picked them up last Saturday night in town." He beamed. "What do you think?"

"These are pretty neat, sir. Thanks a lot."

"That's okay," he said, squinting into the sun. "A man's got to have work gloves to drive machinery, and it looks like you got some driving to do."

"I suppose I do at that," I agreed. I looked down at Mr. Pierce. Sweat ran down his temples and fell onto his plaid shirt, making a dark circle inside the sea of squares. The sweltering sun beat down on the poor man, and he looked as though he might be thinking about a cold beer. But so far he'd stuck to the now lukewarm tea from our shared Mason jar.

I eased the throttle forward with my newly gloved right hand, then listened as the motor's pop-pop-popping grew louder and louder. Holding the clutch in with my left foot, I moved the gear shift lever into first gear and let the spinning clutch out slowly. Mr. Pierce walked away slowly as the tractor started forward.

With both hands firmly gripping the shiny black wheel, I steered to the left toward the uncut acres of prized wheat. With twenty feet to go, I glanced over my shoulder at the large blades rotating on the giant gray combine behind me. When I faced forward again, I was just about to run over the tall shoots of wheat. Quickly, I maneuvered to the left, placing the big blades of the combine in position. Again I glanced back and watched as the blades were only chopping about three-quarters of a row. I moved over slightly, then a bit to the right—perfect.

From then on, the main thing I needed to do was concentrate on keeping the tractor directly ahead of the combine while lining everything up. It took a while to learn how to turn corners, but I got a little better each time I went around the big field.

When I had finished the fourth load, Mr. Pierce drove the truck alongside again. I was tired and hungry and didn't hesitate when he asked the magic question, "We'll have a full load with this one. Do you want to go into town?"

"You bet."

#

Mr. Pierce guided the big truck out to the dirt road, and I quickly closed the gate and jumped in the passenger seat. He had a pleasant look on his face as I climbed up and took off my new gloves. I opened the glove compartment, gently placed my new treasures in it, then carefully closed the compartment door.

"Matt," Mr. Pierce said. "Taking care of your equipment is a good thing. He shifted gears and the big truck, straining with the weight of the wheat, lumbered toward the main highway.

"Yes, sir," I said. The feel of the wind was warm but pleasant as it crossed through the open windows of the cab.

"You know something," Mr. Pierce said. "You might not believe it now, but when I was in the Army, I was one of the best MPs in Camp Alva, and I kept my uniform in tip-top condition."

"Really?" I asked, trying to sound sincere, though he was right when he said I might not believe it now. Mr. Pierce glanced over, and I guess my eyes must have given me away. He grinned in that sly way he did sometimes. He held the steering wheel with his left hand, wiped his mustache with his right and snorted.

"Guess I don't blame you," he said, "the way every darn thing has gone around here during your stay. But it's the truth. After I'd been in Camp Alva for several months and got to know my job, I worked hard and learned a lot from Sergeant Swim. He was a tough old guy, but he knew how to soldier."

"Did you ever have to fight anyone?" I asked a bit too bluntly. But a sidelong glance from Mr. Pierce told me the question didn't hurt his feelings.

"There's more to soldiering than fighting, Matt. We were there to keep the Germans locked up in prison and to keep the Americans safe in town. Sure, there were times we had to get rough, but the important thing was to be alert at all times. That was the key to knowing what was going on around you. But I was lucky I had a great teacher in ole Sergeant Swim. He made sure everyone paid attention. I remember one time . . ."

CAMP ALVA

Thanksgiving was right around the corner, and most of the MPs at Camp Alva were trying their best to get a three-day pass to go home. And if that wasn't possible, they tried to find a local family in Alva that might invite a soldier in for a home-cooked turkey dinner. Henry Pierce, thinking about one of the local girls he had recently met, stood near the back of a classroom in Camp Alva. Sergeant Swim was at the front of the room, giving an indoctrination session to a group of MPs that had arrived the day before. Because Henry would be training one or two of the "new guys," he sat in on the class, ready to help his sergeant if asked.

"We now have over 4,500 POWs here at Camp Alva," the imposing sergeant said, looking at his new men and making certain they were listening. It was well known throughout the camp that you stopped everything and listened when "The Swimmer" spoke. Fall asleep, and you'd pull some crummy detail like cleaning machine guns or teaching an American history class to the POWs.

"You need to know just who these prisoners are that you're dealing with here," he said. "Primarily these Germans were taken prisoner in two areas of the war: France and Africa. For the most part, they are hard-core, highly motivated Nazis. A few American generals who visited Camp Alva described these men as 'rabid, incorrigible Nazis.' I agree with them, and so will you."

Off to one side of the room, one of the new MPs appeared to close his eyes for just an instant. That was a big mistake. Sergeant Swim reached down, and in a split second the drowsy soldier's desk was ripped from under him, sending the man crashing to the floor. The soldier lay on the floor, embarrassed and shaken. He stood up with his eyes wide open. The rest of the men in the room were barely able to hold back their laughter.

"Soldier," the sergeant said to the sleepy MP. "You think these prisoners here are part of the Hitler Youth or something? You're wrong if you do. These Krauts wouldn't think twice about putting a homemade knife in your back. Soldier, you pay attention when someone is training you, or you'll be leaving Alva in a pine box!"

"Yes, Sergeant," the MP said, now standing at attention.

"As I was saying," the sergeant resumed. "The prisoners here are mostly hard-core Nazis and must be watched carefully. We have a mixture of officers, noncoms and enlisted men." The sergeant looked at the back of the classroom and nodded at Private Pierce. "What is the head count, Pierce, and who is their spokesman?"

"Sergeant Swim," Private Pierce said, standing at attention. "This morning the prisoner count is 464 officers, 2,482 noncommissioned officers, and 1,500 enlisted men. The camp spokesperson for the Germans is First Sergeant Schmitt, and the German senior officer is Colonel Koester."

"Very good," Sergeant Swim said in a more official-sounding military monotone. Then again, to Private Pierce, "What percent of those POWs have some understanding of the English language?"

"Sergeant," Private Pierce said. "About fifty percent of the officers have some degree of English, and only five percent of the enlisted men."

"Excellent," the sergeant said, returning his focus to the new MPs. "So out of the three groups of prisoners here—officers, enlisted, and noncommissioned officers—which group do you think poses the highest risk?"

Several hands went up, including the man who had lost his chair. Those who didn't have their hands up sat up straighter, realizing they'd better think fast or at least look extremely interested.

"The Nazi officers, of course," the sergeant said, putting his hands behind him and pacing in front of the men thoughtfully.

"The German enlisted men work on various labor details and receive a small amount of money as well as a canteen credit. Sometimes we do let them buy a kind of watered-down beer. For the most part, the enlisted Germans stay busy and out of trouble. We have problems with a few of them, but the real trouble comes mostly from the extreme Nazi hardliners. Officers.

"Right now, well over one million German POWs are held in different locations around the world. The US government, in its majestic power and wisdom, has realized these men must learn to rethink their political beliefs. With that in mind, the Army has provided instructors to give classes to the prisoners. They provide instruction in basic English, American history, democracy, and other subjects. The prisoners are also given reading material and allowed a few books from the YMCA."

"How do the prisoners handle that training, Sergeant?" One of the MPs asked.

For the first time, the sergeant grinned and said, "Most of the time, the Germans sit there and listen. They might take some of it in, or they might be daydreaming about kissing their wives. I don't know, and I sure as hell don't care. But just last week we had a visiting instructor who came here from New York. He was here to show us how the cow ate the cabbage. He was a stiff little bastard and thought he knew everything.

"In his fourth class, he drew a handful of intelligent German officers from the African battalion. When he finished his lecture, he stood up at the podium, certain he had reeducated these hard-core POWs. One of the Germans raised his hand and stood up. The German said, 'If you value democracy so highly, can you permit us to know why it isn't working in the United States?'

"'It most certainly is working,' shouted the New York visitor.

"'Then why are Negroes treated so harshly, and why are poor citizens living in the slums? If civil rights and freedom are best for the entire world, why is there a class system in the United States?'

"The German grinned as the professor reddened with embarrassment. The professor was speechless and took the first train back to New York because he had not been prepared for someone to ask tough, disconcerting questions."

Sergeant Swim continued, "Our country isn't perfect, so we can't preach about it being perfect. But democracy, with all of its pitfalls, is better than a nation run by Adolf Hitler.

"So the point is, men, the United States government is trying various methods to change and transform the Germans' outlook. Some of it works, and some of it doesn't."

The sergeant paced a few more times and said, "Another thing the government came up with is a newspaper called *Der Ruf*. It is a US newspaper printed in the German language and distributed in all the German POW camps, including this one. *Der Ruf* means 'The Call.' Some POWs read it and like it and some don't. However, I want you to take notice of the ones who read it. Watch them, men. Watch them without being obvious about it. Sometimes it gives us a better idea of prisoners who are anti-Nazis." The big sergeant's eyes narrowed. "Yes, there are anti-Nazis."

"How are the prisoners taking the news from Europe?" one of the MPs asked. "You know, the way the war is going."

"That's a good question, Private," the sergeant said, looking closely at the man. "They know Germany is losing. They believe if they lose the war, there will never be a Germany again as they know it. They worry about that, and it's a bitter thing for them. But their worst fear is once the war is over they will be shipped out of the United States and sent to POW camps in Russia, where they will become slaves. The possibility of going to Russia scares the hell right out of them."

Sergeant Swim walked over to the podium and picked up a few papers. He looked through them and found the one he wanted. "I told you before they have been ordering books from the YMCA in New York. Sergeant Schmitt, the German's POW spokesperson Private Pierce mentioned, is the one who orders those books." The tough sergeant grinned. "Schmitt is very persistent. Last week, among the books he ordered were the typical ones like 20 copies of *Treasure Island,* 20 copies of *Les Miserables,* three copies of *The New Automobile Guide*, etc. At the bottom of the order, he asked for 100 copies of *The Elementary Russian Reader* and 100 copies of *The Advanced Russian Reader.* [1.] As you can see, they are so worried about going to Russia, they are getting prepared for it. It's amazing when you stop to think of it."

Sergeant Swim returned the papers to the podium and remained there for a moment looking at his students.

"Finally, men," he said. "As you go about your duties here at Camp Alva, remember the United States of America signed the Geneva Convention. That means we treat the prisoners humanely, and we don't torture or starve them. We don't beat them or shoot them unless they try to escape or endanger us in some way. Never be afraid to shoot if necessary, but never forget—our job is to watch them, guard them, and let the government decide what to do when the war is over. Don't let me catch any of you abusing a prisoner or using violence when it isn't necessary.

"Oh, and one more thing. I want to make sure you understand we represent the United States Army when we are off duty as well. You conduct yourself as gentlemen in town. I will not tolerate any trouble in Alva or any of the communities nearby. Are there any questions?"

It appeared the men were either afraid to ask any questions or, more likely, just needed to smoke a cigarette. No one raised his hand.

"All right, then," Sergeant Swim said. "I think that's enough for this morning. Sergeant Baker will hand out your duty rosters, and I'm quite certain that after one night here, you won't have to be told where the mess hall is located."

The soldiers laughed out loud, happy the session was over and always interested in talking about food.

"Private Pierce, front and center," the sergeant called out. The young private hurried along the edge of the classroom and waited for the sergeant to speak.

"Got one more thing here," the sergeant said, handing a stack of papers to Private Pierce. "See that you put these up on all the POW bulletin boards."

A faint grin crossed the burly sergeant's face, and Private Pierce knew what that meant—another "lemon letter." The American camp commander had recently written a series of sarcastic memos to the Nazi prisoners, and the MPs at Camp Alva affectionately referred to them as the lemon letters. Sergeant Swim handed Private Pierce the latest installment.

"Yes, Sergeant," Private Pierce said.

As the new men filed out of the classroom, they reached for their cigarette packages and began talking. Private Pierce followed them out into the open area between classrooms. Some of the POWs were standing at the end of the barracks, about thirty yards away. The new MPs couldn't resist the urge to glance at the prisoners while they chatted. Private Pierce stepped over to the two men he was assigned to train: Spencer and Cook.

He said, "When you finish your smoke, go to the armory. I'll meet you there, and we'll check out your weapons."

"Will do," the two men replied.

"See you there in five minutes," Private Pierce added. He left them and glanced around the area in between the buildings.

A tall American walked among the new MPs, introducing himself and welcoming each one of them to Camp Alva. Chaplain Jordahl was a gentleman, soft-spoken, and well respected. He had a reputation for being well educated, caring, and thoughtful. He never pushed religion, but he was always willing to talk about a soldier's personal problems like homesickness, temptation, fear, and most often, about their faith. Raised in the Midwest, a first-generation Norwegian American, Camp Chaplain Jordahl was American to the bone, but he possessed a somewhat European worldview. While most people were concerned with the war's effect on the United States, the chaplain also understood the bigger picture. He could see beyond the surface and recognized the hell which the prisoners were going through. He was in favor of punishing the troublemakers, but he worked hard to develop a healthy relationship with the German chaplains. Through his tireless efforts, the prisoner population was able to establish contact between POWs and their American relatives in the United States if they had any. To some of the Americans, this had been an unpopular accomplishment, but after a while, most of them could see the POWs who were able to communicate with relatives were less troublesome and more cooperative.

The chaplain also worked to identify Lutheran chaplains among the POWs to divide the groups into congregations. For these and many other reasons, he had become well known to the

German POWs and a person that Private Pierce respected. The
hardworking chaplain ministered to both American and German
needs at Camp Alva, and he somehow managed to be respected by
both sides.

"Chaplain, can I speak to you a moment?" Private Pierce
said.

"Good morning," Chaplain Jordahl said. He seemed to
recognize the private. "You seem to be getting along fairly well,
Private. How long have you been here now?"

"Almost ten months, sir."

"That's good," the chaplain said. "What did you wish to see
me about?"

"Well, sir, I've been watching your German counterpart,
Chaplain Werner."

"Yes, I see. What is it about Major Werner?" The
chaplain's tone was gentle, and he had a way of speaking that put
anyone at ease.

"I've been watching him when he's in the enlisted
prisoners' compounds. You know, just watching him now and
then."

"Yes," the chaplain said, showing a trace of impatience
now. "Did he do something wrong?"

"Oh, no, sir," the private said, trying to choose his words
carefully. "It's just sometimes when he talks to the men one-on-
one like you do, that looks normal. But sometimes he goes into a
group of men, say 10 or 15 of them, and he seems to get more
emotional. Some of the prisoners look like they might be arguing
with him. I don't know if it's anything or not, but I just wanted to
mention it to you."

The chaplain smiled and put his arm on Private Pierce's
shoulder gently.

"That's very perceptive of you, Private Pierce. It has come
to Colonel Richardson's attention that Major Werner has been
using his position as the POW chaplain to create trouble. We know
his meetings with the POWs have become more political than
religious. Recently he even managed to pressure some of the more
religious German chaplains into stepping down."

"Sir?"

"What I mean to say is the truly religious chaplains who are POWs are intimidated by Major Werner. Right now they aren't ministering to their POW brothers. Major Werner's agenda and dominating presence has silenced them."

"What can I do, sir?"

"Just keep watch, like you are right now. Let me know if you see anything else going on with him."

"Yes, sir, I will."

"Good," the chaplain said, ready to leave. He stood there a moment, seemingly pleased that this young man, relatively new to his job, had been able to see what was going on and had the courage to report it. He shook hands with the private and said, "Good job, son. Oh, and by the way, didn't I see you the other day in town? That was a very pretty young lady you were with at the dime store."

Private Pierce grinned, visibly embarrassed, but pleased by the compliment.

"Yes, sir," he said. "Her name is Jewel. She's a telephone operator at the camp hospital. I met her last month, and we've gone out a few times."

The chaplain smiled warmly and glanced at a few of the new MPs, anxious to speak to them all.

"Well," the chaplain said. "I have to run now, son. You keep a close eye on Major Werner." Then he smiled and said, "While you're at it, keep a close eye on Jewel, too."

"That I will, sir. That I will."

POW BULLETIN BOARD
Post Immediately in English and German

ARMY SERVICES FORCES
HEADQUARTERS PRISONER OF WAR CAMP
Office of the Commanding Officer
Alva, Oklahoma

It has been noted that a rather alarming number of Prisoners of War on work details are unable to do a full day's work. They march slowly going to work, but rapidly when going to meals. They appear to have lame legs and lame feet, which require them to work slowly and need rest periods, sitting down periods, etc. Frequently they are seen leaning against buildings, their rake handles, and on their shovel handles for support. They also appear to be afflicted with shortness of breath but have a miraculous recovery and an incredible appetite by mealtime. This interesting phenomenon will be studied by Your Camp Commander for future reference and recommendation.

6 A DRUNK FARMER

was still thinking about the German POW camp when Mr. Pierce drove the last block or two near the railroad tracks and steered the red truck into the Cooperative Grain Elevator, where we would be unloading the wheat after it was weighed in. I had to snap back into reality quickly, and I was glad to see there were only two trucks in line ahead of us. That was good news for sure. It didn't take long before we were motioned forward onto the scales, and we got set up to weigh in with our first load of wheat.

Mr. Pierce drove onto the huge scales and switched the motor off. The sun had been down for over an hour now, leaving the grain yard in semi-darkness. The lights above the scale were bright, and I watched closely as the attendant took a scoop full of wheat into the office. Mr. Pierce explained the procedure since I had never done anything like this.

"He takes that in and does a moisture check on it before they weigh us in. If there's too much moisture, like more than 20%, then they might adjust the price. Or if it's even wetter, they won't pay for it at all. There shouldn't be any moisture on this load, but there might be some tomorrow. That's why I always wait until almost noon before cutting."

The man returned, handed Mr. Pierce a piece of paper, and smiled, but said nothing at all. I guess there wasn't too much moisture. When the rear of the truck was in the right spot, the attendant gave us the signal to dump. Mr. Pierce put the transmission into neutral, used his left hand, and pulled a lever on the dashboard, which started the pump motor. The little engine whirled loudly and engaged the dump. We looked behind us through the rear window and saw the front of the truck's storage bin slowly rising into the air. As the front of the container went up, the rear went down, and the wheat tumbled slowly into the wheat collection station. Dust and wheat particles drifted around the cab as we heard the loud rushing sounds of the wheat plummeting behind us. It must have been like the sound of money in the bank to Mr. Pierce. His eyes beamed with pride, and it was infectious.

After we emptied the truck, we drove back to the scale, and there the attendant took the empty weight of the truck. The difference between the truck's full-of-wheat weight and its empty weight was the amount of wheat we had delivered. That's how they determined how much they would pay Mr. Pierce.

The quiet, dusty granary attendant stuck another piece of paper through the open window, then waited for us to drive forward. Mr. Pierce thanked him, proudly, and we drove away. As we passed the post office, I noticed two men standing by the front door; one was a stranger to me, but the other I recognized as Thurman Spencer.

I started to tell Mr. Pierce but changed my mind. Mr. Pierce was happy and proud of our work today, and I didn't want to ruin his mood. He was even humming a song. He glanced at me as we bumped across the railroad tracks.

"Matt," he said. "We're going to eat at Lana's Café tonight and celebrate the first load of wheat. Unless you want another fine meal of pinto beans back at the house, that is." His face beamed with a wide grin.

I smiled and decided to forget all about seeing Thurman Spencer. "You don't have to twist my arm," I said. You could see the delight on his sunburned face as he drove up Choctaw Street and turned toward Lana's Café.

#

Lana's Café was crowded that night, and after a tough day in the wheat field, it was good to smell real food and be around real people for a change. We sat at a table near the entrance. It put me in an excellent position to watch the customers as they came in and out of the front door, a pastime I always enjoy. On our table was a red-and-white checkered tablecloth, a bottle of ketchup, and a shiny chrome-topped jar of white sugar. When they brought our food, one look at my plate and it was easy to understand why the place was so popular. I had chicken fried steak with gravy, mashed potatoes, and homemade rolls. On the edge of my crowded plate were corn, green beans, and yam, and it tasted just as good as it looked. It was easy to see why Lana's was the most popular café in Alva.

Gulping my second glass of iced tea, I noticed a large waitress standing beside our table. I don't know how long she had been there. The woman was taller than Mr. Pierce, with arms bigger around than my waist, and she chewed a wad of gum in a way that kind of reminded me of Mr. Pierce's horse, June. The waitress wore an apron so dirty you would have been hard-pressed to find more than an inch that was clean anywhere on it. Her face and hair were wet with sweat, and she had an unpleasant odor about her. A dreadful combination of food smells that mixed together on her clothing.

But I noticed that in spite of her sweaty, unattractive appearance, the hefty woman had a sincere, sweet smile. She stood right beside me grinning, as if she was trying to figure out who I might be. I tried to speak, but my mouth was full.

Mr. Pierce, seeing my dilemma, grinned and spoke to her warmly, "Lana, this is my top hand, Matt. Matt, this is Lana, the best darn cook in Oklahoma."

The other customers paid little attention to our conversation until Lana spoke. When she opened her mouth, her booming voice commanded attention, and, immediately the other customers turned in our direction.

"Well . . . Hello . . . Sweetie," Lana said. "I bet under all that wheat dust, you're a real cutie-pie!"

I felt my face heat up with embarrassment, and I imagine it turned bright red. I reached for my glass of iced tea. Lana slapped me on the back, causing me to spill my drink, but she didn't seem to care. She pointed to my plate and said, "Looks like you needed a good meal. I see you're trying our famous chicken fried steak and enjoying some of my fresh vegetables. You make sure after eating all that healthy food that Henry buys you a piece of my banana cream pie. All right, sweetie?"

"Yes, ma'am," I said, wiping my face and wishing the other customers would get back to worrying about their own meals and stop looking at us.

At that point the bulky woman strolled away, quickly mixing in and entertaining her other customers. She seemed to know everyone by name, and she took great pleasure in giving each of them a snide remark, which they thoroughly enjoyed. Each of Lana's zingers was only a hair short of an insult. Like Mr. Pierce, they seemed to appreciate "Lana the woman" as much as "Lana the cook."

"She's something, isn't she?" Mr. Pierce asked.

I nodded my head, happy that another poor fellow nearby was being called "sweetie." On the other side of the restaurant, Lana had her pad out taking her next order. But she didn't walk back to the kitchen; she looked across the room at a large open window where a thin colored boy faced her from inside the kitchen

"Gimme one fried chicken, Texas toast!" Lana bellowed. "Two specials, hold the hominy!" She glanced back at her customer, a shy little lady. A wife of one of the farmers, it appeared. "You want fries instead of hominy?" Lana asked. The woman nodded shyly; the fingers of her left hand toyed with her necklace and her eyes darted around the room. Beside her, her husband looked like he was about to bust a gut as he smiled openly, anticipating Lana's high-pitched shriek. And Lana didn't disappoint.

"Turn the hominy into French fries, Sam!" Lana roared. "We got someone out here with class for a change." That comment brought laughter from everyone but the farmer's wife, who rolled her eyes, then flashed her amused husband a dirty look. In the kitchen, the Negro cook showed no emotion, as though he had heard all of Lana's one-liners a hundred times.

I couldn't finish my chicken fried steak or all the fresh vegetables, but I gave serious thought to some pie. I was just about to mention it when a couple walked out the front door. Through the open doorway, I glanced across the street at some people walking along the sidewalk. There were only a few, but one of them surprised me enough that I completely forgot about the pie.

I couldn't tell for sure, but it looked like Carol Rudy. I reached for a napkin and wiped my hands and mouth. Mr. Pierce looked up from his food.

"How 'bout some pie?"

"No. I, ah . . . I need to go across the street for a sec."

"What for?" A curious look on his face. "What could ever be more important than a piece of Lana's homemade pie?"

"I need to pick up a package of . . . um . . . ah . . . gum. Yeah, I need some chewing gum. Be right back in a minute." I stood up, tucked my dirty T-shirt into my jeans, and walked the two steps toward the front door. When I pulled it open, Carol Rudy walked into the café with another girl. I stood there dumbfounded, trying to think of something to say.

"Hi. Remember me?" she asked.

"Sure. How are you?" I asked, as I tried to look anywhere but at her lips or her cute blouse. I felt my face get red.

"Great," she grinned. "This is my friend, Sandra."

"Hi, Sandra," I said. "You guys here to eat? Try the chicken fried steak."

"No," she said. "We already ate. Sometimes we come to Lana's for a Coke." Carol looked behind me, into the café. "Isn't that Mr. Pierce?"

"Oh, yeah," I said. "But I was going out to walk around town for a while. Want to go for a . . ."

"Well," she interrupted. "Let's all sit with him and have a cherry Coke."

I glanced at Mr. Pierce, who looked like he had spilled about half his dinner on his work shirt. He looked up and grinned.

"Sure," I said reluctantly. "Let's go sit with Mr. Pierce."

I led the two girls over to the booth where Mr. Pierce was still eating. The old farmer stood and nodded politely to the girls.

"Mr. Pierce, this is Carol Rudy and her friend, Sandra. Got room for a few more?"

"Any time," he grinned.

I slid in beside him while the girls took the other side of the cramped booth. Carol's friend Sandra was cute and wore her blonde hair longer than Carol's, but I could see right away that while Carol was more of a serious young girl, Sandra was a giggler. When she looked down at my empty plate, she giggled. I moved it out of her way, and she giggled again. Then the smiling teenager glanced at Carol, and it looked as though it was all she could do not to burst out laughing for some reason. Carol nudged her, and finally her laughing tapered off—but only a little.

"So, what are you men doing in town?" Carol asked, glancing sharply at Sandra.

Mr. Pierce smiled and looked over at me, allowing me to respond, "We brought in the first truck of wheat tonight," I bragged, "and we're celebrating."

"That's neat," Carol said. She started to ask another question and was interrupted.

"Well, well, well," a loud voice beside us interrupted. I looked up, and Lana was standing by our table. *Just what we need,* I thought, as I leaned back in my chair.

"All right, you girls!" Lana said too loudly. "Now you stay away from this good-looking boy. I saw him first."

I appreciated the compliment, but somehow the way Lana said it made me want to crawl into a hole. I put my hand over my face to cover the redness I could feel creeping up out of my dirty T-shirt again.

"What can I get for you?" Lana asked the girls.

"Two cherry Cokes, please," Carol said. Before Lana had a chance to make me feel even smaller, a man across the room motioned to her. She saw him but was in no hurry to leave our table.

"I'll be there in a second!" she bellowed. "Keep your powder dry!" Then she hollered at the cook, "Sam, where's my fried chicken? Don't worry about plucking it. Just bleed it and throw it on a plate. These folks are hungry! They might chow down on the menus any minute."

I still had my hand over my face as the enormous waitress lumbered away. Instant relief flowed through me like a warm bath. Even though it had embarrassed me, the girls didn't seem bothered by Lana at all. Everyone else seemed to think Lana was great.

Hoping I might get a minute without our hostess, I leaned over to Carol. Whispering right next to her ear, I said, "I'm sorry about the other day. You know, at the park."

Carol leaned a bit closer, smiled, and the silky smooth skin on her face seemed to glow. Maybe I dreamed it, but it seemed for an instant the two of us were alone in that crowded restaurant. Everyone else disappeared. There was no Mr. Pierce, Sandra, or even big Lana. Just Carol and I, and that's all.

"My aunt saw what happened," Carol said. "She didn't blame you."

I smiled, feeling a lot better about the whole thing, so I said, "Your aunt sounds real nice." I gazed into her blue eyes.

"She is," Carol said. "And she was kind of interested when I told her you worked for Mr. Pierce."

I glanced over and saw Mr. Pierce was leaning in across the table. Well, so much for my fantasy about being alone.

"Did you get into trouble with the deputy?" Carol asked as Mr. Pierce listened in.

"No," I said. He just took me down to his office and let me go after he gave me a lecture. One thing he did mention— something I wanted to talk to you about."

"Yes," she said. "What was it?"

Before I could tell her, someone was standing by our table again. It seemed to me that Lana wouldn't let us have a minute to ourselves. I turned to say something to her and went stone-cold as I looked up at none other than the infamous Thurman Spencer. This time he was close enough for me to get a good look, if you could call it that. There wasn't anything good about being that close to Thurman Spencer. He wore a short-sleeved shirt that exposed large, hairy, muscle-bound arms, and his chest stuck out like that of a weight lifter.

"Big party?" he asked, chewing on a toothpick. "This isn't a bad place if you like food and flab."

I wanted to say something, but I didn't have the nerve to say a word. He stood so close that I felt even more intimidated than I had the night he surprised us on the farm. I slid down in my seat, and I'm sure Carol noticed how frightened I looked.

"Henry," Thurman Spencer said, looking over at Mr. Pierce. "I was just down at the granary, and I watched you pull through. By the looks of it, this might turn into a bumper crop this year."

Mr. Pierce stuttered, "Yeah . . . it . . . ah. It looks pretty good."

"You haven't forgotten our meeting at the bank next week, have you?"

"I haven't forgotten about it," Mr. Pierce said, his face showing his bitterness.

Carol looked across at Mr. Pierce and back at me. She knew something wasn't right, but I had no opportunity to explain things to her—just like at the park the other day. The silence lingered between us while we waited for Thurman Spencer to leave.

The huge, unwelcome visitor had his hands on our table, right beside me. They were bigger than our empty plates, and on his right hand, a brilliant diamond ring fit snugly on his middle finger. A long shiny fork rested in my right hand about three inches from his left hand. I visualized stabbing Thurman Spencer several times with my fork, him writhing in pain, blood spurting up into Sandra's face. I wondered if she would giggle about that.

But then reality set back in and ended my fantasy as Thurman Spencer glanced down at me suspiciously, then over to Mr. Pierce.

"You remember our agreement?" Thurman Spencer asked. Mr. Pierce started to answer, but big Lana suddenly appeared and cut him off.

"Move over!" Lana ordered, bumping into Thurman Spencer like a linebacker. Our table got slammed by the man's bulk, and the two girls grabbed their Cokes instinctively and held them above the table. Looking angry, Thurman gave Lana the space she demanded.

"You men!" Lana said. "All you think about is work. How about a good meal for a change, Thurman?"

"No thanks," he mumbled, still looking agitated.

"Put some meat on you," she added. Several of the folks around us laughed, and Thurman Spencer's face grew angrier.

"I'm afraid I might wind up looking like you," Thurman said.

Lana's face showed the sting from his insult. For a moment, the silence hung in the air thicker than the humid smells from the kitchen.

But Thurman wasn't finished, "Now go back in the kitchen where you belong and leave us alone," he said.

For the first time, Lana looked both hurt and surprised. She leaned forward as if she were about to snap back at him, then she hesitated. She glanced around our table at the sober looks on our faces, then back at the crude, evil face of Thurman Spencer. The woman may have been large and blunt, but she could read people. She didn't know why we were sitting there like sheep, but she seemed to understand she might make it worse for us if she said what she wanted to say to Thurman Spencer. A confident smile returned to her wet, chubby face.

"Thurman!" she declared, in her loudest order-calling voice. "Why is it you never come around here anymore, honey? Years ago, you used to stop by all the time." She slid her bulky arm around his waist as he stood there, turning red. His evil eyes showed a hint of embarrassment. "Yeah," she went on as she pulled him away from our table. "I remember one time you waited for me to get off work. I can't remember what kind of car you drove back then, but it doesn't matter now. The important thing is, it had a real comfortable back seat. Yeah, it was so soft and comfortable, wasn't it, Thurman?"

One second Thurman was standing there with a look of outrage on his mean, ugly face, and the next instant he was shoving two customers out of the way as he tried to beat them out the front door.

Spencer was gone before Lana could pull her fleshy arm back. Everyone in the café laughed as she shook her head, strutting away from our table. Even the Negro cook seemed to enjoy seeing the town bully getting burned. I glanced around the table. The girls were smiling, but Mr. Pierce wasn't.

"I guess we better go," Mr. Pierce said.

I hated to leave when we had just started having fun, but I knew from experience when he said "go," he was ready right then. I let Mr. Pierce out of the booth. Then I stood for a moment looking down into Carol's blue eyes.

"Carol, can I call you sometime?" I asked.

Her silly friend giggled, turned to Carol and said, "I thought you told me Mr. Pierce didn't have a phone." Carol shot her a stern look, so Sandra pulled back and kept quiet.

"How did you know that?" I asked.

"I don't know what she's talking about, but it's okay to call if you want. My number is hickory two five zero five five."

"That's easy to remember," I said. "I'll be seeing you."

Carol waved as I turned and walked away. Opening the front door, I glanced back at Lana, who moseyed down the aisle carrying two plates of food in one hand and a cup of coffee in the other. I smiled at her, but she didn't see me. From that moment on, Lana could count me as another of her many, many fans.

#

I had worked hard that first day of harvest and gone to bed dog-tired, but that strenuous day was a cakewalk compared to the rest of the gruesome week. Each day we woke up at five, worked on the trucks or the old combine, went into the field about midmorning, and stayed at it till well after dark. By the time we drove back to the house for supper, it was almost eight o'clock.

Tired, dirty, and hungry enough to eat anything that didn't move, we trudged in the back door talking about wheat and trucks and how many more days it would take to cut and deliver the rest of the crop. While we ate supper, we listened to the news on the radio. Sometimes Mr. Pierce would let me turn to a station in Enid that played rock-and-roll music, but mostly we listened to his news programs.

That Friday night after work was like most other nights. After we had eaten a meager meal, Mr. Pierce and I went out to the water trough, ready for a much-needed bath. A steady southern breeze blew across the water, its invisible energy slowly spinning the wooden blades of the windmill and cooling our aching bodies. I sat in the fresh well water for several minutes before looking up at the vast heavens overhead. It was a clear night. Thousands of brilliant stars were hanging above me in that enormous sky like floating diamonds on a dark blue lake.

I located the Big Dipper and his Little Dipper brother, and then I gazed at several jewel-studded constellations. It was both relaxing and a bit overpowering to sit in the water and look up at the heavens. A bit earlier, I had felt a bit prideful since I had done a fair day's work and earned my keep. But as the pleasant sensation of cool water surrounded my tired body, I looked up at all the glorious heavens above. Millions and billions of stars and planets so numerous and distant that it gave me an overwhelming sensation of being trivial.

For just a moment, a bright half moon peeked out from behind a large cloud and stood out from all the other lights in the sky. It looked independent and strong in its massive size, yet at the same time so alone and gentle. The moon reminded me of something on the news that night. The radio announcer had reported America's latest step in trying to catch up with the Russians. It was a major victory in the space race.

The announcer had said, "Alan Shepard Jr. became the first US astronaut to achieve suborbital flight when his space capsule was launched 116 miles into space from Cape Canaveral, Florida."

Looking into the heavens, I wondered what it would have been like to ride in that space ship. Once again, I wished Mr. Pierce owned a television so we could watch the news about Alan Shepard, but he didn't. So I had to imagine it all in my head.

The announcer had made the astronaut sound like a courageous man, and I had no doubt he was. I had seen films about rockets being fired, but I had never seen a spacecraft launch. Alan Shepard was certain to become a national hero, but to me, he would never replace Mickey Mantle, the famous New York Yankees slugger from Oklahoma.

"Mr. Pierce, do you think they'll have more flights like that one Alan Shepard was on?" He took a minute to answer because he was carefully trying to light a cigarette while sitting in three feet of water.

"I guess they will," he said. "I was over at my sister's house one night, and they were watching the television. President Kennedy was saying he's going to catch up with the Russians in this space thing."

"Do you think we can?"

"I don't know, Matt. Lots of folks don't like Kennedy in Oklahoma. Just about all the districts here voted Republican. They think he's got more important things to worry about."

"What do you mean?" I asked, as Mr. Pierce sent blue smoke into the night air.

"Well, for one thing, he's been in office less than a year and already has gotten into big trouble with that Cuban invasion. Another thing, every day we hear more about civil rights problems."

"Yeah, my dad has his own philosophy on all that," I said, thinking about the discussions we often had in our house. I expected Mr. Pierce was going to sound off about the colored people just like my dad.

"What's your dad's theory about colored folks?"

"He says we should keep things the way it's always been. Let them do the dirty work and send them to school on the other side of town."

"Is that right?" Mr. Pierce asked. "What do you think, son?"

"I don't know," I said, thinking about his question. "I worked with a couple of Negroes up at the grocery store last summer. They were pretty nice guys. They did their jobs and kept to themselves. I guess there are good and bad coloreds, just like good and bad whites. But I can't discuss it with my father like we're talking right now. I've found the best way to handle him is to avoid the subject of colored people. I don't bring it up."

Somehow we got off the spaceship subject, and that's what I wanted to talk about. So I tried to get back on track and said, "But what about this guy who went up in the space capsule today, Shepard? Think he got close enough to see the stars?"

"Matt, I don't know," he said, sounding a bit irritated.

"But what do you think?" I asked, pressing him by using the same question he had asked me.

"Boy, I told you I don't know," he said, starting to sound more irritated. "I got all I can think about right here. I don't give the moon much thought these days."

I kept quiet as Mr. Pierce got out of the water trough and dried off. He walked away without saying anything else. I guess the conversation bothered him, but I didn't know why.

I watched the glow of his cigarette as he went into the barn. After a moment, the light in the tack room came on. Maybe he was getting something for June.

Alone in the water trough, I started thinking about those rockets we heard about on the radio. It was so hard to believe anything or anyone could fly that high. I thought about some of the movies I'd seen where "spacemen" had found creatures on Mars or the moon. Sometimes there were green, slimy, snakelike creatures on Mars that crawled up to the spacemen without making one sound.

As I continued to sit in the water, it seemed so quiet all around me. Too quiet. I looked toward the house. Nothing. I turned to look behind me. Something large and wet scraped my arm. I jumped up, slipped, then crashed into the water trough backward. When I regained my balance and stood up, I looked around frantically trying to see what had touched me.

There, leaning through the fence was June with her giant tongue sticking out, trying to lick me again. It wasn't a snake or wild animal trying to bite me, it was June just being friendly.

"June, what in the world are you trying to do? I was going to take you for a ride tomorrow, but not now." The bulky horse stared at me, and I knew she couldn't understand a word I was saying. But that didn't bother her.

"You should be glad that I didn't have a carbine rifle. I might have shot you right between those giant eyes of yours."

That didn't bother her either. She stuck her big snout down into the water and slurped the cool liquid. I stepped out onto the ground and struggled, trying to pull my jeans onto my wet legs. Frowning once more at the silent horse, I let her have the water all to herself. I figured I should go over to the barn and see what Mr. Pierce was doing.

I pushed back the large wooden barn door slowly. As I walked a few steps inside, the dark interior of the barn seemed a bit frightening after the scare June had given me. A strong stench of cow manure and horse feed hovered in the muggy barn. It was quiet except for a constant breeze rustling through the loose boards of the roof.

The light from the tack room made a white line across the straw-covered floor. I walked toward that light, careful of each step. Every day, while driving the tractor, I had seen rats and field mice—I could only imagine what might be hiding in the barn. I thought of the rattlesnake I'd driven over with the tractor that morning and had thoughts of similar creatures lurking in the straw nearby waiting to catch a mouse, or maybe a teenager. Those thoughts caused me to hurry along toward the door of the tack room. I peeked in.

"Mr. Pierce," I said. "Are you in here?"

Sitting on a small stool, Mr. Pierce leaned back against the rough wooden beams of the barn. One hand rested against his face. At first, I thought he was asleep, but then I noticed a bottle of whiskey sitting on the floor beside him.

Without looking up, Mr. Pierce answered. It was more of a plea than an answer.

"Just let me alone tonight, Matt. I need to get a few things straight in my mind."

"Mr. Pierce, I know you're worried about the money you owe Thurman Spencer, but this isn't going to help. Come on, let's go in and get some sleep. That's what you need, sleep."

The farmer stayed silent and didn't move.

I walked over and grabbed his callused hand. He pushed me backward, and I fell on my backside, then looked up at him. His eyes showed his pain. And then the quiet rage he kept buried deep inside surfaced.

"I said, get out! I didn't ask for no nursemaid out here! Can't a man have a little time to himself without somebody telling him what to do?"

I got back on my feet and brushed off my jeans. His harsh words took me by surprise and hurt me more than falling. This wasn't the quiet, polite farmer that I knew.

"I only want to help you, Mr. Pierce."

"You do?"

"Yes, sir."

He looked as though he was ready to yell again, but managed to suppress it.

"Good." His voice grew louder with every word. "Then go on up to the house and leave me alone."

He took a long drink from the dark bottle, spilling a little of the whiskey on his chin. The stench of liquor filled the narrow room as the copper-colored liquid trickled down his chin and fell onto the white hairs on his heaving chest.

"Mr. Pierce, don't you want to come in and get some sleep?"

"Leave me alone," he shouted. "Leave me to hell alone!"

I took a few steps toward the door, then turned and said, "I'll bet Sergeant Swim would be real proud of you right now. If only he could see you feeling sorry for yourself because you lost your girlfriend and now you're losing part of your farm."

The old farmer looked up, grunted, then pointed toward the door and growled, "Get the hell out of here!"

"You know something?" I asked. "There might be a way out of this, but you're not going to find it in that bottle."

Mr. Pierce looked at the bottle in his hand and took another long drink. He squinted as the bitter taste burned his throat. His wrinkled face became flushed, his sparkling eyes hostile.

"I'll tell you a way out of my problems," he said. "A bus leaves every day going east to Tulsa. Son, you get your butt back to the house right now or you'll be on that bus tomorrow."

Feeling wounded, I left him sitting there and walked out of the tack room. Somehow, the walk through the silent, unlit barn didn't bother me as it had just a few minutes before. I stood near the barn for a moment, looked up into the sky and thought about the courage it would take to be the first man in space. I couldn't give up on Mr. Pierce, and I needed a shred of courage just then. Taking a deep breath of night air, I turned around and walked back to the tack room door.

Seeing me enter again, the old farmer shook his head and closed his eyes.

"You forget where the attic is?" he grumbled.

"No, sir. You said you wanted to forget your problems. I know a good way to do that."

Mr. Pierce held the bottle up and said, "So do I."

"Okay, but how about we talk about something else while you forget your problems?"

"What?"

I changed my tone, trying to sound friendlier, and said, "Let's forget about the farm a minute. Tell me what happened next at Camp Alva. Did the German prisoners try to trick you again?"

Mr. Pierce looked at me suspiciously, then he slowly took a short sip of whiskey.

"They were always up to something," he said. "We had to watch them and try to figure out what they were really up to. Most of the time they were up to no good . . ."

7   WATCH OUT !

By late fall of 1944, Camp Alva's inmate population had grown to almost 5,000 German prisoners. It was now the largest POW camp in the United States and was known to many as "Little Alcatraz" due to its reputation for having the worst troublemakers from all the other camps. But though they were hard on the German POWs, the United States government and the camp's commanding officer continued to follow the Geneva Convention, something the German and Japanese governments refused to do. It was widely known that American soldiers who had been taken prisoner by the Japanese in Asia or the Germans in Europe were being beaten, tortured, forced into slave labor, and were dying by the thousands due to malnutrition, exposure, and malaria. The Geneva Convention clearly stated POWs were to be treated humanely. But given the hate Americans now had for Germans, those weren't easy orders for the MPs at Camp Alva to follow.

In October, Private Henry Pierce had been in Camp Alva ten months and was quickly becoming an experienced guard. Sergeant Swim had taken a liking to the Texan, and he would often throw him into tough situations as part of his development.

In the evening, after the prisoners had eaten their evening meal and were in the barracks for the night, Private Pierce and his buddy Private Spencer walked their beat inside the POW officers' compound.

The outside air was cool and crisp, and a breeze carried the thick, sooty scent of burning coal. Between the rows of prisoner barracks, MPs, working in pairs, walked their beats, looking for any prisoners outside of their barracks or any sign of trouble. Randomly and with no prior warning, the MPs would enter a barracks to perform a bed check and look for anything unusual. According to Sergeant Swim's instructions, they should have no set pattern as to which barracks they entered; they were to pick one, then enter at the last moment. One of the many procedures to keep the prisoners off guard.

The two MPs walked their beat that night, talking about Thanksgiving back home and what the cooks at Camp Alva might come up with for Thanksgiving. Henry Pierce was training one of the new men, Private Spencer, and he had enjoyed Spencer's company. The new guy was a large, thick-framed Southerner, with black hair, brown eyes, and a willingness to inflict pain when needed. The kind of guy who would try most anything.

It was almost midnight, and they looked forward to getting a mug of coffee and a sandwich at one a.m. The heavy, overpowering smell of mutton being cooked in the mess hall met Private Pierce as the two men strolled past a dozen or so barracks. Private Pierce tossed his cigarette butt on the ground and grunted, indicating that they were going into this one.

"Here we go," Pierce said, as he walked toward a small door. Both men knew these nightly checks were the hardest part of their job, and they also knew anything could happen. With Spencer behind him for backup, Pierce opened the door, moved in, and listened for any unusual noises. The barracks, which had only minimum night lighting on, was dark and quiet. A few prisoners whispered in their native language. Standing near the door, Pierce handed Spencer the flashlight and told him to carry out a bed check. With his flashlight in his left hand and a Smith and Wesson .45 caliber pistol in his right, Spencer walked a step or two in front of Pierce. The rounded light beam moved slowly from one bed to the other as Spencer made sure there was a man in each bed and that none of them were smoking. Since several thousand prisoners were housed in 120 wooden barracks, fires were a dreaded hazard.

Walking on the left side, Henry Pierce carefully held his .30 caliber M1 carbine with both hands. Henry loved his rifle and often argued with other MPs. Some said it didn't pack enough punch, like the more powerful .30-06 Garand. But Henry enjoyed the light, capable feel of the carbine and thought it was the perfect weapon for short-range work like guarding a prison. Gripping the smooth wooden stock, Henry Pierce felt a sense of pride and a trace of confidence.

The two MPs walked cautiously along the middle of the barracks, between crowded rows of bunk beds which housed sleeping Germans. The flashlight's beam revealed the light-skinned faces of the sleeping Germans and occasionally the blue eyes of one who couldn't or wouldn't sleep.

"Avoid their eyes if need be," Sergeant Swim had said. "They want you to fear them and think about them. Don't. Just look around and focus on the big picture, then you'll finish your watch alive."

Right about the halfway point, Pierce glanced across the remaining bunks of sleeping prisoners toward the far end of the barracks. Because it held only German officers, Pierce knew the last bed was reserved for the barracks commandant. As he glanced in that direction, he spotted a glowing orange dot he recognized immediately—a cigarette. It was a clear violation of prison regulations, and the prisoner, commandant or not, would be punished.

"Spencer," Pierce said quietly. "End of the row on your side, I've got a cig. Do you see it?" Spencer turned his flashlight toward that bunk and there, lying in bed like he never had a care in the world, was Fritz Wolf, one of the meanest Germans to ever wear a swastika.

The two MPs stood about 30 feet away from Fritz Wolf, and when Spencer saw the cigarette, he immediately shifted his weight and started to run toward the end of the row. Just as he leaned forward to run, he felt a hand grab hold of his webbed belt from the back.

He heard Pierce say, "Wait a minute, Spencer. This is too easy."

"What?" Spencer said. "Let go of me. I'll show that Kraut what happens when you break the rules."

But Pierce didn't let go. He held onto Spencer's belt as the young private grew even more upset.

"Stand right there," Pierce said. "Let's take a look around. Shine your light across the floor near those bunks right there." Spencer, breathing hard now, relaxed and followed Pierce's advice. He had been told that the POWs could be tricky, so he walked forward carefully, aiming the light toward the floor in front of them. The beam swung back and forth from one bed to the other. And then they saw it—only five feet in front of them, right in their pathway. A thin, silver-colored wire was stretched neatly from one bed over to another bed directly across the aisle. The wire was ten to twelve inches above the floor, low enough not to be seen, but high enough to trip a running MP.

"Son of a bitch," Spencer said. "Son of a bitch!"

"OK," Pierce said. "Let's get 'em up." Spencer walked carefully to the wall and turned on the remainder of the lights, and the barracks, now fully lit, was filled with groans and complaints. But now the MPs could see clearly, and they weren't at all concerned about disturbing anyone's sleep.

"How about we check those two beds right there?" Pierce said. "Let's see if they have any other surprises up their sleeves."

While Spencer covered him with his .45, Pierce pulled the covers off the two beds the wire had been tied to. Now the MPs could see that the two prisoners in those beds had been hiding long two-by-fours which they had planned to use as weapons. The prisoners gripped the boards defiantly and muttered something.

The man on Spencer's side offered little resistance and gave up his weapon without a fight. But the German on the other side—an ugly, muscle-bound, evil-looking Kraut with arms as thick as tree trunks—that was another story. The indignant German jumped out of bed, yelled something at Private Pierce, then pulled the board back and held it in the air like a major league batter, ready to swing at the next pitch. The room went crazy as the prisoners screamed their encouragement to their defiant hero. The German yelled at Pierce, taunting him, daring him to fight.

As Spencer nervously surveyed the situation, Pierce took a small step forward with his left foot. Sweat formed on the German's chin and dripped onto his T-shirt. The German's two-by-four went back a fraction of an inch, signaling the start of his swing, then swished through the air horizontally. Private Pierce froze in place as the lumber zoomed toward his head. An instant before it found its mark, Pierce ducked down, stepped forward and lunged toward the batter. As the German finished his swing, two things happened: Private Pierce's hat flew across the barracks like a home run, having been hit by the two-by-four, and at the same time the butt of Private Pierce's carbine smashed into the right side of the German's ugly face. For a second the prisoners thought their hero had smashed the MP, but as reality set in, the Germans fell silent, and the only sound in the barracks was the pathetic cracking of a broken jawbone.

Quickly, the two MPs regrouped and stood back-to-back in the middle of the barracks, then pointed their weapons at the prisoners they considered the most dangerous. Pierce blew his whistle several times, and within minutes the barracks was filled with MPs—including one large and angry staff sergeant.

Seeing the two-by-fours on the floor, the trip wire, and the bloody face of the German prisoner, Staff Sergeant Swim grasped the situation instantly; his MPs had averted a craftily devised trap and had possibly prevented an escape attempt. The sergeant took control of the barracks and quickly shouted orders to his MPs. His orders were clipped and direct—not only for the MPs' benefit but for the intimidation of the prisoners.

"Give me three men down at the other end of the barracks!" the sergeant yelled. His face remained calm, his voice matter-of-fact and his posture, his military bearing, perfectly poised, erasing any doubt as to who was in charge.

"Get the rest of these Krauts out of bed! I want every prisoner in here taken outside. Have them kneel in the dirt. Give me four men to stay inside and check for other weapons. Spencer, you and Pierce get your prisoners over in that corner. Use your come-alongs on them."

Come-alongs were a kind of double-handed chain-style handcuff which required no key and wrapped tightly around a prisoner's wrists.

"Yes, Sergeant!" Pierce yelled as he motioned for the German with the bloody face to turn around. Defiantly, the German looked straight ahead and stood at attention, his chin held high, as he refused to turn around. Private Pierce shook his head, knowing that it wasn't going to be easy to cuff this giant of a man.

"Which other men were involved?" the sergeant asked.

Private Pierce turned toward Sergeant Swim to answer, "Just these two and Fritz Wolf." Then, without warning, Pierce spun on his heels, brought his full body weight forward, and slammed his left fist into the defiant German prisoner. The surprised German staggered backward, coughed, but didn't go down. The other two MPs scrambled forward, grabbed the prisoner's bulky arms, and then brought his hands behind his back while Private Pierce got behind the German and tried to put his come-alongs on the man's wrists. But it wasn't easy; even though the MPs outnumbered the massive prisoner three to one, he was able to scuffle and resist to the point that it was almost impossible to subdue him. Other prisoners shuffled past the fracas and grinned openly, seeing their German pal dominating the Americans. Private Pierce noticed them and glanced at Sergeant Swim. He knew he had to get control of the situation, and he had to do it fast.

Dropping his come-alongs to the ground, Private Pierce quickly put his left arm around the thick, sweaty neck of the prisoner. With the crook of his left elbow under the man's chin, Private Pierce grabbed the bicep of his right arm and pressed against the German's neck. At the same time, he used his right hand to press down on the German's head, which compressed the carotid arteries and jugular vein. The prisoner struggled, his eyes wide and fearful. Then he went limp as the air, and blood flow was curtailed. As the helpless man fell to his knees, Private Pierce released his sleeper hold and watched the other MPs put the come-alongs on the gasping prisoner.

Sergeant Swim nodded his head, acknowledging the excellent job Pierce had done, then watched as two MPs helped the bulky German stagger toward the front door. The sergeant walked over to Private Pierce, then glanced toward the end of the barracks.

"Now," he said. "Let's deal with the other German bastard." Both men looked toward Major Wolf.

"I'm not surprised that Fritz was in on it," the sergeant said. He marched to the end of the barracks, Private Pierce a few steps behind him, where a very casual Fritz Wolf was standing. The German prisoner, a well-known troublemaker, was tall, with broad shoulders, blond hair, and steel-blue eyes. He had a grin on his handsome face that gave the impression that he was in complete control of the situation. He removed a clean white cigarette from his shirt pocket and put it into his mouth. With the unlit cigarette dangling from his lips, he looked deeply into the eyes of Sergeant Swim. Grinning even more now, he said, "Time to 'brig,' sergeant?" He glanced at Private Pierce and smiled, "I like za brig, sergeant."

The sergeant gripped the long black nightstick he had been holding onto since running into the barracks. He stared into the German's blue, defiant eyes, and in them, he saw the tortured faces of American GIs who had died in battle or suffered at the ruthless hands of Nazi bastards like Fritz Wolf. Sergeant Swim breathed a bit harder as he visualized slamming his nightstick into Fritz Wolf's blond-haired skull. He wanted to pounce on the defiant German with every ounce of muscle and strength he could muster, but he knew that he couldn't under these circumstances.

The gruff-voiced sergeant was silent, the room quiet, and his MPs stared at him, waiting for him to hit the German or issue his next order. And Fritz Wolf, baiting his keeper, knew the American wouldn't hit him in front of his precious MPs. He knew it, and so did the sergeant. The prisoner removed his unlit cigarette and smirked, "Sie müssen lauter sprechen."

"What did you say, you Kraut bastard?" the sergeant said as sweat trickled down the back of his head onto his massive neck and shoulders. He pulled his nightstick back, ready to strike.

From across the room, Luke Reed said, "He told you to speak up, Sergeant Swim." Luke was the only German American

MP at the camp. He wasn't perfect at German, but could get by, and had been quite useful in the camp.

"Ja, Ja," the sneering German agreed.

The sergeant glanced at his young MPs in the barracks, with the faithful looks of men ready to follow his lead. He knew that if he struck the prisoner under those conditions, his men would follow suit, and that wasn't what he wanted. So far, the camp had stuck by the rules of the Geneva Convention, and he would try his best to be a good example to them. As much as this hardheaded, tough-talking sergeant wanted to crack this guy's head, he knew he couldn't—not that night anyway.

Sergeant Swim spun the sneering prisoner around and wrenched the man's hands behind his back. Fritz Wolf gasped as the burly sergeant tossed a pair of come-alongs around his wrists with such speed the MPs who observed it talked it about it for several days. Carefully, he herded Fritz and the other two prisoners out of the barracks and saw to it that all three of them were securely in separate cells in the brig.

Later that evening, in a small, smoke-filled office, Staff Sergeant Swim conducted a debriefing session, commending Pierce and Spencer for a job well done.

"Fritz Wolf," the sergeant said, "and his two German buddies will rot in the brig a little while. But I know it won't change their defiant attitude. And it won't keep them from trying to escape."

"Yes, Sergeant," Private Pierce said.

"But let's not dwell on that," Sergeant Swim said. "Let's talk about how you men performed tonight. What went right and what went wrong."

The MPs were tired and hungry, so the sergeant kept the meeting short. Most of all he complimented privates Pierce and Spencer for a job well done. Neither of the two men knew what to say, so the sergeant wrapped up their meeting. "Now get your skinny butts out of my office!" the sergeant said.

As the two MPs left the sergeant's office and stepped out into the night air, they beamed with pride. It wasn't easy to please Sergeant Swim, but when you did—it was worth a month's pay.

Out of habit, Pierce checked his watch, though a watch was never as accurate as a soldier's appetite. If they hurried, they still might be able to get a hot cup of coffee and a cold sandwich.

It would be a lot more than three rebellious German prisoners would get that night.

POW BULLETIN BOARD
Post Immediately

ARMY SERVICES FORCES
HEADQUARTERS PRISONER OF WAR CAMP
Office of the Commanding Officer
Alva, Oklahoma

Recently the undersigned removed the beer from Compound No. 2 because the German workers made frequent and long visits to the latrine. Apparently, the drinking of beer has a very bad effect on their kidneys, particularly during working hours. It is also possible that the food is causing considerable belly aches and looseness of the bowels. Another alarming factor about this looseness of the bowels is that many fail to lower their trousers while sitting on the commodes. Such indifference to personal hygiene and sanitation is most unique. Perhaps they are copying the habits of their oriental Aryan friends the Japanese, who tie strings around their trousers, defecate in their trousers during the day, and empty the contents on their gardens in the evening. Another remarkable feature of their behavior is that many appear to regain their full health and vigor when confronted with a square meal or when engaged in sports. In fact, about the only time their afflictions are in evidence is between Fatigue Call and Recall and on other occasions when cooperation with the United States authorities is desired.

8   SMALL TOWN DANCE

Saturday morning, Mr. Pierce moved a little slower than usual, apparently suffering from the debilitating side effects of a hangover. Quietly, we drove out to the little field to the east of his house, hoping to cut and haul the last of the wheat. Mr. Pierce hardly spoke at all, and I felt guilty about some of the things I had said to him the night before.

That afternoon I sat on the noisy tractor while the sun grew almost unbearably hot on the back of my neck. As usual, I daydreamed about Carol while cutting row after row of ripe wheat. I kept thinking about calling her. Maybe I'd get the chance to call her soon.

I could still see her looking across the counter at me at Lana's Café. Her long hair brushed back perfectly and her skin smooth and delicate. And those lips of hers; full, moist, and begging to be kissed. I could almost taste her mouth pressing against mine and her sweet-smelling hair in my face. In my mind, we were holding hands as I kissed her. We were alone, somewhere, anywhere. Anywhere except on a tractor in the middle of a wheat field.

Suddenly something shiny flashed in front of me. A barbed-wire fence crossed my path four feet in front of the tractor. I was headed right toward it with no time to turn. Gripping the steering wheel, I turned to the left as my heart beat faster and faster. The wheels of the tractor spun at a sharp angle, and the combine followed grudgingly.

Coming out of the turn, the tractor's huge right tire pressed against the jagged fence, almost crushing it. I jerked the steering wheel to the left again, this time bringing the tire away from the fence several inches. I shook my head in relief. Then, just as I thought my troubles were over, I noticed two of the meanest eyes in the world staring at me. Standing right in the path of the tractor, bold, defiant, and angry, was the gigantic red bull, Pluto.

His massive shoulders were arched forward as he stood like a creature completely devoid of fear, ready to charge the tractor, the combine, and me. Now the front of the tractor was only ten feet from the stubborn bull and closing on him rapidly. For a split second, I thought of turning away, then changed my mind. What the heck, it's my turn to call his bluff.

Pushing the throttle forward, I steered directly for the ornery animal. If he was stupid enough to stand in the way of a noisy John Deere tractor, I could care less. It was time to teach that bull a lesson.

A narrow distance of five feet separated the bull from the oncoming tractor. Then three feet, two, one, and I felt chills run down my back as I chickened out, grabbing the wheel to turn away. But before I turned the wheel, Pluto sidestepped the oncoming mass of steel like a skillful quarterback escaping from a bulky lineman.

The cranky animal ran along with me, snorting, darting back and forth, and then circling the tractor and combine, always watching me. It looked as though he was looking for a place to attack. But if he did, my escape plan was simple; I would cut the engine and hop onto the combine, which stood several feet above the bull's head. Fortunately, my escape plan was never put to the test. Pluto ran off across the field, back where he came from, and I didn't have to evacuate the tractor.

Pluto loped across the wheat stubs, then disappeared over a small hill as I wondered how in the world the stupid animal got into the wheat field in the first place. I looked behind me and felt relieved that Mr. Pierce wasn't nearby. Breathing easier, I decided to pay more attention to my driving and give up the daydreaming.

The rest of the afternoon, I kept expecting to see Pluto standing in the way of the tractor, but he never came around again. The only other obstacle to finishing that day was the rain which threatened to end our work. For a while large black clouds materialized off to the west, cooling the late afternoon, but it didn't rain, and our work went on.

By six o'clock, we had hauled the last of the wheat to town and were back at the house. There was only one thing on my mind: calling Carol. As soon as Mr. Pierce parked the truck, I jumped out and ran to the house for a towel. I heard him shout as I went through the back door,

"Hey, I thought we were going to start plowing tonight."

I knew he was kidding, so I ignored him and grabbed a well-used towel off the cabinet. In ten seconds, I ran back out the door toward the water trough. I was going to town, even if I had to hitchhike. But, like most weekends, Mr. Pierce wanted to go almost as much as I did, and by six forty-five we were clean, fed, *sort of,* and headed for Alva.

#

On the west end of Alva, about a block away from Lana's Café, there was a Hudson filling station, which had four gas pumps, a small office, and a garage with two greasy work bays. Most of the time, you would see farmers or city people standing in the office, passing the time talking about politics, wheat, or sports. Mr. Pierce and I had stopped there a few times to fill his big truck, and I'd noticed a payphone on the wall right beside the red Coke machine.

The only problem was the fact that the crowded little office didn't allow much in the way of privacy. But my other choice was Lana's Café, and if I went there, I would run the risk that Lana might pull the phone out of my hands and say something crude. Private or not, I decided it would be the Hudson filling station.

When we got to town, Mr. Pierce let me off near the pool hall, and I headed for the Hudson station. Inside the office, there was a powerful stench of oil, which caused me to question my decision not to use Lana's phone. Only an hour before I had taken a bath in the horse trough, and the last thing I wanted was to smell like a can of 10W-40 motor oil.

Two idle farmers sat on rickety chairs, talking and laughing with a man who appeared to be the owner. The owner wore a tan uniform and a crumpled bus driver's cap and stood near the cash register, smoking a cigar. Of course, he noticed me right away.

"Can I help you, son?"

"Oh, uh, just need to use the phone, sir."

"Sure," he said. "It's right over there." He pointed across the room, then went back to his discussion with the farmers. I fished a dime out of my pocket, then put it into the coin slot on top of the phone. Hearing the tone, I placed my finger in the black ring, but instead of dialing Carol's number, I stood there for a moment. All I could think of was my phone number back home in Tulsa.

"Problem, son?" the owner asked, as the two farmers stopped talking and stared at me. I shook my head but felt like an idiot. A loud bell clanged twice, signaling a customer's arrival out at the gas pumps. Without saying another word, the owner pushed in the drawer of the cash register, grabbed a red grease rag, then walked out the front door.

The farmers went back to their business of discussing local and world issues, and I glanced up at a calendar above the phone which advertised a local insurance company. There was a colorful picture of a little boy walking down a dirt path toward a pond. The boy wore a pair of coveralls and carried a cane pole, and at his side, his trusty dog walked along, making the nostalgic scene complete.

On the bottom of the calendar, the insurance company had its address and phone number. The phone number didn't matter, but the prefix, Hickory, was the same as Carol's. Seeing that triggered my hazy memory and I dialed her number. My heart began to beat faster with each ring and then, "Hello," a lady said.

"Hello," I replied weakly. "Is Carol there?"

"No. She left about an hour ago. Who's this?"

"This is Matt Turner," I said, knowing she wouldn't recognize my name. "I met Carol a few weeks ago, and I just wanted to talk."

"Yes," she interrupted. "Carol told me about you. She said you might call."

"She did?"

"Yes. And anyway, she's at the teen dance with Sandy and her Uncle Bill. It's over at the VFW club."

"Where?"

"The Veterans of Foreign Wars."

"OK, bye," I said, abruptly. "I mean, bye, ma'am. And ... thanks a lot." Carol's mother giggled as she hung up.

A moment later, one of the farmers, who told me that he was a member of the VFW, took pleasure in giving me detailed directions to the club.

"Thank you, sir," I said.

As I turned to run out the door, the farmer grabbed my arm and said, "Son, I'm a member of the Veterans of Foreign Wars because I was in the infantry during World War II. See, one time when I was in France, our outfit was moving through this big forest."

"Yes, sir," I said. "Maybe you could tell me when I get back. I have to meet someone ..."

"No," he said, ignoring my plea. "It wasn't in France. It must have been Germany. I don't remember. We were trying to move through these woods when one of those German tanks, an uh ..."

"Panzer," the man sitting near the farmer said. The man was reading the newspaper and didn't look up.

"Right," the farmer said. "Panzer. Anyways, we went through this thick forest, and we heard the sound of the darn tank off in the distance as it was trying to make its way through the trees. Now the trees and woods were mighty thick, and I wasn't too worried because there was no road and the tank would never catch us."

"Yes, sir," I said. I tried to pull away, but the old farmer wouldn't let go of my shirt. The manager of the store came back in and stood by the cash register and the man reading the newspaper grunted, but never looked up.

"So," the farmer said. "My buddy Bill, eh …"

"Parker," the newspaper reader said.

"Right," said the farmer. "Bill Parker. Me and Bill were walking fast when the Panzer tank got off its first shot. The shot didn't have a chance in hell of hitting any of us, so I giggled and Bill, uh …"

"Parker."

"Right, Bill Parker. Well, he stopped and looked back at the tank. And about that time the round hit a couple of large trees near us and the trees fell all around us but were no danger. Then the tank fired again, and this time it was a HE shell, and it caused one hell of an explosion at the top of the trees close to us. It scared the hell out of me, and I started running. We were showered with wood fragments and splinters as small as your finger and as big as a fence post. Everywhere you looked, there was wood falling to the ground, and shrapnel too. After I ran a few yards, I looked around for Bill Parker. When I turned around, I saw him all right. He was dead as a doornail. He lay face down, pinned to the ground by a piece of pinewood the size of a baseball bat. I grabbed his dog tags and ran as fast as I could to get away from there."

"That must have been pretty rough," I said. "Thank you, sir. I need to get going."

The farmer let go of my shirt. "Sure, son," he said. He had a kind of puzzled look on his wrinkled face and asked his friend, "Why did they call some of those tank shells HE rounds?"

This time the man looked up and shook his head. "I don't remember."

"High-explosive rounds," the gas station owner said. "High explosive."

"That's right," the farmer said. "And I can tell you, they sure as hell were."

#

When I got to the VFW club, I told the guy at the door that my grandparents were there, and he let me in. Inside the big hall the sound of rock and roll vibrated throughout the room. After weeks of near-silent days and nights on the farm, the magical, musical sounds gave me chills, and for the first time in my life I listened to the words, not just the rhythm, and they spoke to me. Standing there in the dark, smoky club, waiting for my eyes to adjust to the dimly lit room, the simple lyrics of an Everly Brothers ballad went right to my heart.

Walking past several groups of teens and grown-ups, I strained my eyes, looking for Carol and Sandy. With the interior lights turned low, it had a shadowy, romantic effect on the room, as the band played one of my favorites,

> *Never felt like this until I kissed ya.*
> *Never knew what I missed until I kissed ya.*
> *Never had you on my mind,*
> *Now you're there all the time.*
> *Never knew what I missed until I kissed ya.*
> *Until I kissed ya.*

Leaning against a steel beam, away from the crowd and feeling almost invisible, I listened as the music and a solid drum beat continued to weave a magical spell around me. One second it gave me such powerful confidence, then it seemed as though I was alone in the middle of an endless desert.

> *Never knew what I missed until I kissed ya.*
> *Until I kissed ya.*

And with that thought in mind, I finally spotted Carol sitting at a crowded table. She was drinking a Coke and looking right at me. Her face seemed to radiate in the murky smoke-filled light of the dance hall, and I had hopes that the Everly Brothers ballad had cast the same musical spell on her that it had on me.

I was fifteen years old, and love was an expression that I'd heard all of my life. But until that moment words like love and government and atmosphere had always had a kind of secretive meaning. I never expected to know their purpose, and I never dreamed of using one in a personal sentence. But now that was all changing. *"Until I kissed ya."*

Carol raised her hand, motioning for me to come over. I don't recall walking across the room, but I must have. I only remember sitting next to her and looking into her eyes, wishing that we could dance.

As I approached her table, Carol stood up and appeared very dressed up in an off-white two-piece outfit that looked terrific on her. It was a matched set with a tiny floral design along the edge of the pants and a similar design on the top. The pants were mid-calf, and kind of tight around her hips, and the top was sleeveless and barely touched her waist. Very cute. I wasn't expecting to be at a dance and had worn a pair of clean jeans and a T-shirt which looked a bit too casual.

"You look dressed up," I said. She smiled as she introduced me to some of the grown-ups at her table, most of which were related to her. Sandy sat with a boy, and it looked as though they were on a date.

Carol adjusted her blouse and smiled. "My grandmother bought me this outfit from the catalog. You like it?"

"I like it a lot," I said. What kind of blouse is it?"

"It's not a blouse, silly. It's called a pop-top."

"Well, you look like one of those rich girls in Tulsa, except that you're not stuck up like them."

Carol's cheerful smile faded a bit, and I realized she wasn't sure how to take my comment. And once again I remembered something my grandmother always said: "Choose your words as well as you choose your friends, and you'll never get in trouble."

Before this summer, I don't think I ever realized what a wise woman my grandmother was. Neither Carol nor I spoke for a few minutes, and I was happy just to sit and look at her, but then I got a little nervous and thought I should say something, but not about clothing.

"I called your house," I said. "And your mother told me you would be here."

"I'm glad you called," she said. She looked at me shyly as the band switched over to a slow song by Elvis Presley. Hopefully, an Elvis song could make her forget my stupid rich-girl comment.

I will spend my whole life through loving you, just loving you.

"Say, that's a pretty good band," I said. "Wanna dance?"

Her friend Sandy, who was now right beside Carol, stood up and said, "Sure, I thought you'd never ask." As I sat there in shock, Sandy grabbed her boyfriend and they went out to the dance floor laughing.

Carol smiled good-naturedly and walked past me, following the others, then she glanced back at me over her shoulder. Feeling a bit shocked by her sudden response, I quickly hurried to catch her. The next thing I knew we were on the dance floor looking at each other, my arm around her thin waist, and my hand touching a tiny island of silky smooth skin along her back. I was beginning to like those "pop-tops" after all. The band continued the slow, romantic song which swirled around us, blending deeply with Carol's perfume.

And they played on, just for the two of us …

Winter, summer, springtime too, lovin' you, just lovin' you.

With my face next to hers, our bodies touching gently, I prayed that the band would play that same song forever and only stop if the Russians invaded the United States, or if modern science invented a cure for zits. There must have been other couples dancing near us, but I didn't notice them. I could only see the girl in my arms.

Makes no difference where I go, or what I do. You know that I'll always be lov…ing…you.

Then Carol's adorable little nose touched my face as she looked up at me. She grinned as if she knew some deep, dark secret.

"What's wrong?" I asked.

"The song's over," she said. "Let's sit down before people think we're crazy." I glanced around the dance floor, and sure enough, people *were* staring at us.

Quickly, I released my arm from around her waist and stepped back. We laughed as we walked back to her table. Sandy sat with her boyfriend, and I finally got a good look at him. He was tanned and husky and looked like he might be the son of a farmer. I nodded to him as we joined them at the table.

"Howdy," he said, in a thick country accent. Then, without waiting for a reply, he and Sandy were lost in their own conversation again. I couldn't have been more pleased. Carol sat across from me and exchanged a few secret looks with Sandy. I could see that country girls and city girls know how to tell things to each other without saying a word. I had seen girls do this before, and I always wished I knew their silent code. Boys were different. Instead of little eye signals or head movements, boys relied more on punching or jabbing each other, each blow signifying something completely different. Since most of my friends were bigger than me, I always wished that we could switch to the girl's less painful code.

But it didn't matter, because the guy Sandy was with didn't have much to say to me. He was busy telling Sandy something about the Peace Corps, an organization I had heard about on TV but one I knew nothing about.

Carol smiled again, then took another drink of her Coke. I tried to think of something to say, something impressive.

"We finished up the harvest today," I said, proudly. "We start plowing tomorrow."

"Neat," Carol said. "Did Mr. Pierce have a good year?"

"Pretty good," I said, thinking about his problems.

"What do you mean?"

"Oh, it's just that he has some things that he can't seem to work out." Then trying to forget about Mr. Pierce's problems, I said, "That doesn't matter tonight. Let's talk about you. What's your favorite band? Bet I can guess. Brenda Lee? How 'bout Bobby Darin?"

"Wait a minute, Matt," she said. "What did you mean 'things he can't seem to work out'? Mr. Pierce is such a nice man, and my aunt always says good things about him. What happened? Did he borrow some money or something like that?"

"Kind of like that," I said.

"Well, tell me," she said, now looking at me with an expression I had never seen on her before. I could see now that this girl could get serious about stuff. I figured I'd better ignore the music and try and not look at her face too often since it only kept me off track. I glanced at her one more time. I only wanted to talk about her a little while longer. Was that asking so much?

After a moment, I started to think clearly, and when I did, it made me care about her even more. To think that a young girl like Carol might worry about an old guy like Mr. Pierce, it was pretty nice. I took a deep breath and decided to get to it. To tell her everything I knew. It may not have been the right thing to do, dragging an innocent girl into that mess, but I needed some help and Carol had a very helpful look on her cute little face.

#

The next few hours flew past us in a beautiful blur of dancing, talking, and silly stuff like sharing a Coke. Carol was a good listener who seemed to have a keen sense of understanding, which went far beyond the simple things I talked about with her. After I had told her everything about Mr. Pierce's dilemma, we danced our last dance of the night. "Last dance," because Carol had a strict curfew, and she had told me her father was not a patient man. I looked over at the clock and asked her the magic question, "Can I walk you home?"

Carol looked at me with a mysterious look on her face and said, "Only on one condition."

She grinned.

"Anything," I said with a mock bow and a sweep of my arms. "What dragon must I kill for the beautiful princess?"

"You're silly," she said. "Just take Sandy and me to Lana's for a cherry Coke, then you and I can walk home from there, and Troy can walk Sandy home."

"Sounds great!" I said, beaming, but trying not to look too anxious. If she had looked closer, she would have seen just how excited I felt.

9   SHERIFF'S OFFICE

L ana's Café was pretty crowded by the time we arrived, but not as bad as the time Mr. Pierce and I had been there. It was Saturday night, and Lana's was the only place open, except for the pool hall. So many of her customers were teenagers.

Because all the booths were occupied, the four of us agreed to sit at the counter. Troy hadn't said much at the dance, but somewhere between the VFW and Lana's Café, he overcame his shyness. We sat on bar stools that swiveled and faced the counter. Troy spun around a couple of times on his seat, then grabbed the sugar container during his third spin. When he stopped, he unscrewed the shiny chrome top of the sugar container and turned it back slightly. It was an old trick to fool the next customer who would tip the container into a cup of coffee or glass of tea and spill the entire contents either into his drink or onto the counter.

Sandy giggled, but Carol ignored him. He seemed to be enjoying the attention Sandy freely offered him, and she didn't seem to care that his pranks were better suited for grade school kids. Now that I got a good look at the guy, I could see he probably didn't know much about girls. Of course, I didn't either, so that part was okay. But watching him a bit more closely, I noticed something about his eyes. He wasn't just silly; he was more spiteful, and maybe a bit mean. Sandy didn't seem to notice.

I ignored him, thinking any minute big Lana would show up and drop a tray of fried chicken in his lap. But, unfortunately it turned out Lana had the night off and another waitress came over to take our order. This woman didn't have Lana's personality, but it looked as though she had experience in handling people.

Wearing a pink, short-sleeved uniform with a food-soiled white apron and crumpled white cap, the thin waitress gave our group a glance and said, "Okay, what's it going to be?"

"We're not in here to eat," Troy spouted.

"Oh, yeah," the waitress said. "What are you here for?"

Troy stood up and faced the waitress. Then he spoke loud enough for everyone to hear, "We heard there was a dance here tonight, and we're going to show this town how to rock around the clock." As he made the announcement, he grabbed the waitress's hand and pretended to spin her around. Instead of joining in, she jerked away—leaving him standing alone. His little show didn't get much of a positive reaction from the other customers either, and Sandy seemed embarrassed.

The thin waitress stuck her pencil into her ratted brown hair and cracked her bubble gum a couple of times.

She smiled a kind of fake, overly friendly smile, looked right at the girls and said, "You better tell your friend here if he doesn't quiet down, he's going to be rocking around the kitchen back there washing pots and pans." She raised her voice slightly and took complete control of the situation, "Now what do you kids want to eat?"

We gave the waitress our orders, and she disappeared into the kitchen. Troy's cheeks were as flushed as if he had been called out by the school principal. What was supposed to be funny turned out to be embarrassing. I tried to think of something to say, but I decided to keep quiet. Evidently, Troy felt differently.

"I don't have to take that crap from her!" Troy said indignantly.

"Come on, man," I offered with a smile. "Don't sweat it. Everyone gets told off by a waitress sooner or later. I remember one time in Tulsa I was . . ."

"Well, I don't!" he interrupted. "It ain't right."

I started to say something to smooth things over when a young Negro cook came out from the kitchen with a large pie in his hands. As he walked, he continually looked down at the floor. I had seen him back in the kitchen the first time we ate at Lana's, but now I could see him up close.

He was taller than me, around six-foot tall, I guessed. He had broad shoulders and wore white cotton work slacks and a food-stained, white T-shirt. A dirty apron was wrapped around his slender frame. His nose was thick, his skin light brown, and his eyes were dark, brooding, inquisitive. He appeared self-conscious now that he was out of the kitchen and into the crowded café—teeming with noisy white customers. I tried to think of how I might feel working in an all-Negro café. It wouldn't be easy.

The young cook placed the pie on the counter and began to cut it, his back to us. I glanced over at Troy, who was looking closely at the black worker. He stuck his index finger out, then slowly pushed a sugar container forward. The glass container was less than an inch away from the edge of the counter. In hushed tones, Sandy whispered to Troy, "Stop it, Troy. Just stop it." The cook continued to cut his pie, seemingly unaware of the situation behind him. He held the large knife in both hands and moved it clockwise around the pie, dividing it into generous pieces.

Troy glanced at Sandy and smiled pleasantly, and it seemed like he might listen to her. But then the husky teenager grinned, nudged the sugar container slightly, and a second later the hideous sound of glass crashing against the concrete floor was heard all across the café. The young cook jumped forward and spun around with the butcher knife gripped tightly in his hand. Everyone watched as the frightened cook surveyed the mess on the floor and looked up at the four of us at the counter. Before he could say a word, the waitress was there with her hands on her hips.

"Sam, put that knife down!" A scowl across her hollow face. "What did you do this time, boy?"

Sam stood shaking his head, and blood from his left hand dropped onto the floor. The young cook wrapped his dirty apron around his hand and glanced at the red stain on top of the snow-white pile of sugar.

"I didn't do anything," he said. "I was puttin' them pies up just like you said, then I heard that glass breakin'." He looked accusingly at Troy and said, "'Bout cut my finger off, too."

Troy stood up and rose to the challenge. It was one thing to get told off by the waitress, but he wasn't about to have a Negro stare him down. "Boy, you better tell the truth," Troy shouted. "And you best quit eyeballing me."

The humiliated cook looked down at the floor again, his face betraying quiet anger. The waitress glanced around the café, at the all-white customers who seemed concerned with the incident and the shock of seeing a colored boy holding a butcher knife. You could see in the waitress's face that she knew she needed to get things under control. People in Alva were nice folks, but they wanted to enjoy their food and didn't care much for the civil rights movement. She looked at Troy suspiciously, and I guess she knew who was wrong, but she also knew she better not accuse the white boy or there would be hell to pay. She glanced around the restaurant at her customers again, then took a deep breath and looked at her cook.

"Sam," she said indignantly. "You know I'll have to tell Lana about this. And you can be sure she *won't* be happy. Now you clean up this mess and get back in the kitchen. You're done out here for tonight."

"Yes'm," he agreed. He stood for a moment with his shoulders slumped and his head down. It was the posture of submission I had seen so often by Negroes who worked for tough white people. The waitress started back toward the kitchen, but before she got to the door, I blurted something out.

"Wait a minute."

She turned around. "Now what?"

Troy looked at me and whispered, "What the hell are you doing?" I ignored him and looked right at the waitress, who wasn't at all happy to turn around.

"Ma'am," I said. "I was playing around and knocked the sugar off the counter. I was being stupid. I'm really sorry." She looked at me suspiciously and shook her head.

"Well, just be more careful next time. Okay?" She glanced at Sam as though she might apologize. Sam looked at me and then at the waitress, a slight look of hope on his face. The waitress glanced at the dull stares of her customers, and something, perhaps the mood in the room, must have made her want to end it. Without another word, she turned and went back into the kitchen a few steps in front of the colored boy, who looked back at Troy. Just as the waitress was out of sight, Troy said, "What are you looking at, boy? I told you not to stare at me."

"Just cleaning it up here," the cook said, holding his dustpan in one hand and a broom in the other hand. The black dustpan had a bright red bloodstain around it from the cut on Sam's hand.

"That's what I thought," Troy said.

The cook never looked at any of us again, and soon he was back in the kitchen and safely away from Troy. From time to time, I saw him back there, and down deep, I hoped he would give me a knowing gesture or an approving glance, but he never looked my way.

"Hey, look," Sandy said. "There's Kate and Suzie."
Two pretty girls walked over and stood behind us. They chatted away with Sandy and Carol, talking about the dance and some of their other friends. After a few minutes, everyone seemed ready to leave.

Sandy clutched the arm of one of the two girls who had joined us and said, "Are you guys going home?"

"Sure," the girl said. "Want to walk with us?"

"Okay," Sandy said, to Troy's obvious disappointment. I'm sure he wanted to walk alone with Sandy, but I had the feeling she didn't want to be alone with him. Troy and the three girls went out the door, leaving Carol and me alone at the counter.

"Matt," Carol said. "I'm glad Kate and Suzie came along. I wasn't going to let Sandy walk home alone with that boy. Do you think he was drinking?"

"Maybe so," I said. "Just enough to feel tough. If you want, we can catch up with them."

"No, that's okay. We do need to start for my house pretty soon though."

"Sure," I said, happy we would be walking alone.

"You know, we never did finish talking about Mr. Pierce and Thurman Spencer," Carol said. "I was thinking, maybe there is some way we can get into the police records and find out the name of the person in the car that night. They must have had some report on that accident."

"I don't know," I said. "I'm worried the police may be in on it. I met one of them that night at the park. Remember?"

"Sure," Carol said. "But he's a good guy, and he'll know if something happened that night. Maybe we could stop off at his office and talk to him on the way to my house?"

What I wanted to do was stop off and sneak in a kiss or two along the way. But checking out the serious look on her face, I figured stopping to see the deputy was a pretty good idea. With Carol along, the deputy might be a little more helpful. We hurried out of the café and walked down the street toward the police station.

Several teenagers were driving their hot rods and pickups back and forth on Main Street as we walked along. It was a small-town ritual they called dragging Main. Time after time, cars passed us driving one direction, then they turned around and drove the opposite direction. As an old Ford drove by, an older boy whistled at Carol.

"Hi, Larry!" Carol shouted as they went by. The car kept going along Main Street, the boys inside laughing loudly.

"I'm gonna get a car next year," I bragged.

"Really? What kind?"

"I don't know, but my sister's boyfriend is a good mechanic. He told me if I bought a car, he would help me with the engine and stuff. I want to raise the back end, put in a floor shift and maybe get tucked and rolled leather seats. It's going to be a hot car, very hot."

Carol smiled but didn't say anything. I tried to think of the other things I had overheard the older boys say about cars, but Carol seemed reasonably impressed, so I let it go. About that time,

I noticed we were getting close to the police station, and I forgot all about cars and began to worry about the police.

We walked up the steps of the station together, and it looked like Carol might be a little anxious too. I reached for the door handle and looked into Carol's eyes once more. She gave me a cute, confident grin, and we walked in. I liked her self-assurance.

Inside the police station, the Indian deputy sat at his desk reading the newspaper. His office was located a short distance from the jail, obviously near enough for him keep up with what might be going on there. It was a small room with one cluttered desk, a beat-up swivel chair, and two old chairs placed in front of the desk for visitors. There was a single light fixture suspended from the ceiling, providing enough light to see the deputy, but leaving most of the office in shadows. The only decorations were a couple of things on the wall. On one wall, there was an iconic picture of Will Rogers—cowboy hat, head tilted, right hand scratching the back of his head. On the other wall, there was a worn-out, stained poster announcing "The Chickasaw Nation Annual Meeting in Ada, Oklahoma." And adding to the depressing atmosphere was the faint smell of urine mixed with cigarette smoke which drifted through the bars of the jail and ended up in the office. It wasn't a pleasant place to work.

The deputy wore the same khaki uniform, shirt sleeves rolled up to his elbows and his black hair freshly cut—military style. When we walked in, the deputy looked up, and a smile formed on his rugged face. For a second, I felt a lot better. Maybe Carol's idea was going to work.

"Well, well," he said. "How in the world did a pretty girl like you wind up with a city boy like this?" The deputy grinned.

"She's just picky," I said.

"Not picky enough," he said. Then in a more serious tone, "Now what are you two kids doing in this place when you could be out roaming around town?"

Carol cleared her throat and said, "We were walking by and wanted to come in and say hello."

The deputy's eyes narrowed. He stood up and walked around the desk, then leaned against it, his arms folded. "Oh, is that right?" he said. "So you came in to do your civic duty and see how the police station is running?"

"Well, kind of," Carol said.

"Okay," he said. "I'll give you a full official report." The tall, sturdy deputy stood up straight, his face more serious, and instantly he was transformed into a professional police officer speaking to some unseen supervisor.

"Sir," he said, his voice deep and tough, like one of the police officers on television. "Tonight we have had no major crimes—no stolen cars. There were two drunks picked up around 4 p.m. They were released after they consumed one pot of black coffee and spent four hours in the drunk tank. We had one minor accident involving a tractor and street sign. And there was one stray dog picked up over at the campus after scaring the crap out of a janitor." The deputy, seeing the surprised look on our faces, grew even more professional as he continued his report.

"Oh, one more thing, sir; one of the kids dragging Main was watching a pretty girl in a pair of tight short shorts. He failed to stop at the red light on Choctaw, and his car bounced off the back of a wheat truck. The collision smashed the front of his Dodge, but barely scratched the wheat truck."

The deputy grinned and relaxed, his report finished and his two visitors visibly impressed.

I saw this as an opportunity and grabbed it.

"Deputy," I said. "That's what we wanted to talk to you about—a car wreck."

"You mean you didn't come in to hear a police report?" he said. Then more seriously, "I thought there might be something else."

"Yes, sir," I said. "Do you keep records of all the accidents that happen in town?"

"Sure, but why?"

"Well," I continued. "One night last year, around . . ."

Just as I was about to ask him the most important question of all, two men walked through the front door, then into the hallway.

"Oh," the deputy said. "Here's the sheriff."

124

A short, fat man in his forties, the sheriff led the way, and right behind him, Thurman Spencer strolled in, smiling like a snake oil salesman. The sheriff, noticing visitors in the deputy's office, joined us, and both he and Thurman Spencer frowned when they recognized me. Neither of them seemed too pleased.

"Well," the sheriff said. "What's going on here? Why are you kids here? Is something wrong?"

"Sir," the deputy said. "They came in to pay me a courtesy visit. We were talking about how we maintain records at the police station." Then he turned to me and said, "Now, son, what was it you were asking?"

I didn't like the nasty look on the sheriff's face when he looked at Carol, and Thurman Spencer looked mean enough to tear the plaster off the wall. We had lost our opportunity, and it was time to get Carol home.

I smiled and said, "Oh, I just wanted to come in and say hi, that's all. I've got to get Carol home now. Thanks a lot."

I grabbed one of Carol's soft hands and led her to the door before anyone had time to ask more questions. Glancing over my shoulder, I noticed the deputy standing in the middle of the office, scratching his head while the other two men watched us suspiciously.

Thurman Spencer followed us to the front door, and I felt his penetrating stare as Carol and I walked down the steps and out to the street. We hurried along toward Carol's house.

Ten minutes later, in front of Carol's two-story, wood-framed home, we stood quietly on the sidewalk for a long moment. Thankfully, during the walk to her house, we talked about other things, and it seemed as though we had put the sheriff's office far from our minds. Now, finally alone, we were drawn into the subtle magic of a summer night. In the sky above us, a million stars flickered while a milky-white moon looked down on us, and the sweet smell of honeysuckle swirled around the narrow porch. Then, the lonesome whine of a little kitten broke the silence. It was mewing under the porch.

"Is that your cat?" I asked. "What's her name?"

"No, she's our neighbor's cat, Biscuit."

"Little thing sounds pretty lonesome," I said. "Do you have a pet?"

"No, Daddy won't let us. How 'bout you?"

"I guess I do," I said. "I have a horse, or I should say Mr. Pierce has one. Her name is June, and she's kind of like a cat in some ways. You know, she's easy to get along with as long as you let her have her own way."

"Listen," she said, glancing at her front porch. In an instant, her face changed from caring to concern. "I have to get inside pretty quick. My father's probably standing inside the front door, watching us. If I'm not in by exactly 10:00, he's not too happy and will flash the porch light on and off."

"All right," I said. "Hey, I'm glad you told your mother about me and glad she told me where you were tonight. I had fun at the dance—and something else."

"What's that," she said. She glanced nervously at the front door.

"It did me a lot of good to talk to you about Mr. Pierce."

"That's okay," she said. "Maybe you could call me again. I mean, since I wasn't here when you called tonight; that call didn't count."

"Sure thing," I said, smiling.

Carol stood facing me with her back to the house. Glancing over her shoulder, I thought I saw her father's outline through the front door. I wasn't sure. Even though I didn't want to get her in trouble, I felt an urge to kiss her. The feeling was so strong, so powerful, that even if her dad walked out and stood between us, I knew I just had to kiss her.

Something inside of me, something I had never felt before, took total control of my emotions. At the dance, I'd had similar feelings, but standing so close to her in the night air, smelling her hair, holding her soft hands, and looking into her innocent, beautiful eyes—I knew I had found love. Nothing on earth was going to block it—not even her dad.

I took a deep breath and gently pulled her closer to me. Her eyes closed for a second, and I moved forward. Suddenly she opened her eyes and turned toward the house. Two porch lights, as bright and unsettling as prison searchlights, blinked steadily. Romance turned into fear, and the soft touch of Carol's smooth hand turned into moisture. On the fourth blink, Carol's hand slipped away almost as fast as my resolve to kiss her evaporated.

"Well, I guess you have to go in now," I said, feeling weak and cowardly.

"See ya," she said as she walked toward the door.

"See ya," I said with about as much enthusiasm as a condemned man.

With Carol safely inside, the porch light flickered for the last time and then went out. The darkness enveloped the front of the house as I stood alone. A little calico kitten circled my legs, purring softly and rubbing against my jeans affectionately. She softly meowed as I knelt and touched the smooth fur on her narrow back. At that moment, Biscuit and I had a lot in common.

"That's okay, Biscuit," I said. "Someday when we finally grow up, they'll let us in."

Biscuit followed me a few steps, then she sprinted across the lawn to the safety of her porch. Walking alone in the dark streets, the stars above my head gleamed brightly—each one a silent reminder of the twinkle in Carol's blue eyes.

10   WRONG SIDE OF TOWN

As I continued walking, the streets grew darker and less familiar, and then I passed through areas with fewer houses and more open fields. Here and there a dog's bark shattered the silence momentarily, and I was careful not to trip on the bumpy dirt road. During the first few minutes of what was turning into a hike, I could only think about one thing: the kiss that wasn't. Like my grandma used to say, "Getting close only counts in horseshoes."

But after a while, I stopped thinking about Carol and started to consider the possibility I might be lost. Nothing looked familiar, and I knew right then I should have paid more attention when I walked to Carol's house.

The lights of the town square were not visible ahead of me, and I couldn't see the train station or the lighting framing the top of the granary. Nothing broke the endless darkness. I worried about the direction I was walking, and it seemed as if my vivid imagination expanded every noise I heard. Every sound became a threat of some kind.

In a way, it felt silly to be frightened about walking around in town at night after several weeks of walking around the farm every night. But an acidlike fear developed in the pit of my stomach and rose slowly, steadily into my throat.

Just when I was losing my nerve to go a step further, I noticed something; a single streetlight surrounded by trees shined like a beacon in the night. It was only one block away, so I walked a little faster, hoping to read the street sign on the corner. In the dark nearby, a dog sprinted across a yard. I started to run, then heard a thud as the angry animal struck the inside of a fence. I felt my heart pounding as I scurried toward the safety of the streetlight, happy the dog's owners had installed a fence. "Sorry, boy," I said as I scrambled along the street.

The snarling dog continued to bark as I crossed the street. On the other side of the road, an old car was parked with its hood up. As I walked closer, the muffled sounds of laughter came from the other side of the car. *Maybe I can get directions*, I thought. I listened carefully and strained my eyes in the dark to find out if it was someone I knew.

As I walked around the front of the dusty, battered car, all laughter stopped completely. Steam rose from the car's overheated radiator, and on the other side of it stood three angry-looking colored boys who were frowning at me through the rising mist. It was the first time I'd ever been alone, face to face with a Negro. The expressions on their black, sweaty faces ranged from disgust to hatred, and at that moment, I realized what the word minority really meant. My knees quivered, my mouth seemed unable to move, as I tried to think of something to say.

The tallest of the three boys grunted, and the short guy in the middle elbowed him—egging him on.

"Well, well," the tall boy said. "I think this young cracker is lost."

He was a tall, muscular kid and seemed to be the leader of the group. He took a small whiskey bottle from his hip pocket, removed the cap, and took a swig. Wiping his mouth, he gave the bottle to the short boy and stepped toward me. Before I had time to run, the large boy stepped closer to me, so close I could smell the liquor on his breath. His face was dark and brooding, and there were small orange and brown freckles all along his cheeks. When he spoke, his deep, stern voice gave the impression of a grown man.

"Yeah, he's lost all right," he said. "Or maybe he be messing with the girls on this block. How 'bout it? Maybe you the white boy who tried to pick my sista up the other night."

"Hey, man," I said. "I don't know your sister. I was just walking a . . . uh . . . a white girl . . . home. She lives a few blocks from here. Now I'm trying to get back to town."

"Oh, you tryin' to get home?" the shorter one said in fake sympathy. Then he slapped his tall buddy on the back and said, "Tell'm how to get to town, Speck."

"Yeah, I'll tell him where to go, all right," Speck obliged, now standing even closer. His mean, dark eyes glared as if he had captured some hated soldier behind enemy lines. A mixture of cheap whiskey and body odor swirled around the tall Negro as he grabbed my shirt and pushed me down to the ground. "Get up," he said. "Then get your ass back to your own part of town."

The third boy, who up to that point had been silent, moved in closer. I stood up, expecting at any second one of them would throw a punch—or worse yet—pull a weapon out of his pocket. Like most white kids, I had heard the stories of Negroes who carried knives, guns, and everything imaginable. Kids around our neighborhood liked to tell and retell far-fetched tales of the Negro bootlegger near Tulsa who kept a bazooka in the trunk of his car. Some kids even said he had a flamethrower at his house. At that moment, I was ready to believe anything, and I didn't want to find out what these three boys carried in their pockets. I needed to run. I needed to hightail it out of there, and quick.

Sweat formed on my forehead, trickling down my cheeks as I faced these three angry guys who looked mean enough to make me wish I'd never been born white. Then Speck, the leader of the group, reached into the back pocket of his jeans and pulled out a long thin switchblade knife. My heart pumped adrenaline so fast I thought it would explode. Speck touched the tiny lever, and the knife's blade snapped open.

For some reason, the quiet boy's expression changed.

"Wait a minute, Speck," he said, grabbing Speck's wrist.

"Man, don't be grabbing me," Speck said to his friend. "What's wrong with you, Sam? We ain't gonna do nothing except teach him a lesson."

"No," the quiet one persisted. "I think I know this white boy."

"What?" Speck asked in amazement. He shot Sam another angry look.

"Yeah, I know this white boy," Sam repeated.

"You do?" Speck and I said in unison, equally amazed. Then Sam asked, "You came to Lana's tonight with three other white kids, didn't you?"

"That's right," I said, finally recognizing him and slightly relieved that I did. "I sure did, and you're the cook, aren't you?"

"Yeah, he's the damn cook," Speck grumbled. "But that don't mean shit. You shouldn't be on this block. We walk around your neighborhood and they'd have our asses in jail."

"It's okay, Speck," Sam said. "This guy took up for me tonight. See, some white smart-ass smashed a sugar jar on the floor and tried to blame it on me. This white kid here spoke up. Maybe we ought to let him go just this once."

"This guy didn't stand up for you," Speck said. "I don't believe it."

"Sure did," Sam said.

"He did that in front of white people?"

"In front of a room full of white people," Sam said.

Speck looked back and forth between the cook and me and shook his head. He closed the switchblade carefully and put the long knife back into his pocket. He examined me with disbelieving eyes, squinting as if seeing something very unusual for the first time. He made a quick decision and said, "He's just a cool cat then. You help my buddy? That makes you a cool cat up around here."

"Thanks," I said as relief swept over me. My knees were still knocking slightly, but starting to settle down.

Speck and the other boy laughed and went back to working on the car. Sam stayed with me. He held out his hand and smiled, "I'm Sam," he said. Sam was slender, but not at all frail. His shoulders were solid and his arms muscular. When he smiled, his eyes had a tinge of sparkle to them, and his young black face looked truly happy.

"I'm Matt," I said, feeling a lot better. "Thanks. I was getting a little worried about your friend."

Sam grinned, "He's a pretty good guy when you get to know him."

"Yeah, I have a few buddies like that. They can come on pretty strong with people they don't like, but they'll do anything for a friend—I'd do the same for them."

"Yeah, I bet you would," Sam grinned. "Say, where you from anyway?"

"Tulsa. I'm working the summer out on Mr. Pierce's farm."

His expression changed again, like it had just moments before when he had recognized me.

"What's wrong?" I asked.

"Oh, nothing," he said unconvincingly.

"No, man, there's something wrong. Did Mr. Pierce bother you?"

"No, that old farmer seems nice to everybody. He's been eating at Lana's as long as I been working there, and always polite. But there's something I heard . . ."

"What was it?"

"This is nothing but trouble, man," Sam said. "And I don't want no part of it."

"Please," I said. "If he's in trouble, I need to help him. If you know something, tell me. I promise I won't let anyone know where I heard it."

The young boy looked down at his feet for a moment while his two buddies were laughing about something nearby.

When Sam was sure they weren't listening, he took a deep breath and sighed, "If I tell you, you got to promise you won't ever say I told."

"I won't tell," I said, and I stuck out my hand to seal the promise. I glanced down as we shook; one black hand and one white, joined together over a wheat farmer. My father would never believe it.

Once again Sam glanced over at his buddies, who seemed to be getting nowhere with the overheated car. The shorter boy they called Clyde attempted to put the cap on the steaming radiator, but he fumbled it and cussed.

"Let's go over there and sit on that rock," Sam whispered. I followed him to a spot behind the car, where we sat under the streetlight. The isolated street was dark, and the only movement seemed to be the two colored boys fixing their broken-down car and a lot of mosquitoes buzzing around my face looking for a good place to land. Sam's expression showed his concern as he began.

"I've been working for Lana for three years now, and you hear a lot back in that kitchen. Sometimes I hear people tell lies so big I want to go out there and call them on it. Sometimes we get married folks who come in and never speak a word to each other. Kind of makes me wonder what it's like to be a white person. At our house, you can't get a word in without someone interrupting you. Except you better not interrupt my pa, or you'll wish you didn't."

"That's the same in my house," I said. Again, I thought of what my dad would think if he saw me sitting on the curb beside a Negro. The thought of my dad's face made me grin.

"What's so funny?" Sam asked.

"Oh, nothing. You were about to tell me something."

"Well," he continued as he studied my expression. "The other day, these two white boys come in and sit at the counter where you were tonight. They had more grease on their hair than I use to fry a chicken—looked like a couple of hoods. The one boy, the big one, he's talking 'bout what a great trick he and Linda's uncle played on a drunk farmer last fall. I thought I heard him say Pierce."

"No kidding? What did he mean?"

"Didn't hear much. But he said something like 'car wreck out by the graveyard.' I didn't get the rest. Just sounded like some prank, but they aren't nice kids."

"I think I know what they were talking about, Sam."

"You do?"

"Yeah, but it's a long story. Like you said, nobody should know we talked."

"You right about that."

"Oh, something else, too," I said. "I know who Linda's uncle is."

"Who is he?"

"Thurman Spencer."

Sam looked at me with fear in his eyes. The name Thurman Spencer seemed to have an equally unpleasant effect on everyone—black or white.

"I don't want to go up against Mista' Spencer," Sam said. But if I ever get the chance to spit in his coffee, I'll do it."

I grinned, thinking about Sam spitting into Thurman Spencer's coffee. "What'd he do to you?" I asked.

Sam took some time answering, and his face showed his hate for Thurman Spencer. A heavy thud broke the silence as a large tool crashed against metal. Then I heard Speck cuss out loud. When it was quiet again, Sam answered my question.

"A couple of years ago, my daddy was working down at the wheat silo. Back then, he always taught us to respect the white man and do whatever it took to get along. Daddy would say things is gonna work out some day, and we gonna live right and have good jobs.

"Well, one day Mister Spencer come into the office over at the granary and asked my father to fetch some papers out of his truck. Daddy took those papers into the office and went on back to work. Later, the boss and Mista' Spencer came out to one of the silos where Dad was shoveling wheat. They were mad. They said Daddy stole a pistol out of the glove box of Mista' Spencer's truck.

"Daddy told them he never seen no pistol. But while everybody watched, they searched Daddy and looked every place for that pistol. They never found no gun, but that didn't matter none. Daddy came home that night and sat down at the supper table like he'd lost part of his soul. 'I been fired,' he said. 'Fired for stealing.'"

Sam tossed a rock into the road and shook his head. "Daddy never missed church a Sunday in his life, and he never took a nickel didn't belong to him. But that didn't matter. A white man said he stole a gun, and they fired him. And of all the things Daddy could have said that night, what he said next surprised me the most.

"My dad said that he was lucky, because they almost sent him to jail, if it weren't for the boss standing up to the sheriff." When Sam finished, he took a deep breath and shook his head again.

"Sam, I think we share the same opinion on one thing," I said. "Thurman Spencer is one man this town would be better off without. We should ask President Kennedy to ship him off to Cuba or Russia. Somewhere far away like that."

"Cuba's too close," Sam said. He shook his head. "Russia would be better."

"What's your dad doing now?" I asked.

"He doesn't have a job. That's why me and my brother works so hard. But he's going back East in a couple of weeks. My uncle lives in Pennsylvania, and he has Daddy all excited 'bout something they're doing up there."

"What is it they're doing?"

Before he answered, he looked closely into my eyes. It was as if he was trying to see if he could trust me. I guess he decided he could, because he said, "My uncle Hollis is spending a lotta time with this civil rights stuff back East."

Those words "civil rights" were on the radio every day, and everyone had an opinion about it. But I wasn't sure which side to take. To tell the truth, I thought Negroes had been pushy during the past year with all the boycotts, demonstrations, and marches. But sitting there talking to Sam, I wasn't sure what was right. He seemed like a good guy, and if he had been living in my neighborhood back in Tulsa, we would probably be buddies. At least we would be if older people stayed out of it.

"So what's your uncle going to do?" I asked.

"He's been writing to tell Dad about this trip they're taking in a couple of weeks. They're going to have three or four busloads of our people go from Washington, DC, all the way down to Atlanta, Georgia. Then they go from there over to Jackson, Mississippi. He says there are also some white people going along with them."

"Wow! Is your dad gonna do it?"

"Yeah, I guess so. Something else, too," Sam said, looking at me with a suspicious look on his face—a look I didn't particularly care for.

"Don't tell me you're trying to find some more white people to go. Cause I'll tell you right now, I'm not going."

"No, that's not it," he said with a grin.

"Then what's the something else?"

Sam pulled a long piece of grass out of the ground and stuck one end in his mouth for a second. He gazed at me again. This time he had a look of simple determination and maybe a trace of fear on his young face.

"I might go with him," he said. "I might ride on that freedom bus."

It was one thing to hear someone's father was about to become a freedom rider, but it was another thing to be face to face with a young Negro boy and find out he was a civil rights guy—or whatever it was they called those demonstrators on TV. Over and over again, I had seen black people getting beaten by the cops and chased by the snarling German shepherd dogs.

"What's wrong?" Sam asked. "You don't think Negroes should be doing something like that?"

"No, that's not it."

"Then why you look like someone who just took hold of a hot skillet?"

I wasn't sure what to say. The entire conversation had taken a serious turn, and now we were talking about something I knew nothing about.

"Never met a civil rights actor before," I said.

Sam laughed and said, "The word is 'activist,' 'rights activist,' and I'm not one of those people. I won't be protesting. I'm just going to go on the bus with my uncle and stay out of the way."

"You said a few minutes ago you didn't want to mess with Thurman Spencer. Now you're talking about going on one of those freedom-rider buses halfway across the United States. You know there are going to be people who don't want to see a caravan of buses go through their town loaded with colored people. I'm not saying there's anything wrong with what you're going to do, but you know what happened before. Man, back in May I saw it on TV when the bus stopped in Birmingham, Alabama, and the freedom riders got off. The cops and white people were right there waiting. Hundreds of people yelling and screaming, and they beat the crap out of the freedom riders, white and black. It was horrible. Tell you what, I would have stayed on that bus. But they didn't; they walked right down the steps into the crowd, knowing they were about to take a beating. I couldn't understand it."

"Yeah, I saw that on TV," Sam said. "But I'm not sure I understand it either. And don't think I ain't scared. The thing is, I'm not even sure my mother will let me go."

"But, man, you could get your head bashed in."

"Hey," Sam interrupted, "I know all about that, and I might know why those guys walked off that bus, knowing they're going to get beat. They do it because they believe black people and white people should have the same rights. They do it to show the world they believe in something enough to walk with their heads held high even if they might get beat up for doing it."

It was quiet for a minute or two. Neither of us spoke. I was so confused, I didn't know what to say, and Sam seemed to have said all he wanted to say. Then Clyde broke the silence.

"What are you two going to do?" Clyde asked, walking up from behind. "Sit here all night talking like a couple of girls?"

"Might as well," Sam said. He winked as if to remind me that our conversation was a secret. "Because you two are about the slowest mechanics in Alva."

Speck grinned and said, "Hey, white boy, you need a ride?"

"I sure do," I said, jumping up and wiping the dirt off the back of my jeans.

Before I knew it, everyone began piling into the old, worn-out Plymouth.

"You can sit in front," Speck offered.

"What about me?" Clyde whined. No one answered him, so he grumbled a bit getting into the back seat. It was quiet inside the car as we drove toward town.

Just before we stopped, Clyde whined, "I still don't think we should let him ride shotgun. Next thing ya know this white will say he wants to drive, and you fools will probably let'm."

"Shut up, Clyde," Sam said. "Every time someone else rides shotgun, you whine like my little sister trying to get into the bathroom."

Speck turned the corner at Main Street while the three of us laughed at Sam's remark and Clyde grumbled under his breath.

The streetlights had never seemed as bright as they looked right then. We had left the darkest part of town behind us. Speck stopped the car about midway down the street, but he didn't switch off the engine. After I got out, I faced the car for a moment and bent down, looking into the front seat.

"Thanks, guys," I said. "I hope I can return the favor some time."

"There's one way you can," Sam said as he grinned. "Send that white trash we were talking about to Cuba in a leaky boat."

I laughed as the old car drove away, its engine knocking loudly and more steam coming from the hood. They turned north at the next intersection and moved out of sight behind a brick building. Across from the pool hall, Mr. Pierce's pickup sat among the cars belonging to the other diehard Saturday-nighters. I didn't feel much like going into the bar to get him, but the only other option was walking home. Just before I crossed the street, I glanced at the pickup once again. This time I saw movement.

From the driver's side window, a hand waved. Walking several steps closer, I recognized the farmer's grinning face and worried that he might be drunk—or worse, about to pass out. But to my surprise, Mr. Pierce appeared sober. His eyes were clear, his expression happy and alert. Relief flowed through me like a cool midnight breeze. It was time to go home, and I wouldn't have to drive after all.

"So what have you been doing this evening?" Mr. Pierce asked casually, as he put the transmission into first gear. The engine groaned, giving us just enough power to head toward the highway.

"Oh, nothing," I lied. "Just another boring summer night." The night had been too special and too personal to share. I decided to keep it to myself for a little while longer.

#

The red mud in the corral oozed with each noisy step I took, and June waited silently by the fence with a look of anticipation on her long gray face. Our Sunday evening rides had become a regular thing, and each week I gained a bit more skill at riding. I scraped my muddy boots against the bottom slat of the wood fence and hoisted myself into the creaking leather saddle.

A feeling of exhilaration flowed through me the instant I mounted her. My legs gripped the horse's thick middle, sending a silent signal I was ready to move. She eased forward, her head swaying with the rhythm of her gait, and she trotted slowly out of the corral.

Just ahead of us, Mr. Pierce was by the fence, leaning casually there with his ever-present cigarette dangling from his dry, cracked lips. He stood facing west as if waiting for the sun to set behind that little knoll he called the Indian Hills. June brought me right up to him, and I think it broke his concentration. He turned toward us and grinned as June came to a stop.

"You two going off to a nighttime rodeo?" he asked.

"No, we're just going out to see if Pluto's keeping the cows satisfied."

He grinned, mockingly, "Now how would you know one way or the other what that bull is doing?"

He was right, of course. I wouldn't know one way or the other. My reddening face must have shown my ignorance, but I didn't feel like giving in. "Oh, you can tell," I lied. "You can always tell."

"Right," he smirked.

"Okay, I guess you got me on that one," I confessed. "There's a lot I don't know about animals. Come to think of it, there are a few things I don't know about you." That brought a frown to Mr. Pierce's wrinkled forehead. "Mr. Pierce, you still owe me an answer."

He exhaled, and gray smoke clouded his face as he said, "Give me a little time, son."

"I know, sir. I know you've got to think it over. But next week you're going to the bank, and after that it'll be too late to do anything. If we're going to find out the rest of this thing, we need to go into town and get some answers. Maybe we can go tonight."

The tired old farmer frowned, and I knew I had pushed too far.

"Matt, I know you mean well. But I can't do anything about this crazy yarn you heard. You haven't even told me who you heard it from. In a way, I want to believe you, but I've got an obligation. When a man gives his word, he needs to keep it. Never forget that, son. Your word is your bond, and it's more important than some bank account."

"I won't forget it, but . . ."

"No buts. Just remember I've given my word to Thurman Spencer. He promised to keep this thing quiet, and I'll give him half the wheat crop. So far, he's kept his part of the bargain, and I plan to keep mine. That's the end of it."

When he finished his little lecture, I knew by the look on his face that he meant it.

"What about the story I heard?"

"I just told you, son. I don't know who started that foolishness. So, let's forget it."

"But how are you going to manage with only half the wheat money?"

"My worry," he said, turning back toward the Indian Hills. Before he turned, I knew from the stern look on his face that our conversation was over. What else could I say? If I told him I had heard it from a Negro teenager, it would appear even less believable to him. This might be one of those times when "Silence is golden," as Grandma used to say.

So I left him as he climbed up to sit on the wooden fence. He had that look of quiet resolve on his face, and I knew I had gone as far as I could go to try and make him do something he didn't want to do. He was just one of those people who seemed to accept things the way they are. Like everything else in his lonely life, he had no will to fight. No desire to change things.

But I did.

June walked slowly into the east pasture, her head bobbing up and down like a pump handle while the pesky horseflies droned around her jet-black mane. Grass and cactus appeared to blush in the sun's fading crimson light. The peaceful evening mixed with the gentle rhythm of June's gait, and I enjoyed the quiet moment.

The sure-footed horse walked with muffled steps as the sun dropped below the tree line behind us. The clean, fresh smell of rain swirled in at us from somewhere off in the distance. I truly loved this rugged farmland. I wanted to learn more about the land and the man who had spent his life working it. Mr. Pierce, for all of his faults and stubbornness, seemed like a wonderful man. I didn't agree with his philosophy on how far a person should go to keep his word, but I did admire his sense of honor. It took me a long time to figure it out, but the strange thing about him keeping his word had everything to do with me being there. It might have been the same sense of honor that caused him to hire me for the summer also kept him obligated to Thurman Spencer. When I showed up unexpectedly and he remembered talking to my dad, he must have felt compelled to help me. And now when he had so many problems, there seemed to be nothing I could do to help him.

The sun was fading slowly when June decided to walk back to the corral without a word or any coaxing from me. The farm was quiet and peaceful, and a cool breeze from the north strengthened the expectation of rain. In the darkened sky an evening star emerged directly over the barn. Its brilliant form added beauty to the night, though unlike the moon, it had no special purpose. The little star seemed to be there to make the night less lonely. Gazing up at it, I thought about Mr. Pierce and wondered if in some way I could try and be an evening star to him. Maybe I could make his life a bit less lonely—at least I could do that.

\#

Later that night after I brushed June down and gave her a few carrots, I went in and helped Mr. Pierce with supper. I knew he was concerned about our chat out by the fence, so I changed the subject, thinking it might improve his gloomy mood. I stood beside him at the sink and started cleaning potatoes. He passed me a pan, so after I peeled and cut the potatoes, I placed them on the stove to boil.

"Mr. Pierce," I said.

"Son, I don't want to talk about the bank anymore. Okay?"

"Oh, I forgot all about that," I lied. "I want you to tell me something about Camp Alva. Did you ever have to shoot at any of the German prisoners?"

Mr. Pierce seemed surprised by my question, but he went ahead and placed two fairly clean dinner plates on the table. Unlike most people who stored things in kitchen cabinets, he kept almost everything on the tabletop. As usual, the center of his cluttered table had an assortment of canned goods, boxes of crackers, a bag of sugar, a sack of flour, a can of coffee, and a variety of other things piled together, taking up almost all the space. When I first got there, I thought it was pretty strange, but after a while, I got used to it. In fact, I added a few items to his little assortment, like a bottle of dish soap, a container of insect repellent, a coffee mug we used to store clean silverware, a box of matches, and a flashlight. When we were in his house, the kitchen table was the center of our world.

With one arm Mr. Pierce shoved all the junk toward the middle of the table, making a place for us to eat. While I waited for the potatoes to cook, I sat down and used my elbow to push several cans forward. I was desperately trying to glean a little bit more room. The flashlight fell on the floor, and I quickly retrieved it to lay it on top of the bag of flour.

Mr. Pierce leaned back in his chair and took a knife out of the coffee mug. He held it for a moment, looking at his reflection in its shining blade. I waited for him to speak, knowing anything he told me would only come when he was ready—only when he wanted to tell it. The potatoes on the stove were boiling, a familiar fly buzzed around the bare light bulb over the table, but otherwise, the kitchen was quiet.

"Before I answer your question about shooting someone," he said, "I need to tell you something else that happened at Camp Alva. It was just before Thanksgiving, and it started like every other day. Then . . ."

11   WHAT HE DIDN'T SAY

Two days before Thanksgiving, privates Pierce and Spencer patrolled one of the compounds housing noncommissioned officers. That afternoon a meeting was held in the compound chapel, with several prisoners leaving through the chapel's main entrance.

When Private Pierce noticed Sergeant Schmitt in the group, he walked over to say hello. Unlike most of the German POWs, the stout German sergeant often had a good word and seemed to cooperate with the American authorities. Although some disagreed, the sergeant was thought to be anti-Nazi. Private Pierce respected him and spoke to him when the opportunity arose, always remembering Sergeant Schmitt might face reprisals from the Nazi officers and other noncoms if he was suspected of brownnosing the Americans. So Private Pierce remembered to keep the discussions short and not overly friendly.

"Where are you men going?" Private Pierce asked firmly.

The POWs stopped, turned toward the two MPs and hesitated.

Sergeant Schmitt walked closer to Private Pierce. He answered for the group, "Finished chapel meeting," he said in broken English. "Now to barracks."

"Don't walk bunched up together," Private Pierce said. "You know better than that." The Germans grumbled something under their breath and walked away. Sergeant Schmitt stood for an extra moment. He held up a copy of a Bible.

"Show best verse," he said. "Show please, best."

The two MPs looked at each other and shrugged their shoulders.

"Come on, Henry. Let's go," Private Spencer said, looking at the German sergeant with disgust.

"Wait a minute," Private Pierce said. "I want to know his favorite." He touched the Bible and asked the sergeant, "Show yours?"

Sergeant Schmitt opened the Bible and found his place. He pointed to Job 28:10. Pierce didn't read the verse carefully, but noticed it said something about rocks and eyes.

"Should have known it was Job," Private Pierce said, sarcastically. "That's too depressing for me. What else do you read, sergeant? What books do you like?"

Sergeant Schmitt said something to one of the other prisoners, and the man stopped walking as if he was waiting for the sergeant. "Looking home angel," Schmitt said as he glanced back at Private Pierce.

Private Pierce smiled slightly and said, "You mean *Look Homeward, Angel*."

"Ja, Ja," the sergeant said. "Ja, Ja, 'Looking Home.'"

"Move along," the private said, faking an angry look for the sergeant's benefit. The good-natured sergeant walked away and joined several other German soldiers as they strolled toward the prisoners' mess hall. Watching the sergeant for a moment, the young private thought about the similarities between Swim and Schmitt. Both of them were hard as nails, and both of them were built like linemen on a football team. What a shame Schmitt had been born German instead of American, Pierce thought.

The sound of a shrieking whistle came from the other side of the compound, and a moment later Pierce and Spencer were breaking up a fight between prisoners. Lately, the fights had become more frequent, and the camp commander had not been pleased about it. The MPs were instructed to be on the alert. They were warned against getting caught in the middle of a fake fight organized by the prisoners in order to beat up the MP.

"If they don't stop when you blow your whistle," the camp commander had said, "use your nightstick. If they don't stop when you hit them with your nightstick, then use your sidearm. Under no circumstances are you to step in between two men fighting."

Henry Pierce always remembered that advice and had been successful at breaking up several fights. This time the two prisoners stopped fighting the moment they saw a nightstick in the MP's hand, realizing only a few seconds separated them from getting clobbered. As the two prisoners backed away, privates Pierce and Spencer looked around the area to make certain there was no other sign of trouble. Private Pierce was relieved the two men had broken up their fight, but Private Spencer was disappointed—it showed all over his face. He wanted to see some action, and he wanted to use his nightstick on a German.

#

On Thanksgiving night, Private Pierce walked into the little town of Alva with a couple of his buddies. Pulling the day shift had prevented him from accepting an invitation to Thanksgiving dinner at Jewel's home, but he was looking forward to having a drink or two with her. They had gone out several times over the past few months, and he was crazy about her. He wasn't sure how she felt about him, but she had never turned him down for a date—that was a mighty good sign.

Soldiers walked along Seventh Street between several of the bars and restaurants new to Alva since the camp had been built. Crossing the street, Henry could hear the loud music coming from inside Tootsie's, the little bar where he planned to meet Jewel Criswell.

Inside Tootsie's the music was loud, the dance floor was packed, and the beer was cheap. *Another great night at Tootsie's*, Henry thought. It was one of the most popular places in Alva, and he had taken Jewel there several times already.

Pierce saw Jewel right after he walked in. She sat at a table surrounded by three of her girlfriends as well as two soldiers, men Private Pierce didn't know. But he wasn't worried or jealous, because people had fun when they could during the war. If he had any concerns about her, they were dispelled the second she looked up and saw him. The look on her face clearly told Henry she was keeping room for him at the table and a place for him in her heart.

But before he had a chance to sit down, someone turned up the jukebox, and the air was filled with Glenn Miller's "Chattanooga Choo Choo." He knew that fast-paced song was Jewel's favorite, and he figured there would be no sitting down for a while.

"Hi, Henry! Let's dance, Henry!" she said. Jewel's quick greeting caused the other people at the table to laugh, and Henry couldn't keep from laughing himself. He put his heavy Army overcoat across Jewel's empty chair, took her hand, and walked her to the little dance floor. He maneuvered for a spot as close as he could get to the jukebox.

They danced wildly, and Henry laughed as he thought about Jewel; her beauty had attracted Henry, but it was her personality that kept the relationship going. She was fun to be around, nice to everyone, and she threw herself wholeheartedly into anything that was going on—including dancing the jitterbug. She never did anything halfway. She could jitterbug better than anyone Henry had ever seen. The fact is, his dancing had improved considerably since he had been going out with Jewel Criswell.

After several dances, Henry escorted Jewel back to their table, where the population had grown. Now three soldiers and four of Jewel's girlfriends were laughing and having fun while the Mills Brothers sang "Paper Doll" on the jukebox.

"I'll get us a couple of chairs," Henry said. But before he could walk away, Jewel took his hand. "Don't bother," she said, and smiled secretly at him.

Jewel leaned down and whispered something to her best friend, Linda. A moment later, Jewel and Henry were walking out together. The Mills Brothers were harmonizing on the chorus of "Paper Doll," but Henry didn't notice. He was wondering if it was too cold to stop by the park.

Outside in the night air, Jewel invited Henry to walk her home. "But let's walk through the park on the way," she said. He grinned, and she looked back at him and said, "What's so funny?"

"Nothing," he said with a big, silly grin. "I was just thinking about the park."

The couple walked slowly and talked about the war, her work as a telephone operator, and how she wished Henry could have joined them for Thanksgiving dinner. When they got to the park, Henry spotted an empty wooden bench and led her to it. They weren't the only couple in the park that night. But it didn't matter; they had a place to be alone for a while.

Standing in front of the park bench, Henry looked down into Jewel's beautiful eyes. He pulled her thick, wool scarf down around her face and tucked it into her winter coat, trying to make her feel warmer. She looked up at her handsome soldier and smiled. He kissed her softly on the lips, and they sat on the park bench—seemingly unaware of its cold hard surface. From time to time, he kissed her and touched her hair with his gloved hand, but after a while he could tell Jewel was getting too cold to sit out in the open. As much as he hated to admit it, he knew he should take her home.

"I guess it's time to look homeward, angel," he said, making a pun out of the book title.

Jewel smiled as they stood and said, "I loved that book. Did you read it?"

"No, I've never read any of Hemingway's stuff," he said. "But if you loved it, it must be good."

Jewel giggled as they walked along the street and held closely to his arm. "Ernest Hemingway didn't write that book, silly. It was Thomas Wolfe."

"Oh," he said, but he wasn't really thinking about books at the moment. He was wondering if he might be able to get one more kiss before he took her up to her front porch. But much to his surprise, Jewel took care of that situation. She stopped on her corner, two houses down from her own, and looked up at him like she did at the park. It took the young soldier less than a second to pull her into his arms, but it took more than a minute for him to kiss her goodnight.

After their long kiss and warm embrace, Henry walked Jewel to her front porch and gave her a quick peck on the cheek— an acceptable goodnight kiss in case her father or mother happened to be watching. They said goodnight, and Private Pierce—in love and as happy as any man in Oklahoma, walked back to Camp Alva thinking about her the whole way. He wondered what it might be like to be married.

#

When Henry got back to camp, he was too excited to go to sleep. So he walked to the library to see if he could find a copy of *Look Homeward, Angel*. Along the way, he remembered it was Thanksgiving and the camp was at minimum staff level. He noticed fewer MPs in the camp, some of which were returning from town looking a bit tipsy from too much beer.

Inside the camp library, Private Pierce noticed only one person sat at the long reading desk. He was pleased to discover the man was Lieutenant Jordahl, the American chaplain. Private Pierce walked over to the desk and sat across from the chaplain.

"Good evening, sir," Private Pierce said, removing his hat and gloves.

"Evening, Private Pierce," the chaplain said. "Couldn't sleep?"

"No, sir," Private Pierce said. "I thought I would start a new book tonight."

"Very good," the chaplain said. "Anything special?"

"Yes, sir, I thought I would read *Look Homeward, Angel*."

"Afraid you're out of luck on that one, son. I was looking over the list tonight and noticed all five copies are out."

"Well, that's okay," the private said. "Maybe I'll look up a Bible verse, then."

The chaplain smiled and pushed a few books away, exposing a very well-worn Bible. He pulled his Bible closer to him and asked, "Can I look it up for you?"

"Yes, sir. I think he said Job 28:10. Something one of the POWs mentioned."

The chaplain quickly found the verse Private Pierce mentioned. "Want me to read it to you?"

"Sure. I mean, yes, sir," the private said as he glanced around the room, wondering if anyone else was in the library. For a moment he wondered what in the world he was going to take back to barracks to read since they didn't have the book he was looking for. He turned toward the chaplain out of courtesy, but he wasn't terribly interested.

"Okay, then. Here we are," the chaplain said, waiting for Private Pierce to pay attention. "Job 28:10, '*He cutteth out channels among the rocks; and his eye seeth every precious thing.*'" 1 (ASV)

The pleasant smile disappeared from the chaplain's handsome face. Private Pierce let the words sink in, and his face grew red. He had heard it, but he couldn't believe it. "Uh, would you please read it again, sir," he said. This time the chaplain read it lower and softer, making each word clear and meaningful, 'They tunnel through the rock; their eyes see all its treasures.'

"Good Lord," Private Pierce said, his face flushed with concern.

"Good Lord," the chaplain repeated.

12   THE ROAR MASTER

On Thursday morning, the day Mr. Pierce was going into town to sign papers at the bank, he tried to look calm as he went about his morning routine, but anyone could see that he was clearly nervous. Working on his third cigarette since breakfast, Mr. Pierce went out the back door and drove the pickup up to the gate. I finished the dishes, wondering if he would allow me to go into town with him. I didn't ask because it was such a sad occasion, and I figured he might want to be alone. As I finished wiping the soapy water off our plates, I heard the horn honking outside and knew what it meant.

A moment later, the kitchen door slammed behind me as I ran out into the yard toward the truck. The door handle on the old Ford felt hot from the sun as I pulled it open and looked in. Mr. Pierce held onto the faded black steering wheel and looked at me with an expression that fell somewhere between pride and regret. I expect his emotions were battling within him, and I couldn't imagine how he felt. We had brought in one of the largest wheat crops ever raised on his farm, but he would have to give up half the money he had earned.

We were going into town so he could sign the papers giving Thurman Spencer his money. At the foot of the hill, the tired old truck growled as Mr. Pierce eased it out of the dirt driveway and onto the highway. We passed the mailbox when he shifted gears, and the truck gained speed gradually.

I tried to think of something to say that might make things more comfortable for both of us, but it was one of those times when silence felt more natural than forced conversation. I guess we both knew what the other person was thinking since we had gone over it so many times. Fields of cut wheat passed outside my window, silent reminders of the hard work and sacrifices this trip represented. It wasn't fair at all. It just wasn't fair.

The old truck's motor struggled along as noisily as ever, and I glanced over at Mr. Pierce, who appeared deep in his thoughts and probably didn't notice the noise from the truck's straining motor.

It seemed funny how things had worked out. I had just met Mr. Pierce a few months before, and during that time he'd never done anything I would consider all that impressive. But there was something about him—the gentle way he treated people, how he never blamed anyone else for his problems, and the fact you could always believe what he told you. It made the man seem more like a father to me than a boss. He was just an old simple farmer who had nothing to call his own except hard luck, and now he was driving into town to uphold some stupid tradition of honesty. Only a grown-up would do something that stupid. Kids knew better. But it was his choice, and it was about to cost him more than any man should ever have to give up.

#

When we arrived in Alva, I watched the familiar sights of the little country town, but I found it hard to enjoy the usual break from farm scenery. As we rounded the corner toward Main Street, Mr. Pierce parked the pickup in his favorite spot across from the town hall. The city square appeared active as people walked along the sidewalks and a few large trucks hauled their wheat toward the granary.

We stood on the sidewalk for a moment, watching the line of trucks pass by, and Mr. Pierce pointed to the last truck in the little caravan.

The driver leaned out the window, slapped the door with his hand and yelled toward us, "Hey, Henry, wait for me at Lana's and I'll buy you a cup o' coffee!"

"Okay, Bill!" Mr. Pierce yelled back.

We walked down the street toward Lana's Café. Hopefully, going there might help Mr. Pierce's mood. It was such a rare occasion to be in town on a Thursday. On the way to Lana's, we passed the co-op store, a small clothing store, and then Anthony's, which carried a variety of products like furniture, bedding, sewing products and the like.

I looked in through the window at a section displaying men's clothes. There was a blue seersucker shirt with thin white stripes and beside it was a pair of boy's white slacks. I wondered what I might look like walking Carol to the movies in an outfit like that. We kept walking, and a few minutes later, we were in front of Lana's Café.

A couple of older men came out of the front door just as we were about to go in. Like everyone else in town, they knew Mr. Pierce.

"Hear you had a good crop this year," the shorter man said.

"Not too bad," Mr. Pierce agreed humbly. "I guess it wasn't as good as some, but not as bad as others."

The tall fellow grinned and put a half-chewed toothpick back in his mouth. The two men walked away, talking about something I couldn't understand. Mr. Pierce shook his head and walked into Lana's.

Inside the busy café, a delicious smell of fried eggs and coffee met us like an old, familiar friend. We found an empty booth and plopped down. I glanced around at the other customers, hoping Carol might be there, but she wasn't. By the time I finished surveying the place, two cups of steaming coffee were on the table in front of us, and big Lana stood inches away, smiling as if her own sons had come home from the war. She was fanning herself with a small green order book and chewing her ever-present wad of gum.

"Now where have you two handsome boys been lately?" she flirted. Then she stared at me and spoke loud enough to be heard two blocks away, "I bet you went and got married since you were in here last time, didn't you?"

I smiled in my embarrassment as I reached for the coffee cup on the table. Mr. Pierce, who would normally enjoy seeing me embarrassed, just smiled politely. I think Lana noticed his mood. She started to say something to him, but I spoke first.

"No, ma'am," I said, "I didn't get married."

"Well, I bet it won't be long," she said. Then to Mr. Pierce, she said, "Henry, what are you and this young man going to have this morning?" While I waited for Mr. Pierce to reply, I stared at Lana for a moment. I'll bet she and my grandmother would get along pretty well if they knew each other.

That's when Mr. Pierce spoke up and surprised me. "How 'bout a short stack of pancakes for me and whatever the boy wants."

"Wow, thanks," I said. After all, we had already eaten a bowl of cereal. "I'll have the same thing."

Lana walked away, but she did it without finding out what was bothering Mr. Pierce. I watched her disappear into the kitchen, where she clipped the green order form onto a nail-size chrome holder. A black hand reached for the order, and then his face appeared. It was my buddy, Sam.

The young Negro cook was sweating from the intense heat in the kitchen, his face and arms shiny with perspiration. When our eyes met, he tilted his head toward the back door of the café. I didn't know what he meant. I frowned, but then he made a circling motion with his finger, then scratched his head. From that, I figured he wanted me to go around to the back of the café. I nodded slightly. Sam went back to filling the orders in front of him.

A little later after we had finished our breakfast, Mr. Pierce and I stood at the front of the café. Mr. Pierce paid Lana and thanked her for a good breakfast. The front door opened, and the farmer who had invited Mr. Pierce for coffee walked in. He had gold wheat dust all over his coveralls and a warm smile on his rugged face.

"So you ate without me, huh?" he said in his deep, gravelly voice. Before Mr. Pierce could answer, Lana butted in.

"Yeah, they did, but we saved enough to keep you quiet,Bill"

Mr. Pierce led the dusty farmer back to the same booth, and I got ready to sneak out, as I figured it was as good a chance as any to find out what Sam was up to.

"Thanks for breakfast," I said to Mr. Pierce. "How 'bout I meet you at the truck after a while?"

"All right," he agreed, looking at his watch. "It's twenty-five minutes till ten. I'll be going into the bank when they open at ten. I'll only be there fifteen minutes or so. You be back by the truck when I come out."

He smiled, but I could see just mentioning the bank took the sparkle out of his eyes. You could tell he was concerned.

"Yes, sir," I agreed, walking away. Before I went out the door, I glanced at Sam, who didn't look directly at me. I could feel him watching me.

Standing on the sidewalk in front of the café, I wasn't sure which direction I should go to get to the back door of Lana's Café. I walked to the end of the street and turned back toward the alley. Once in the alley, it was easy to find the back of her café. A blind man could have found it because of the horrible smell coming from the kitchen. It was like last week's brown beans and onions were pouring out of an electric ventilator—enough to make me wish I had skipped the pancakes. Passing three or four overflowing garbage cans, I squinted as the stench of rubbish mixed with the repulsive aroma of ventilated food.

In the narrow space between a wooden fence and an overflowing garbage can, a large brown dog leaned across scraps of food protectively. I walked carefully around the wild-looking animal, giving it plenty of space. When I was a few feet away, the mangy animal growled, turned toward me with foam and food dripping from his jagged mouth, and went back to his breakfast.

Relieved to get past the oversized dog, I hurried up the steps of the concrete porch just as the screen door flew open. Sam, looking fearful, motioned for me to get inside.

"Hurry up," he said. "I get caught, and Miss Lana will fire me sure as I'm standing here." Sam pulled me into a small storage room off the kitchen where shelves held a selection of canned goods—cans large enough to hide a basketball and adorned with photos of tomatoes and corn as well as other fresh vegetables. Sam glanced behind him into the kitchen and pulled the door shut.

"What's going on?" I asked.

Sam looked at me as sweat ran down his face and onto his white T-shirt. I thought if I ever had to work in that kitchen, I would probably pass out from the heat.

"I'm glad you come in today," he said, smiling for the first time. "I heard something last night and thought you'd want to know about it."

"What'd you hear?"

"That boy I told you about. The one who bragged about pulling the trick on old man Pierce; they say he's got a job over at the Hudson gas station." Sam smiled. You'd think he had just told me a secret code or something.

"You sure?" I asked, doubtful. "We bought gas there a couple of days ago, and I didn't see him."

Sam's smile evaporated like his sweat hitting the concrete floor. He wiped his forehead with his elbow.

"Am I sure?" he said. "What you think, I'm some kinda fool?"

"Relax," I said. "I don't think that at all. I'm just saying I didn't see him over at the station a couple of days ago. You say he's there. Then he's there."

The young cook stood as if trying to decide if he had done the right thing by telling me. I could see the wheels turning. I glanced at a clock nearby. Fifteen till ten. If I was going to learn something from that guy at the station, I had to get going.

"Listen," I said. "I appreciate your help and I owe you one. But if we're going to be friends, then we have to be honest with each other, right?"

"Yeah, that's right," he said, without enthusiasm.

"Well, don't read something into everything a white boy says. We're not the same color on the outside, but we're a lot alike on the inside. You have doubts, and I have doubts. So if we're going to be friends, then we've got to say what we think."

"Yeah, I see what you mean," he said, a faint smile returning to his face.

"I've got to go," I said, looking at the clock. "Think I'll pay the Hudson station a visit. Thanks for your help."

I put my hand out, and he grabbed it. It was a wet but solid handshake. Once again, the image of my white, callused hand gripping his black, sweating hand made me feel like there could be hope.

"By the way," I said, pointing at the gigantic cans with pictures of tomatoes and corn. "I sure feel a lot healthier after being around all these fresh vegetables."

We giggled like a couple of girls as he opened the door, and we snuck out of the storage room.

Quickly, I ran out the back door, down the steps, and into the alley. But somehow I had turned right instead of left and faced a large wooden fence. I had hit a dead end. When I spun around, I met something much more menacing than a dead end. The mean monster of a dog faced me head-on. He must have finished his breakfast and thought he needed to guard the alley. The mangy animal barked loudly, exposing a set of teeth as large as the fingers on my hand—fingers I was fond of and wanted to keep.

"Hi, boy," I said in my best boy-to-dog voice. "It's okay. I'll just go around this other way." I tried to move toward the street, but the Tyrannosaurus-mutt blocked my way. The angry animal growled, unimpressed with my friendly, nice-guy voice. I reached down carefully and removed a battered metal lid off one of the garbage cans and held it in front of me like a shield. Now, I was ready for anything.

"Okay, Killer, get back," I said, switching to my tough-guy voice. The irritated dog, who now looked more like a bear, ran toward me at full speed. With a mouth large enough to make a shark jealous, the dog grabbed the lid, jerked it backwards, and I stood there with the four-inch lid handle in my hand and a look of fear in my eyes.

The dangerous animal twisted his head back and forth, waving the metal lid from side to side. Next, he tossed the lid across the alley, where it landed in a pile of dirt. I looked for an escape route or maybe something else to use as a weapon. Seeing nothing weaponlike, I decided to make a run for it. I took off down the alley so fast my football coach would have been proud. But even with my Jesse Owens sprint, that bear of a dog stayed right on my tail. Now the dog was only a foot or two behind me. I knew any second he would lunge at me and I'd feel his giant teeth in my butt.

But just as he pounced at me, I quickly sidestepped him, like any good linebacker would have done, and I quickly crossed over to the opposite wall. Nearby I spotted several wooden crates, slightly smaller than the trash cans stacked beside them. I ran up those crates and across the garbage cans as the dog followed inches behind. As I crossed the last garbage can, I leaped onto the tall wooden fence—barely reaching the top with my fingers.

Dangling from the ten-foot fence, I felt the dog bite into my right foot. The sharp pain was just enough to give me the determination I needed to pull myself up onto the fence. I looked down at the mangy animal who barked furiously below me

"Listen, Snaggletooth," I said. "Yes, you. You got big teeth and bad breath, and you're about the ugliest dog I've ever seen. Did you ever hear about the Russian space program they call Sputnik? They use dogs like you as passengers in their spaceships. Better learn to be nice or that's where you're going to wind up."

#

After my run-in with Snaggletooth, I hurried toward the filling station as the morning sun rose higher in the sky. As a result of my struggle with the mangy mutt in the alley, I could feel the dampness of sweat sticking to my back. Though I only had a few blocks to run, I felt the familiar sense of panic set in as I tried to think of what I might accomplish by talking to the jerk at the filling station. With no idea of what to say, I pushed on. I had to find out the truth about the "accident" near the cemetery.

A couple of pickups sat near the gas pumps in front of the Hudson filling station. Inside the station's cluttered office, the foul smell of gasoline and oil filled the air. My eyes quickly scanned the unorganized office with its magazines and old newspapers stacked on the floor as well as the glass counter. There was a black cash register on the counter and beside it several open boxes of car parts. A tall man, dressed in oil-soaked green khakis, leaned against a Coke machine and frowned when he noticed me.

"What do you need?" he asked.

"I'm looking for John. I heard he's working for you— drives a baby blue Chevy."

The guy shrugged and pointed toward the back of the station. "He's out back working on his car."

"Thanks," I said, hurrying through an open doorway and into a long, narrow garage.

In the rear section of the garage, a black Chevy was parked with its hood up. Beneath the Chevy, someone lay across the floor, their feet sticking out the front, and by the looks of it, there wasn't much room to move due to the car's lowered frame. The person under the car wore shoes that sported shiny taps along the front. It was John all right, and seeing those taps brought bad memories flooding back. The way he lay under the car, it almost looked like he had been run over, and I wished that he had.

The familiar sounds of rock-and-roll music came from a radio nearby, and cars and trucks passed along the street from time to time. John was alone in that part of the garage, except for one farmhand that he wasn't yet aware of.

I stood near the front door waiting for John to see me from under his car. As I lingered there, I glanced across the street and noticed a 4th of July firecracker stand a few doors down. It gave me an idea.

Five minutes later I was back near the Chevy, squatting down and ready to talk. Looking under the car, I saw John's grease-covered face not far from the transmission's oil pan. It was John all right, the same greaser who had tried to beat me up that day at the park.

From under the car, John noticed me right away. When he did, his mouth formed the same ugly sneer he'd sported the last time we'd met. From the small space under the car, John could barely move his head. When he spoke, he sounded short of breath.

"What do you want, creep?" he asked. "The key to the bathroom?"

"No, I came to return a favor."

John moved his head for a better look and seemed to have a tough time moving in the cramped space between the pavement and the bottom of the transmission.

"Come on, what do you want, jerk," John said. "I don't have time to mess around under here."

"I don't have much time either," I said. "I have a question for you."

John flipped a fly off his nose and said, "Cut the crap, punk."

"I'll tell you exactly what I want," I said. "I want to know if you tricked Mr. Pierce one night out by the cemetery. I want to know if you are in cahoots with Thurman Spencer to make Mr. Pierce think he killed someone in that phony car wreck."

John chuckled. His dark eyes narrowed when he answered. From the radio I heard Jerry Lee Lewis singing his big hit:

You shake my nerves and you rattle my brains.
Your kind of love drives a man insane.

"Now, punk," John said. "I'm going to tell you something. You hit the road before I crawl out of here. 'Cause when I do, I'm going to be mad as hell, and there won't be no one to stop me this time. You were lucky the first time; there won't be an Indian cop to save you today."

"I'm glad you brought that up," I said. "That day in the park, you showed me a trick with a cigarette, and I'd like to return the favor."

I held up a chrome gas cap I had taken from his car. "Recognize this?" I asked.

"Hey, you little punk! Put that back right now!"

I tossed the gas cap on the ground and pulled something out of my pocket. John's eyes flashed in recognition as Jerry sang on,

You broke my will
Oh, what a thrill.

John struggled as he tried to get out. Somehow, he was pinned in under his car and every movement seemed to make it worse.

"Hey!" John yelled as he bumped his head on a solid piece of metal. "That's a cherry bomb. Quit messing around, man!"

"I'm not messing around, and this isn't a cherry bomb. It's an M-80. It's like three cherry bombs in one."

I lit a match and squatted down so he could see clearly, as I held the flame about an inch from the thick green fuse. John's oil-covered face grew more fearful as he helplessly tugged at the bottom of the car, attempting to pull himself out.

"You have about ten seconds," I said. "You either tell me what happened or this little baby is going into your gas tank. See, that's my trick, making your car disappear."

"You're already gonna get your butt whipped when I get out of here," John grunted, struggling to move. "You light that thing and you're dead. You hear me? Dead."

With my hand shaking with fear, I held the glowing match against the tip of the fuse. In less than a second, the fuse sputtered, its orange sparks crackling onto the cement floor. John's feet kicked about under the car, his chest heaved up and down, and his wild need to get out made it more and more impossible for him to move.

"Throw it away, kid!" he shouted. "I'll tell you! I'll tell you!"

"Good. Tell me quick, or she's going up in smoke. I got nothing to lose here."

"Okay, I did it. Like you said, I did it," John was panting now. "Get rid of that thing!"

From a pile of tools on the ground, I grabbed a pair of pliers and jerked the short, burning fuse out of the M-80. John relaxed for a split second, then the evil grin returned to his sweaty face.

In the background, the music continued to play.
I laughed at love, I thought it was funny

But you came along and moooved me, honey.

"Now I'm going to kick your butt, punk!" John looked as mad as the dog back in the alley, and I knew I was about to get beat up.

An instant later, the smirk on his ugly face disappeared and a look of intense fear replaced it. John stared at the astonishing object I held in my right hand. In a cautious voice, filled with fear and disbelief, he asked, "What . . . is . . . that thing?"

"You mean this?" I said. In my right hand, I held a foot-long firecracker that looked more like a stick of dynamite.

"This," I said. "is a Roar Master, something I brought along in case you didn't tell me what I wanted to know—which you didn't. Now I'm gonna light this baby and ask you one more time how you tricked Mr. Pierce."

I took out another match and prepared to light it. It was intensely quiet under the car, but the silence was broken by the radio playing the chorus of the Jerry Lee Lewis song:

I've changed my mind
This love is fine
Goodness, gracious, Great Balls of Fire!

The faint smell of gasoline hung under the car, adding another layer of danger. I was starting to lose my nerve a little, but I wouldn't let him know it.

"If you don't start talking," I said, "you're gonna have great balls of fire in about ten seconds."

Without waiting for John's answer, I lit another match and slowly moved it near the fuse of the long, thick firecracker.

"Okay, okay!" he shouted. Still stuck under the car, John's eyes looked as though he was trying desperately to figure a way out. "Put that match out!" he demanded.

"No, you talk first."

"All right," he agreed finally. "Mr. Spencer and I waited for old man Pierce to get drunk. When he left the bar, we followed him and ran him off the road easily. He passed out in his car after he ran into the ditch. We parked a wrecked car in front of his truck like there had been an accident. I put a couple sacks of feed across the front seat with a coat around them and poured a bottle of ketchup on the coat to make it look like someone was all cut up. When we got him up, the old-timer was so messed up he fell for it."

"What did you get out of it?" I asked. At that moment, the match burned out.

"I'm not sayin' no more, man," John said.

"Fine," I said. I tossed away the burned-out match and lit another one, holding it to the fuse of the Roar Master. Sparks danced along the white fuse, making a familiar crackling noise. John's face turned as pale as a ghost. Mine must have been white, too, since the last thing I wanted to do was to start a fire under that car—but I needed the whole story.

"I'll ask you again," I threatened without raising my voice. "What did you get out of it?"

"Okay, okay," John said. "Well, uh, when Thurman Spencer gets the wheat money from Mr. Pierce, I get the title to this car. That's it, that's all there is. Come on, little buddy, put that thing out!"

I heard someone behind me and figured it was the filling station manager.

"Hey! What the heck are you doing with that thing, boy?" The manager said. "Put it down right now!"

John's boss stood directly behind me, looking very upset, but he kept his distance because the fuse was only seconds away from disappearing into the top of the explosive. He shouted at John, "Get out from under there, you idiot!"

"I can't! I'm stuck!" John yelled, scrambling with his feet and bumping his head. John's boss rushed around to the other side of the car and pulled the angry boy free. I glanced at the firecracker, its fuse now disappearing into the body of the explosive. John, on his feet now, rushed around the front of the car as I threw the Roar Master toward the open door, aiming for the empty driveway.

The long, thick firecracker flew through the air with the speed and accuracy of an NFL football, but sometimes even a well-thrown football gets blocked. If John had just kept his big hands down, the Roar Master would have landed harmlessly in front of the garage. Instead, the giant explosive was struck by John's right hand and deflected into a large barrel of oily rags, assorted garbage, and grimy car parts.

While John and his boss stood frozen in shock, I ran out the door as fast as I could.

A few steps outside, I heard the massive explosion behind me, and it sounded more like an atom bomb than a firecracker. I was afraid to look back, so I just ran as fast I could toward the bank.

"Come back here, you little maniac!" John yelled. I glanced behind me as a giant cloud of gray smoke rose into the air over the garage like a scene from a war movie. Out of that smoke, an enraged teenager ran toward me. John's shirt was ragged and torn, only one leg of his blue jeans remained attached, and his long black, greasy hair stood on end with tiny puffs of black smoke piping in rings above it. The angry teenage boy looked like he'd been trapped in a barbeque grill, and he ran as if he'd just escaped from the psychiatric hospital.

I had a lead on John, but from the way he was running, I figured he would catch up soon. Suddenly a truck drove down the street past me, so I chased it and jumped on the running board. The truck was heavily loaded with wheat, so I figured it was headed toward the grain elevator. I wanted John to think I was going there.

The truck went around the corner, and luckily several buildings blocked the truck from John's view. Spotting a good opportunity, I jumped off before the truck made a left on its way to the granary. I ran as fast as I could into the dime store, and when John sprinted by, I scrunched down beside a display of ladies' shoes. When John chased the wheat truck, I went back outside and darted down the street in the opposite direction toward the bank. I expected the sheriff would be looking for me any minute now, but that didn't matter, I had to catch Mr. Pierce before he signed any papers. I knew the truth.

#

When I made it to the bank, I stood in the lobby for a moment, trying to catch my breath and hoping I wouldn't look too out of place. The bank looked much larger on the inside than I had expected. There was a group of desks near me, and on the other side of the long foyer was a long counter connecting two cashier workstations. Several customers stood in line in front of the cashiers, making deposits or getting change—whatever grown-ups do when they go to the bank. I searched for Mr. Pierce and glanced at the clock. It was five minutes after ten.

"May I help you, young man?" I heard someone ask. Turning to my left, I saw the frowning face of a lady who looked old enough and grumpy enough to be in the Witch's Hall of Fame. It's not that I have anything against older people, but this old bag looked like she hated everyone. Sitting behind a shiny wooden desk, she wore a long-sleeved black blouse buttoned all the way to her neck. Her hair was bluish-gray, worn in an old-fashioned pompadour hairstyle popular in the '40s. Her face was wrinkled and her expression rigid, and her brown eyes were magnified twice their normal size by a pair of gold rim bifocals. With her stork-like chin held high and her long, skinny hands folded in front of her, the woman spoke to me again with the accent and arrogance of British royalty.

"What do you want, young man?" she said frostily.

"I need some help," I said.

"Of course you do," she said. "Go over to the cashier's windows where they will change your quarter for you."

"No, ma'am. I'm looking for Mr. Pierce. He has an appointment with one of the managers this morning. It's really important."

"Yes, I see," she announced with no added friendliness. "Unfortunately, Mr. Pierce is upstairs with Mr. Thompson. Do you see that chair by the rail? Sit down and wait." Without waiting for a response, she immediately returned to her paperwork.

"Thank you, ma'am, but I need to see him right now."

I started walking up the stairway and didn't look back.

"You. Young man!" the old lady shouted. "Come back here this minute!"

I hurried up the wooden stairway toward a very important-looking office with a large door and a frosted glass window in the middle. I tried to open the door, but it was locked. When I glanced behind me, the grumpy old secretary stood right behind me with her arms folded across her chest and a seething scowl on her snarling face.

Reluctantly, I started back down the creaking staircase. I was rapidly trying to think of what to say or what to do. The witch walked behind me on the staircase.

"Young man," she said piously. "I told you to wait, didn't I?"

"Yes, ma'am, but . . ."

"No buts, young man. I told you to sit down and wait until Mr. Pierce is finished. Your manners are deplorable."

I stepped toward her, looking carefully at her face and neck. I thought about the German prisoners at Camp Alva. She would have made a good Nazi.

"Lady," I said, without moving away another inch. "I need to see Mr. Pierce right now. It has to do with the business he's discussing with Mr. Thompson. It can't wait."

"It will wait!" she snapped. Her heavily made-up face was unbending, and her eyebrows arched as if I had asked her for a million-dollar loan from her personal savings.

"Sit down, young man! Sit down this instant!"

I hadn't noticed it before, but someone had joined us at the bottom of the stairs. At first, I thought it had only been a curious onlooker since we seemed to be creating a fuss. Finally, the person spoke.

"My goodness, Lilly," she said pleasantly. "Is this boy a bank robber?"

The intruder was slightly younger than the secretary. But she had a lovely face—dignified, yet openly friendly. Her beautiful blue eyes seemed to have spent a lifetime enjoying the world instead of criticizing it. She was a silver-haired, elegant lady with a golden glow about her.

"Lilly," the nice lady said. "I believe I can handle this situation."

I didn't know who the sweet older woman was, but she seemed to have some influence in the bank. "Luftwaffe Lilly" took a step back. She was visibly upset at me but tried to look calm. She took a deep breath and ended up with an insulted frown pasted on her face.

"No, of course, he's not a bank robber!" Lilly said. "But he insisted on barging into a meeting with Mr. Thompson and Mr. Pierce. Mr. Thompson will not allow interruptions while in a conference."

"But, ma'am," I said to the newcomer. "I need to tell Mr. Pierce something crucial to this meeting. Please, it's very important. I'm not trying to cause trouble; I'm trying to prevent it."

"Young man," the grumpy lady said. "I have tried to be patient with you, and you won't listen. I want you to go outside—immediately."

"But . . . ma'am . . ." I said.

At that point, the nice older lady touched my arm gently and spoke again.

"Lilly, this young man seems to have a good business reason to go up. Why don't you let him? If Bill Thompson has a problem with it, tell him I suggested it."

Lilly gave that same sinister look to this lady that she had used on me several times. Her wrinkled, frowning face stiffened like an old piece of stretched leather. Her face resembled a worn-out baseball glove with hair and eyes.

"No, I will not!" she said. "I know what Mr. Thompson would want in this situation. He would not wish to be interrupted."

"Lilly," the sweet lady said, now changing her tone to a more severe and threatening sound. "Do you think Mr. Thompson would want my husband's account moved over to the new bank in Enid? I understand there's a new Sears and Roebuck opening in a few weeks. Banking there would give me a good excuse to do a little shopping every Saturday. What do you think?"

The angry secretary picked up the phone and spoke to someone, presumably upstairs. As she spoke, she clenched her free hand into a fist. For some reason, she seemed to lose her British royalty accent.

"Ida, open the door. There's someone here to see Mr. Pierce." There was a pause, then she said, "Yes, yes, I know there's a meeting going on. Just do it, Ida."

I smiled at the lady beside me.

"Thank you, ma'am," I whispered. "I'm Matt Turner." She put out her delicate hand and smiled.

"I know who you are, Matt. My niece told me all about you. I'm Jewel Rudy."

Surprised isn't the right word to describe how I felt. Maybe I was shocked, or better yet, astonished. But I didn't have time to chat; I had to move fast.

"I hope I can return the favor someday," I said.

"There is a little something, Matt. I'll explain it to Carol, and then she can tell you. Would that be all right?"

I grinned. "That will be very all right. That will be neat."

I heard a groan from across the room, and the grumpy lady said, "Teenagers today should learn proper manners and proper English."

Hurrying up the stairway, I smiled and wondered how I might be able to put a proper tack in that old woman's proper chair, so she could scream her proper head off.

Once upstairs, I glanced below me. The nice lady, Jewel Rudy, looked up at me and smiled. Behind her, I noticed the front door open. The police chief walked into the bank and looked around the lobby. I quickly darted into Mr. Thompson's office and closed the door behind me, hoping the police didn't see me.

Mr. Pierce sat in front of a large oak desk, a small stack of papers in front of him and a ballpoint pen in his hand. The frown on his face was enough to tell me that he wasn't happy to see me. Across the huge desk, a heavyset man in a dark suit scowled at me as if I had interrupted the signing of a peace treaty. The banker's office had bookshelves on each side wall, several leather chairs for visitors, and behind the banker, a large window which ran the width of the office and offered an excellent view of the street below. It was an office that the president of the United States might be proud of. Glancing over the banker's shoulder, I caught a glimpse of a tall teenage boy sprinting along the sidewalk; his shirt and slacks were torn and his long black hair was smoldering. People on the street stopped and stepped out of the way as he passed them.

I looked back inside the office as both men frowned at me, and I felt as out of place as goldfish in the Sahara Desert. Hoping to say the right thing for a change, I said, "Hi there, Mr. Pierce."

13   THE TUNNEL

n the base library, across the table from Private Pierce, Chaplain Jordahl stared at the young soldier in disbelief. Private Pierce felt his heart beat rapidly as the word "tunnel" echoed in the empty library.

"Who gave you this verse?" Chaplain Jordahl asked.

"Sergeant Schmitt," Private Pierce said.

"All right then, let's not panic here. Think for a moment. What else did he say?"

Private Pierce tried to remember the conversation, but he couldn't remember much else.

"I've got to go and tell the sergeant of the guard," the private said. "I have to go right now. They might be in the tunnel tonight," he said as he stood.

"No, sit down for just one more moment and let's think this out. The camp is too large to try and find a tunnel tonight. We need to know more. What else did Sergeant Schmitt say to you?"

Private Pierce knew the chaplain was right. "That was all, he just told me his best Bible verse and left."

"Nothing else?" prompted the chaplain.

Private Pierce looked at the stack of library books on the table and looked back at the chaplain.

"There was one more thing," he said. "Sergeant Schmitt told me his favorite book was *Look Homeward, Angel*, then he turned and walked away with some other German soldiers."

The two men looked at each other, in thought.

"Nothing in that book has anything to do with escape or tunnels," the chaplain said. "That was the book you were looking for tonight, right? Why were you looking for it?"

"Jewel, the girl I'm seeing, said she loved it. Well, to tell the truth, I thought I'd read it to impress her. I thought the author was Ernest Hemingway, but she corrected me and told me it was written by Thomas Wolfe."

As he said the name "Wolfe," both men looked at each other in astonishment, then jumped up and bolted toward the front door.

#

Sergeant Swim was sleeping like a two-hundred-pound child as the unlikely pair of worried men stormed into his unlit barracks. Private Pierce raced across the wood floor, tripped over someone's bed, recovered, and stood by the sergeant's bed. Chaplain Jordahl stood behind him.

"Sergeant Swim! Sergeant Swim!" Private Pierce yelled. "Wake up, sergeant! Wake up!"

The sleepy staff sergeant opened his eyes and shook his head, obviously trying to understand what was going on. He sat up in bed and looked at the chaplain, then over at Private Pierce. His expression was a mixture of drowsiness and anger.

"What the hell is going on?" Sergeant Swim asked gruffly. Then he changed his expression slightly, as he noticed the chaplain.

"Pardon my French, chaplain," the rugged-looking sergeant said with a fake smile. He frowned again and said, "Pierce, what the hell is going on?"

"It's pretty unusual, sergeant," the private said.

As several other men in the barracks woke to the intrusion, a frightened Private Pierce related the story of the possible tunnel. After he let the story sink in and tried to get his wits about him, Sergeant Swim stood and put his trousers on. Without saying a word, the thoughtful sergeant pulled his boots out from under his bed, squatted down, and put them on. He put on his shirt, then stretched and yawned. Private Pierce was amazed at the size of the Sergeant's chest and arms.

"So, we go after Major Wolf, and we go now," the burly sergeant said, buttoning his shirt.

"Chaplain," the sergeant said, "I'm not sure what part you play in this, but you can tell me later. For now, I would like for you to go and alert the front gate as to the situation, then go and wake Colonel Richardson. Tell the colonel we will start our search in Major Wolf's barracks and several barracks in that part of the officers' compound."

The chaplain looked around the room, noticing the attention they were getting.

"Yes, sergeant," the chaplain said, looking a bit intimidated.

"Go now, chaplain," Sergeant Swim said, "Go now."

#

Ten minutes before midnight, Sergeant Swim and seven MPs entered barracks number 302, the barracks where Major Wolf and 39 other German officers were housed. Sergeant Swim walked in first and turned on all the lights. Immediately the German soldiers began to grumble and cuss in their own language, but once they saw Sergeant Swim was in their barracks, they climbed out of bed and stood sleepily by their bunks.

Quickly, two MPs walked in opposite directions along the three-foot-wide aisle that ran from one end of the barracks to the other. The remaining five MPs and Sergeant Swim stood in the middle of the room with machine guns and pistols at the ready.

As the MPs walked between the bunks, they searched for any sign of a missing prisoner. The German POWs stood lethargically and pretended not to care, but it was obvious from their expressions that they knew what was going on. Several prisoners complained, but the Americans ignored them.

Before he reached his end of the barracks, Private Pierce looked at the end bunk and there, looking right at him, was Major Wolf with his standard evil grin on his face. Private Pierce felt a sudden lump in his throat and a horrible feeling in his stomach. The man he had accused of trying to escape was right next to his bed, exactly where he was supposed to be. From the other end of the barracks, his fellow MP gave his report, "All present and accounted for, sergeant."

Private Pierce stared into the blue eyes of the German major, the man he thought he would catch tonight. The major looked at the private; a slight grin crossed his face, showing the contempt he obviously felt for the lowly American soldier.

"All present and accounted for, sergeant," Private Pierce yelled as Colonel Richardson and several MPs entered the barracks. Private Pierce felt a deep knot in his stomach as he saw the sleepy-eyed camp commander.

"What's the situation here, Sergeant Swim?" Colonel Richardson asked.

"We just completed a bed check, sir, and it appears everything is normal."

"Velcome to barracks, colonel," Major Wolf said in broken English and fake friendliness.

"Quiet, Major Wolf!" Colonel Richardson said as he walked over to Sergeant Swim.

"Anything . . . unusual to report?" Colonel Richardson whispered as he stood face to face with the burly Sergeant Swim.

"No, sir," Sergeant Swim said, reluctantly.

Private Pierce stood nearby and knew there was going to be hell to pay for getting Sergeant Swim, Colonel Richardson, and half of Camp Alva up on Thanksgiving night with nothing to show for it. Nothing, that is, except for the righteous indignation of one despicable Nazi.

"Then let your men get back to bed, sergeant," Colonel Richardson said, "We can discuss this tomorrow morning."

"Yes, sir," the sergeant said, now looking at Private Pierce as if he might strangle him.

"Okay, men," the sergeant said, "You heard the colonel. Out you go."

The MPs shuffled out of the barracks as several German prisoners giggled, now pleased that the American surprise inspection had revealed nothing. Sergeant Swim, still looking at Private Pierce, turned and walked toward the door. As he walked along the aisle, he glanced down at the barefooted German POWs beside him—men who seemed anxious to get back in bed.

On his left, the sergeant noticed two men standing side by side with a third man behind them who seemed a bit nervous. As the sergeant walked past them, the two men in front seemed to move with him and block his view of the third man. The sergeant stopped and turned to the left. The two German soldiers in front did not move. The sergeant took a step toward them, and the men moved slightly closer to each other, filling in the gap between them. Only a tiny movement on their part, but it appeared intentional. The prisoner behind them looked the other way as if he were reluctant to look the sergeant in the eye.

Sergeant Swim took his nightstick and stuck it between the two men in the front, then he roared, "Move!"

When they did, the sergeant saw what they were trying to cover up. The prisoner behind them had on one army boot, which by itself wasn't strange, but looking closer, the sergeant was able to make out a line of red mud along the toe. There had been no rain or snow in Camp Alva for over a week, and when it did rain—the mud was never red. That mud came from somewhere else.

"Men," Sergeant Swim said. "Let's not get in any hurry here."

The MPs, seeing the look on their sergeant's face, gathered around him and waited for orders. Sergeant Swim looked around the room and seemed to be assessing the reaction on the faces of the German POWs. Across the aisle, several of the prisoners appeared a bit nervous, where before they had been cocky.

"I want all prisoners moved to the other end of the barracks, double-time," the sergeant said. As the MPs herded the German prisoners to the other end of the barracks, there were complaints and jeering from most of the prisoners. The sergeant commanded, "You three men right here, move these beds out of the way!"

The MPs went into action immediately. This was not the first time they had searched the prisoners' barracks, and they knew what to look for. The last few prisoners, including Major Wolf, were shoved out of the way, the beds were moved, and books and other personal gear got kicked to the side as the MPs inspected the floor for signs of a secret door.

As Sergeant Swim kept a keen eye on the prisoners, his three MPs, including Private Pierce, searched for anything out of the ordinary. One of the MPs took his nightstick out and tapped the floor: tap-tap-tap. He moved closer to the wall: tap-tap-tap. Now he was right beside the wall: tap-tap-tap-KNOCK.

"Well, well," the MP said. "What have we here?"

Removing a small knife from his front pocket, the chubby MP worked one of the boards loose and carefully pried out four other boards that popped up with such ease it surprised him. Under the three-foot boards, he found an earth-colored gunny sack neatly tucked in the empty space there. As he removed the gunny sack, the MP next to him pointed his flashlight at the hole. Sergeant Swim and his MPs stood looking into a perfectly square hole that dropped straight down at least twenty feet. They had found their tunnel.

Three MPs on their hands and knees looked into the entrance of a very deep passageway. Sergeant Swim stood above them. There were only two MPs guarding the now anxious prisoners, so the sergeant, fearing a riot, chose to secure the prisoners' situation before inspecting the tunnel.

"Move out, men!" Sergeant Swim yelled. "Lewis, get more MPs in here and get Colonel Richardson back. You other men, assemble the prisoners outside and put them on their knees. If anyone resists or talks back, take them to the stockade!"

The MPs smiled as they carried out their orders.

#

Twenty minutes later, as the prisoners were closely guarded outside, Colonel Richardson and Sergeant Swim studied the shadowy pit as Private Pierce descended along wooden planks installed as steps. The "steps" looked every bit like the slats which stabilized an army bunk. Of course, that's exactly what they were.

The beam from Private Pierce's flashlight went farther and farther down into the earth, but finally he stepped onto the solid ground at the bottom. He looked up and smiled nervously at the men above him, then took his pistol out of its holster, held his flashlight in his mouth, and squatted down to see the tunnel.

As the flashlight pierced the darkness in front of him, Private Pierce was shocked by what he saw. The end of the long, narrow, tunnel was too far away to be seen, and he could tell that the passageway had been constructed with care and designed with accuracy.

The reinforced walls were oval-shaped, somewhat narrow, and just wide enough for a large person to squeeze through. There were bed slats on several places along the tunnel's walls and ceiling which appeared to be placed there to reinforce the loose soil and prevent the tunnel from collapsing.

Army blankets, the kind which had been requested recently, were shoved between slats in several areas. After his eyes grew accustomed to the light, he noticed a thin black electrical cord that ran along the ceiling. The Germans had tapped into the camp's electricity.

"What do you see, Private Pierce?" Colonel Richardson asked as Sergeant Swim started down the wooden steps.

"You're not going to believe it."

As Sergeant Swim stepped off the last wooden plank, he squatted down and peered into the escape tunnel. He took the flashlight from Pierce and glanced around the tunnel, taking in the wooden slats, electrical cord, dirty blankets, and right above his head, a small piece of wood with a hand-carved name. It seemed to be the name the Germans had given their tunnel,

"Der Ruf"

Der Ruf, German for 'The Call.'

They had named their tunnel after the German-language newspaper published by the American government and despised by the Nazis.

Sergeant Swim pointed to the name above them and said to Private Pierce, "See this? They planned on us finding their tunnel after they escaped. This is to add insult to injury." The burly sergeant looked up through the tunnel entrance to the camp commander.

"Sir, it's long, it's well built, and they have been digging it right under our noses."

14   JEWEL

A cold, thick silence lingered in the banker's office. Its gloominess reminded me of an early morning fog above the east pasture—somewhere I'd rather be right now. While the two men exchanged worried looks, I glanced around and took in the elaborate furnishings. The office was large enough to store a couple of John Deere tractors and still have room for his king-sized desk. It wasn't at all what I had expected in a small-town country bank.

Mr. Thompson's desk was larger and more polished than the puny desks downstairs, and a brown oval carpet covered most of the floor near his work area. At the center of his desk, a lime-green lamp was placed to shine on the more important papers, some I figured had been discussed right before my interruption.

Several paintings hung on the walls—large, expensive-looking works I was unable to see much of. On one wall, I noticed a county map like the one in the sheriff's office. Yet this map was not just another decoration, because it provided more detail about the countryside surrounding Alva

"Why are you here, son?" Mr. Pierce asked, sounding polite but disappointed.

I walked closer to the desk and glanced at the papers in front of Mr. Pierce, hoping I wasn't too late. The bank manager smiled, but it was clearly a forced grin.

"Mr. Pierce," I started. "I know you're here to sign some papers to allow Thurman Spencer to keep half of your wheat earnings, but I have something to tell you that will change all that."

The banker grunted, and the smile on his face disappeared.

"Son," the manager said in a worried tone. "What is it you need to tell him?"

"Well," I said. "Mr. Pierce knows part of the story, but now I know how all this happened."

"Okay, then," Mr. Thompson said. "Go ahead."

"There is only one reason Mr. Pierce is signing over part of his crop: a dirty trick Thurman Spencer cooked up."

"You better explain yourself, young man," Mr. Thompson said.

I told them how the whole thing had been cooked up by Thurman Spencer and how they had used it to blackmail Mr. Pierce. When I finished, I felt pretty good about my detective work, and I expected Mr. Pierce to smile, get up, and walk out of the office with me.

"Matt," Mr. Pierce said, taking a deep breath. "That's enough, son. I told you I wanted to forget all of this."

I glanced at Mr. Thompson. I hadn't noticed it before, but something about the look on his face told me he wasn't hearing this story for the first time. Mr. Thompson took off his glasses, cleaned them with his handkerchief, and put them on again.

"Sounds like a silly prank some of the teenagers around town pulled just for fun," he said, waving his hand and dismissing the whole thing like it was a joke.

"Now, Mr. Pierce," Mr. Thompson said unconvincingly. "If you don't feel like finishing what we're doing right now, we can leave it. I'm in no hurry."

Mr. Thompson glanced at Mr. Pierce over the rim of his glasses to see the farmer's reaction.

Mr. Pierce shook his head and frowned at me.

"No, sir," Mr. Pierce said. "Matt here is just leaving." Then he turned to me, "Matt, I appreciate you trying so hard, and we will talk about this some more back at the farm. But for now, will you wait for me at the pickup?"

"But . . . But, Mr. Pierce," I said. "I forgot to tell you. I just came from talking to the boy who helped blackmail you. He even admitted it."

"What?" Mr. Pierce asked. "He admitted it?"

"Yes, sir," I beamed. "When Thurman Spencer gets the crop money, John gets the title to his blue Chevy."

Again, the two men looked at each other. Then Mr. Pierce smiled as if it all had sunk in.

"Matt, you've done good, son." He shook his head and pulled on his left earlobe, thinking hard. "But we could never get Thurman Spencer to admit to anything. He'll fight and make more trouble; you can be sure of that. But there is some good news to come from this. Mr. Thompson has offered me a deal to take care of Thurman Spencer and still leave me with a large part of this year's wheat money."

The overweight banker looked over at Mr. Pierce with phony humility. At this point, I suspected anything he offered couldn't be all that hot.

"Has the bank bought your farm or something?" I asked.

"No, but he's given me the chance to make up for the loss to Thurman Spencer."

"I don't get it, sir. You don't owe anything to Thurman Spencer." At that point, I felt like Mr. Pierce didn't understand his own situation.

"Son, the bank is buying all the mineral rights to my farm. They will have the right to drill for oil or whatever they want to do on it."

I looked back up at that map behind Mr. Thompson's desk. Now I could see what it was. It wasn't farm activity at all. It was some kind of oil map. Several farms had a red "X" on them, and I took it to indicate they were either owned by the bank or maybe had some drilling planned.

I glanced at the chubby banker again, and something about his shifty eyes told me this whole thing had more cow crap at the bottom of it than Perry's barn.

"Have you signed those papers yet?" I asked, desperately.

"No. We were looking at them when you came in."

"That's great," I said. "I may have an idea or two to help you make up your mind. How 'bout it?"

"No, Matt, no. I want to put this whole thing behind us right now."

"That sounds like a very good suggestion," the banker offered. "If that's the way you feel, I'll have Lilly bring up a check for you right now."

While I tried to think of what to do next, Mr. Thompson lifted the receiver and called "Luftwaffe Lilly" downstairs. The banker smiled at Mr. Pierce and spoke pleasantly into the phone, "Lilly, would you be so kind as to draw up a check for Mr. Henry Pierce in the amount of nine thousand, five hundred dollars? That's right. Bring it up right away, please." The banker looked over at me while he held the receiver, "Well, yes. That young man is still here." He coughed and said, "Yes, I agree, he certainly is a *fine* young man."

Now I knew for sure the man was a liar. He put the receiver down and pointed to one of the contracts on his desk. "All right, while she prepares your check, all we need to do is have you put your John Hancock right here and right here." He handed Mr. Pierce an expensive-looking fountain pen.

"Mr. Pierce," I begged. "Please wait and talk about this. I don't know anything about wheat, and I know even less about oil. But maybe you could hold off a day or so and think this over?"

The quiet farmer frowned, and I knew I was about to be thrown out on my ear. But I couldn't just stand by and let him sign those papers.

"Matt, listen," he said. "Mr. Thompson is trying to help me. I can pay off my note at the bank and maybe get a new pickup to boot. Son, I know you're trying to help. But for now, please go on outside and let me finish this. Please, Matt."

Feeling depressed and hurt, I walked to the door of the large office. I was walking away from what I felt to be the second-biggest mistake Mr. Pierce ever made. I didn't want to give up, but Lilly was on her way up the stairs with a huge amount of money. I wasn't certain what I should do in regard to the mineral rights, and I felt pretty sad standing there.

When the door opened, I looked up expecting to see the glum, wrinkled face of that horrible secretary. But what I saw instead gave me more hope than anything had in years. It was an older lady, all right; it was Jewel Rudy smiling right at me.

The moment Jewel Rudy walked into the room, the cold, gloomy office came to life. Her warm smile brought a cheerful glow to the cool, drab atmosphere, and her quiet confidence carried the first ray of hope into the room.

Mr. Thompson, a large, balding man in his fifties, sat at his desk with his mouth wide open, almost wide enough for him to swallow the papers on his desk.

Mr. Pierce, who had been looking intently at the contract in front of him, glanced at Jewel Rudy, back at his papers, then jerked his head up in surprise. His eyes were wide.

"Excuse me, gentlemen," Jewel Rudy said. She pointed over at me and continued, "This young man told me Henry was in here, so I thought I'd come up and say a quick hello. I hope I haven't interrupted anything."

I slid a little closer to her, but I didn't make a sound. Mr. Pierce stood up to greet the visitor, while Mr. Thompson remained seated, and his surprised expression changed from disinterest to irritation. In fact, from the look on his face, it was obvious that he didn't consider Jewel Rudy a welcome guest. But that didn't seem to bother her. She had entered, and in a split second, she had taken charge.

"Oh, you know you're always welcome in this office, Jewel," Mr. Thompson offered, but his words were flat, insincere. He glanced over at Mr. Pierce and said, "I guess I don't have to introduce you two, do I?"

"No, sir," Mr. Pierce said. He removed his cowboy hat with his right hand and held it against his chest. With a look of pure sincerity and respect, he nodded his head and smiled.

"How are you, Jewel?" he said. "You're as pretty as a picture." He spoke with all the charm of a country gentleman, and it was a side of the man that I had never seen before.

"Thank you, Henry. I'm fine," Jewel said. She gave Mr. Pierce her hand, and he took it gently. "Henry," she said. "I met this hired hand of yours downstairs, and he was in a terrible rush to find you. Is everything all right?"

"Yes, it is," he said.

She held her glance with Mr. Pierce as though she were expecting him to elaborate, but he didn't. When he let go of her hand, she looked at me.

"Yes," she said, smiling toward me. "If I ever have a problem, I want this one on my team. But Matt, it looks to me like you were on your way out when I came in?"

"Yes, ma'am. I'm not needed in here as bad as I thought."

"That's exactly right, young man," the bank manager interrupted. "You can just run along now."

"Yes, sir. I guess I will then," I said, looking down at the floor. "I came in here to talk about wheat farms, and the whole conversation switched to oil. I know a little bit about wheat and nothing about oil."

"Did you say oil?" Mrs. Rudy asked.

"Yes, yes," Mr. Thompson snapped as he seemed to forget his manners. "And we were just about to . . ."

But before he could finish his sentence, Mrs. Rudy cut him off. "That's funny," she said. "I had just mentioned to Matt earlier, I wanted to talk to him about something. But to tell the truth, it wasn't Matt that I wanted to talk to; it was you, Henry."

"Well, what was it, Jewel?" Mr. Pierce asked.

"Just what you're talking about right here—oil. What a silly coincidence! I guess I'm here just at the right time."

"No, you're too late, ma'am," I said. "The bank's going to buy up all of Mr. Pierce's mineral rights. Isn't that the plan, Mr. Thompson?"

"Well, yes, it is, as a matter of fact. We have made Mr. Pierce here a very good offer," the banker said. His words were strong, but he looked like a child who had just taken the last cookie out of the jar. Mr. Pierce followed the conversation, but he still looked as though he were in shock at being so close to Jewel Rudy.

"But, Bill," Mrs. Rudy said. "I might be mistaken here, and God knows I make a lot of mistakes. But wasn't Henry's farm part of the land my husband told you he was interested in?"

The banker coughed again, and the redness rising from under his collar was now visible on his skin.

He said, "I'm not sure I remember what you're talking about, Mrs. Rudy."

Mr. Pierce looked at the banker suspiciously.

"Sure you do, Bill," she said. "You were over for supper last fall, and you two men were speculating on which plot of land offered the best prospects for drilling. My husband mentioned two or three large farms, and Mr. Pierce's place was the only small farm he mentioned. He said it might be small when it comes to acreage, but it had petroleum potential. I think he mentioned some rocks or . . . Oh, what's that term those engineers use? Oh, yes, I do remember—rock outcroppings. I think that's what he called it." She giggled and touched her hand to her face shyly. "I can never seem to get those things right."

Mr. Pierce grinned at her, and I felt like hugging her. But Mr. Thompson wasn't sharing our enthusiasm. It sounded like Mrs. Rudy knew a lot more about oil than she let on.

"Well, maybe he did say something like that," Mr. Thompson said. "I really can't remember that far back. Anyway, we were just about to complete this thing. So if you will wait downstairs, I'll be happy to handle whatever it is you need today, *Mrs*. Rudy."

The bank manager gave an added emphasis to the way he said "Mrs." and judging by the stunned look in the woman's eyes, he may have done more damage than he had intended. Mrs. Rudy was obviously hurt. She glanced at Mr. Pierce, and for a moment, it looked as though he might take up for her, but then he looked away. Mrs. Rudy looked back at the banker and regained her poised expression.

"Why, of course, I'll run along," Mrs. Rudy said, her voice a bit weaker now. "I didn't need anything. I just came up to say hello to Henry and tell him he's lucky to have such a good hand like Matt here."

"Fine, fine," the bank manager said, walking across the office, then hastily escorting Mrs. Rudy to the door. But then Mrs. Rudy stopped and turned to face Mr. Pierce.

"Oh, and one other thing," she said, this time her voice stronger, less friendly.

"What is it now, Mrs. Rudy?" The banker whined like a kindergartener.

"Henry," Mrs. Rudy said. "I'm sure the bank is giving you a fair offer. At least they should. But if you're looking for a backup offer, my husband had mentioned that he is willing to give you $15,000 for your mineral rights."

Mr. Thompson's shoulders slumped dramatically the instant she mentioned the higher offer, and Mr. Pierce stood with his eyes and his mouth wide open.

"I guess that's about all I can say," she said.

The $15,000 figure still echoed throughout the room as Jewel Rudy walked confidently out of Mr. Thompson's office. The troubled, overweight banker returned to his desk, sat down and sneered at me. Without saying a word, I chose that moment to slip out the door and go back to the pickup like I was told.

When Mr. Pierce came out of the bank ten minutes later, I was standing under one of the oak trees lining the perimeter of the city square. He walked up to the pickup as if nothing unusual had happened all morning. Then, looking over at me, he grinned and got into the truck.

We drove out of town and headed toward the farm like we always do. As usual, he didn't speak for a while. I didn't push him. He would talk when he was ready, and that was fine with me.

The wheat fields we passed were almost all cut now, and some had already been plowed over. It was a pretty sight, but somehow I couldn't concentrate on farming.

It seemed like so many things had happened since I came to work on the farm. A mixture of good and bad, but it was mostly good, I thought. Seemed like every time I had worked things out, something else happened to throw a monkey wrench in the works. But now it really did look like things were working out. "Good as gold," Grandma would say.

About halfway back to the farm, Mr. Pierce finally said something, "Have you ever seen anyone in your life who made the world light up like Jewel does?"

"No, sir. Guess I never did."

"You probably won't either, because that lady is one of a kind."

"Well, there are two other people who would run a good race to be 'one of a kind' like that—my mother and a cute girl named Carol."

With the wind blowing through the windows of the pickup, Mr. Pierce looked across the cab and smiled at me. I guess he knew what I thought before I said it, but I said it anyway.

"Mr. Pierce, she's a wonderful woman, but there are other women in the world—women who might be looking for someone." I hesitated and said, "You notice I didn't say looking for a handsome man or anything."

Mr. Pierce chuckled and said, "Well, let's forget about the boys and the girls for now. Let's talk about my farm since you're so all-fired interested in my business."

"I hope you're not too upset at me going into the bank and all. I was only trying to help."

"I know it, son. I'm glad you have been here this summer, and I understand why you pushed your way into the bank today. I guess you're wondering what I did after you went out, aren't you?"

"Yes, sir."

"I told Mr. Thompson to hold on to his offer. I told him I might take some advice I picked up from my hired hand."

I smiled at Mr. Pierce as he continued.

"Well, son, I just told that Mr. Thompson I wasn't signing anything right now. He tried to act like it didn't bother him, but I knew different."

"I bet he was mad. He seemed pretty anxious to settle with you this morning. His offer wasn't nearly as good as the one Mrs. Rudy mentioned."

"Yep."

"So?" I asked.

"So what?" Mr. Pierce said.

"So, will you talk to Mr. Rudy about his offer?"

"Well, I think I will. It seems like an awful lot of money, though. How can my land be worth that much just for them to drill on it? They won't own the land."

"I don't know anything about that, Mr. Pierce. But if you go out to see them, I'd like to come along. Carol might be staying with her aunt."

"Sure. We can drive out tonight if you want to."

"You bet. I'm ready to go right now."

"No," he said. "I need to give her time to talk to her husband and pave the way, so to speak. This isn't going to be easy for any of us. He knows Jewel and I was courting years ago. He may not welcome this little get-together."

"But, Mr. Pierce, would a man your age get jealous?"

"Love doesn't have an age limit, son. Never forget that. If you love someone, then it's just natural to be jealous. But I am not going to kindle the fire. She chose him years ago, and he's been good to her."

"He has?"

"Sure. Around here, you'd know about it when someone isn't good to their wife. So I plan to go out there and try and work out this business. Don't want to open any old wounds."

"Mr. Pierce, I think I understand what you mean. That's pretty cool."

"Cool," he said. "I don't think I've ever been called 'cool' before. Tell me, is that good or bad?"

I grinned at him as he went on. "Because it's so hot outside, I guess cool is good. So, what if it was winter and you called me cool? Wouldn't mean the same thing then, would it? It would be bad then, I expect," he rambled on and grinned.

"I think you know what I mean, Mr. Pierce."

He laughed again as we turned on to the long dirt road that led to his farmhouse.

That night we drove over to Bronson's Corner, where Mr. Pierce used the phone to call Rudy's ranch. I barely had enough time to buy a Coke when Mr. Pierce finished his call and walked out the door toward the pickup. I scurried out the door behind him and jumped into the truck just as he was starting it.

"I guess you got ahold of them?"

"I did," he said. "They're expecting us in fifteen minutes, Matt. You're in luck, too. Carol's over there visiting."

187

I grinned. "Funny how things just seem to work out, isn't it?"

"Sure is, son. Real funny."

It was dark as we drove along the highway and turned southward onto a bumpy farm road. The dim lights from the dashboard shone across Mr. Pierce's face, giving him a gentle radiant glow. In front of us, the truck's bright headlights lit the dusty road, bringing unwelcome light to the night creatures here and there.

In the distance, a pair of glowing orange eyes seemed transfixed as we approached a cottontail rabbit huddling on the edge of the embankment. The frightened animal waited until we were almost on top of it before darting across our path, barely escaping certain death.

Then, a mile or so further south, a large bird flew out of a tree and darted out of sight before I could make out what it was. I thought maybe it was an owl because it flew so slowly, but I never got a good enough look to know for sure.

There is something fun about driving along old country roads at night. Maybe it's the headlights cutting through the darkness, illuminating so many things. You watch carefully since you never know what you might see on the road or along the side of the road. It's the time when animals move around a lot more than they do during the day. I had seen turtles and snakes at night, and one time I even saw a deer. We were about to cross Powder Creek, and the possibility of seeing a deer kept me watchful.

I glanced at Mr. Pierce, who seemed to be enjoying the drive. The dim lights from the truck's dashboard lit his whiskered, wrinkled face, and I knew he had a lot on his mind. Without bothering him, I looked back at the road just as we rounded the corner, just above the creek.

Suddenly a pair of bright headlights came right at us moving faster, and in the opposite direction on the road.

"Watch out," I yelled. Mr. Pierce jerked the steering wheel to the right. Our pickup veered off the road and into the ditch's soft dirt. For a moment, it seemed like he had lost control, but then he guided the truck back onto the main road. Now a thick cloud of dirt and dust swirled around us, blocking our view of the country road, and I was completely disoriented. Mr. Pierce hit the brakes, and when the dust finally cleared, we were on the edge of the embankment about ten feet from the water. If he had driven a few more feet, we would have hit the creek in one of its deepest places.

"Who was that?" I asked.

"Thurman Spencer."

"What's he doing out here?" I asked, my voice quivering.

Mr. Pierce put his callused hands on the top of the steering wheel and stared into the windshield. His face was a mirror of his returning fear.

He shook his head. "He's not finished yet, son."

I watched him as he reached into the glove compartment and pulled out a dark-colored bottle of whiskey. He looked closely at the almost-full bottle and looked over at me.

Not again, I thought. *Not this again.*

"Mr. Pierce," I said. "Please don't do this tonight. Please don't do this. Remember, we're going to the Rudys' place. You can't get drunk. Not tonight."

"How far?" Mr. Pierce said.

"How far, what?" I said. "You mean the Rudys' place?"

"How far?" he asked again.

"I don't understand, sir. 'How far' for what?"

"You told me you play football."

"That's right, but . . ."

"Well," he said, "How far can you throw this thing?"

And then I caught on. I grinned at him, took the bottle out of his hand, and got out of the pickup. We both walked around the front of the truck and stood there for a moment.

"Ever hear of a Hail Mary pass?" I asked.

"I don't think so," he said.

"That's an exciting play a quarterback makes when there are only a few seconds on the clock. It's at the end of the game, and his team is behind. The pass will be a long shot, and lots of people are always trying to block it. But he gives it his best shot, prays someone is there to catch it, and that God will keep the other team off his back."

"That's just the play we need right now," Mr. Pierce agreed.

With Mr. Pierce watching and the pickup's headlights shining toward the creek, I took a few steps back, went into my best quarterback stance and threw that whiskey bottle down the creek as far as I could. Swish, it went, right into the night. After several seconds, the crackle of glass breaking against a rock was heard in the distance. I don't know how far it went, but I was happy when I heard the sound of breaking glass. It wasn't just the familiar sound of a broken whiskey bottle, but the inspiring sounds of a broken man trying to get his life back together.

We got into the truck and drove the last few miles to the Rudy ranch, and during that time, I thought about how proud I was to see a man change the way Mr. Pierce was changing. He might have a ways to go, but he was trying, and I sure liked him for it.

Then I got to thinking about his days as a soldier, when he was young and more confident. I realized that I didn't know what happened after he found the Nazi tunnel. I needed to find out.

"Mr. Pierce," I said. "I was thinking about how great you must have felt finding the tunnel that night during the war. It must have felt terrific. But then I got to wondering why you and Jewel never got married. It seems like you had everything going for you."

Mr. Pierce held the steering wheel a little tighter, then glanced at me and said, "You're right about part of the story; I did feel mighty good after finding the tunnel. But some other things happened, you see. We had to find out everything we could about that tunnel, and I guess we found out a few things about ourselves in the bargain …"

15   HEAD IN THE CLOUDS

For several days, the amazing tunnel was inspected, measured, analyzed, and photographed. A complete investigation was conducted to determine which prisoners were involved and who the leaders were. If that weren't enough to keep the company commander busy, questions also poured in every day from the Prisoner of War Special Projects Division Headquarters.

They wanted to know things like "How did the POWs manage to build a hundred-and-fifty-foot tunnel right under your nose? What tools did they use? How many prisoners were involved? Who planned the escape, and when did they intend to carry it out?"

Reports went out every few hours, and each day brought a hundred other questions. It took almost a week of inspecting the tunnel and searching the camp for evidence. Looking for tools, other escape routes, and at the same time conducting a hit-and-miss interrogation of prisoners to determine the facts. Prisoners often lied while being questioned, and as hard as the MPs tried, it was impossible to get all the facts. Any German prisoner suspected of squealing could expect to be beaten or executed by his fellow Nazis, so it was tough going for the interrogators. In addition, the American government stressed the importance of adhering to the rules of the Geneva Convention, so the investigation was bound by those rigid guidelines.

But little by little, hint by precious hint, the facts started to materialize, and a complete report was compiled. The long, arduous report was sent to the Office of the Provost Marshal General as well as to J. Edgar Hoover at the FBI. The document was sent through the normal channels and signed by the company commander at Camp Alva.

Subject: Report of Investigation—POW Tunnel, Camp Alva

To: Commanding Officer of the Provost Marshal General

    1. The Tunnel discovered on Thanksgiving was given the codename *Der Ruf* by the Nazi planners. It was measured from the inside of barracks 302 and found to be one hundred and fifty feet in length. It ran in an easterly direction, and the exit was located across the main road into Alva. The tunnel was three feet wide in most places and occasionally had areas carved into the side of around four feet. Some of these small pockets of space were used for turning around and others were used to store food and other items needed during the escape. Items found in the tunnel have been inventoried, and that inventory will be sent in a separate report later today. However, the bulk of the items found were foodstuffs, German backpacks, hard chocolate from the German Red Cross, canteens, civilian clothing, and water.

    2. Various tools were found, among which were coal shovels, picks with shortened handles, coal buckets, and a sort of cart used for moving dirt. The cart was made from the bottom of a shower stall and had small wheels. We believe it was filled with dirt, pulled into the tunnel entrance with a rope, and the dirt removed, to be dispersed the next morning.

    The dirt movement was the brainchild of Major Wolf and involved the new soccer field which was being built in a common exercise area, inside the prisoners' compound. Each morning the dirt was hauled to the soccer field and stacked in one particular area, then spread across the soccer field. The prisoners knew when to haul it and when to spread it.

    3. As far as can be determined, there were 21 POWs who took part in the escape plan, and they were to leave through the tunnel in seven groups of three. All POWs in the escape group, regardless of their rank, took part in the digging. They planned to escape on Thanksgiving Day but ran into a technical problem. The exit location was off course by twenty feet and was too close to the road, so another few weeks of digging were required. I do not know if this part of the story is true, but one of the prisoners told us how they were able to determine where the tunnel exit would come out; two men crawled the length of the tunnel during the day while a number of POWs watched from inside the compound. One of the men in the tunnel stuck a long, thin stick up through the dirt with a tiny white cloth on it. When the flag was poked through the dirt, the prisoners in the compound could see it, and they knew it was off course. It was disappointing to the tunnel rats, but they were determined to escape and one or two weeks more wasn't the end of the world. That prisoner has been moved to another camp after his interrogation, to avoid reprisals by the super Nazis.

4. The prisoners were able to tap into the camp's electrical system and came up with a light that aided them in their digging. However, there were several places where water one to two feet deep had to be crawled through, and the electric light often gave our Nazi guests a good shock.

The 21 POWs, less the informant, have been interrogated and are currently spending time in the stockade under the supervision of Major Rodgers. We have carried out and continue to carry out more shakedowns and will encourage prisoner informants to lead us toward troublemakers.

5. While the camp is not quite back to complete order, it runs very smoothly. For this, one noncommissioned officer and one enlisted man under my command deserve credit. You will find a letter regarding these two men and my recommendation enclosed.

Lt. Colonel R.D. Richardson

#

After the discovery of the Thanksgiving tunnel, life around Camp Alva changed for many of the POWs. And it had specifically changed for one very happy MP. Because the Americans feared reprisal from the Nazis, there was never a hint of any assistance from Sergeant Schmitt—the German prisoner who had given the Bible clues which led to the tunnel discovery. As Chaplain Jordahl preferred staying out of the limelight, his name was never mentioned in documents or reports. The result was an outpouring of praise for the astonishing job of Military Police work done by Private Henry Pierce.

The following memo was part of the daily report at Camp Alva:

> *Based on his attention to detail, self-confidence, and unshakeable self-determination, Private First Class Henry Pierce has been promoted to the rank of corporal in the United States Army. Private First Class Pierce has been awarded the Army Commendation Medal, and his outfit, the 401st MP Company, has been awarded the Presidential Unit Citation.*

Overnight, Corporal Henry Pierce had become a folk hero and was also becoming extremely popular in Alva since the "Thanksgiving tunnel discovery." To say the least, he was the talk of the town.

Almost any night Corporal Pierce could be found in one of the many bars or restaurants around Alva. He would need only to walk into a nightspot and he would instantly be surrounded by people offering him drinks or inviting him to a party. A few times he had even been invited to parties in Enid, some 70 miles away. Of course, he could only accept those invitations if he were able to find transportation.

Regardless of where he went, the questions always persisted: "Tell me about the tunnel," or "How in the world did you know it was there?" or his personal favorite, "Why don't they just make you the camp commander?"

So, night after night and drink after countless drink, Corporal Pierce told and retold the story. Of course, like any good soldier, Corporal Pierce embellished a bit here and there, and maybe he left off a critical item or two. He would relate how he had read the Bible Thanksgiving morning and how God had told him Job's line about the "tunnel" was meant for him. Then he would tell how he had been walking in the park on Thanksgiving night and got to thinking about his favorite book, *Look Homeward, Angel*, by Thomas Wolfe. Sometimes he mentioned he was walking with Jewel, but if he was relating the dramatic story to a pretty girl, he might forget to mention Jewel altogether. But regardless of who he was talking to, he would always explain how, on that fateful evening, he had put the two things together, realized what was going on, and convinced Sergeant Swim to let him search Major Wolf's barracks. Of course, in telling and retelling any great story, the line between fact and fiction is often blurred. Corporal Pierce was no exception to that rule.

So, occasionally for dramatic effect, Corporal Pierce would tell them how dangerous it was to crawl into an enemy tunnel alone—or if he had already consumed a few stiff drinks and happened to be weaving the story for a pretty girl, he would lean in and whisper, "When I crawled down into that black pit of a tunnel, I found a filthy German soldier hiding in a little cubbyhole. Of course, I had to shoot the dirty Kraut, but don't tell anyone."

At that point the pretty girl would swear to keep it to herself, then she would slide over a bit closer to the town hero.

As the word spread of his exploits, Corporal Pierce became the local expert on other POW camps, attempted escapes, and tunnel-digging in general. He loved to hold court with a number of rapt listeners as he told, in great detail, stories about the various prison camps in the United States and how the US Army and the FBI were depending on guys like him to keep citizens out of harm's way. One of his favorite stories, the one he saved for fresh faces and generous listeners, was the one about the three POWs from Crossville, Tennessee.

"Three German enlisted men," Corporal Pierce would start his great tale, "escaped from a POW work detail and ran off into the woods. Several days later they came to a small, secluded mountain cabin and started to get water from a pump. This tiny old granny appeared in the doorway, aimed a gun at them, and told them to 'Git.' Unschooled in the ways of mountain folk, the escaped prisoners scoffed at her and paid no attention. A few moments later, she drew a bead and fired, killing one of the men almost instantly. Later on, when a deputy sheriff informed the old lady that she had killed an escaped German prisoner of war, she was horror-stricken, burst into tears, and sobbed that she would never have fired if she had known they were Germans.

"'Well, ma'am,' the deputy asked, puzzled, 'what in thunder did you think you were aiming at?'

"'Why,' she said, 'I thought they was Yankees!'"

That story always got him a big laugh and another free drink. So it went night after night. Corporal Pierce had more stories, gained more attention, and his fame seemed to grow more.

By late January, some three months after the tunnel was discovered, a seasoned newspaper reporter from Oklahoma City fought his way through a mountain of red tape and was granted special permission to visit Camp Alva. He was thrilled to go to the camp and had high expectations of interviewing Corporal Pierce.

On the evening before the big interview, Corporal Pierce and Jewel met for dinner at a small restaurant on Main Street. She had suggested the location because it offered them a more private setting. Lately, she had noticed how Henry never refused to tell his story and had become prone to accepting more drinks than he could handle. In a loving and caring way, she had told Henry she was starting to worry about him. For once, he seemed to take her comments to heart, and it gave Jewel hope.

"Friday night," Henry said, "let's forget the war, the camp, and everyone on earth except you and me. We are going to have a nice quiet evening to ourselves." Jewel looked into Henry's eyes and smiled as he kissed her.

"It's a date, soldier boy," she said. "It's a date."

16   REVENGE

E ntering the main gate of the Rudy ranch, I felt the same emotions people must experience when visiting the White House—a mixture of amazement and fear with just a dab of jealousy. But since I had met Mrs. Rudy at the bank, I also felt a strong sense of admiration.

We passed a white picket fence and drove along a circular drive with tall cottonwood trees on both sides. It was too dark to make out much of the yard, but there was enough light to see it was well-trimmed and lined with a variety of lovely flowers.

Before reaching the house, the gravel driveway passed by a white barn with several new trucks parked in front. Like a couple of kids on Christmas morning, Mr. Pierce and I strained to see every building and piece of equipment around the beautiful ranch. Mr. Pierce pulled up in front of the white, two-story home. There was a long, open porch facing the front yard, with a swinging chair and at least a half-dozen rocking chairs.

After Mr. Pierce parked the pickup, we walked up the steps and onto the front porch. Before either of us had a chance to knock, Carol opened the front door. Her smile caught me a little off guard, but fortunately, Mr. Pierce hadn't lost his manners.

"Good evening," he said. "I think Mr. and Mrs. Rudy are expecting us.

"We sure are," Mrs. Rudy answered warmly, as she and her husband walked up behind Carol. Introductions were made all around, and in a moment we were walking through their beautiful home. I took it all in with no small amount of amazement. We stopped for a moment in the living room.

"Carol," Mrs. Rudy said. "Why don't you and Matt take some lemonade out on the front porch and chat about rock and roll? We old folks will stay inside and bore each other with business."

"Sure, Aunt Jewel," Carol said. "Come on, Matt. Let's go into the kitchen. It's out this way."

"I think I'd rather go out front with the young people," Mr. Rudy said. He took me by surprise with that remark, but everyone else seemed to know he was joking. Mr. Rudy was a tall, bald-headed man with a pleasant smile. If I saw him on the street, I would have guessed him to be a preacher.

"Get three glasses, Carol," Mr. Rudy said. Everyone laughed.

"Well," he said, "I guess I'll come out later. I don't want Henry Pierce to think I'm not hospitable."

"OK, Uncle Bill," Carol said. She grinned at him, and it was easy to see she really cared about her uncle and aunt.

The three adults strolled down the hall, leaving us alone near the kitchen. I didn't see much of it, though I do remember it was clean and well stocked. My attention was strictly on Carol, who wore a pair of dark blue shorts and a white off-the-shoulder kind of frilly blouse. I carried the two glasses of lemonade out to the front porch and tried not to spill them. Carol sat on the porch swing first and looked up at me. I handed her a glass, and then I carefully sat beside her.

Carol rocked the porch swing gracefully and said, "I heard about what happened at the bank today."

"Did you hear that your aunt was quite a hero?"

Carol looked at me with a questioning glance. "What do you mean? She told me you were the one who kept Mr. Pierce from losing everything."

"I didn't do anything special," I said, "and to tell you the truth, there's only one reason we're out here tonight." I went on to explain what happened in the bank while Carol listened. She didn't seem surprised to learn that her Aunt Jewel had stood up to the banker's grumpy secretary as well as the manager.

"My Uncle Bill," she said. "He takes care of most of the business deals and handles everything except the house—but don't let Aunt Jewel's sweet smile fool you. She knows all about farming, and she knows a lot about oil. She can be a real tiger when she needs to be."

"I believe you," I said. "She has a way of handling people without them even knowing what hit them. By then it's too late."

I sipped lemonade and gazed into Carol's eyes. "Hmm," I said. "I wonder if you're like your aunt. You know, people don't know what hit them."

Carol grinned. "I'm not sure," she said. "I guess you'll find out if you ever try to pull a fast one."

For the next hour or so, we sat and talked about her family, and all about the things that had gone on between Mr. Pierce and Thurman Spencer. I told her some of the stories I'd heard about Camp Alva, and she was very interested.

The night was warm and humid, but a gentle breeze kept the porch comfortable in spite of the heat. Carol looked so pretty, that even if the sun would have risen in the middle of the night, I would have stayed right there on that porch, close to her.

"We've talked a lot about my family," Carol said, "but you never say much about yours. How about your parents? Aren't they worried about you being away from home all summer like this?"

"No," I said. I didn't want to volunteer more.

"Not even your mother?"

"Well, I guess my mother is a little worried. She seemed pretty sad when I left. She packed all my clothes, gave me some money, and took me to the bus station. Even my grandmother was a little worried when I called the day I left. But my dad doesn't care one way or the other."

"How do you know?" Carol asked.

"Oh, if I make the football team in high school, he'll care then, but anything else I do won't matter to him."

"Well, I hope you make the team."

"Thanks," I said. Then I started to say something but didn't. She noticed immediately.

"What were you going to say?" Carol said.

"I don't know. It sounds kind of silly, but I have this urge to do well on the football team—just to please my dad. He can be a real jerk sometimes, but I want him to be proud of me. I'm not sure why."

"I'll bet he is proud of you," Carol whispered. She smiled right at me, and her face sort of lit up when she spoke. It had a wonderful, warm effect on me.

The moonlight cast a soft white glow across her face as she looked my way. Everything else in my world evaporated as I took in the sweet scent of Carol's perfume and gazed into the endless depths of her blue eyes.

I had been close to girls and kissed a few of them, but it was never this meaningful or this exciting before. Now I felt something inside of me that felt good and right. Without waiting for anything else to be said, I reached out and took Carol's hand. She gave it willingly and moved closer.

It was a small gesture, but I knew then it was okay. OK when we touched. After a few moments of silence, I sensed she would let me go a little further. Not knowing when the grown-ups might finish, I figured I might not get another chance.

I glanced behind us to make certain they weren't around. The coast was clear. With less grace than I had wished for, I swung my right arm around her bare shoulders, leaned over and lightly kissed her wet, enticing lips.

While we kissed, I closed my eyes and realized in that very moment—I was in love. It was an expression I had heard so many times. All the corny movie stars used the word "love" all the time, but the phrase had meant nothing to me. But now it was different. Now it was personal. Now it was—love.

After I sat back, we just looked at each other. She smiled, and I tried to think of the right thing to say, but I couldn't think of a single thing. So, instead of talking, I kissed her again. This time she leaned toward me a little more, and I felt the incredible softness of her body against me. It was front-porch paradise. While caressing the cool, smooth skin around her bare shoulders with my right hand, I kissed her and inhaled the scent of perfume on her neck. I didn't want to stop kissing, but I did.

Sitting there with Carol in my arms and the lingering taste of her lips against mine, I remembered what Mr. Pierce had told me about him and Jewel when they were young. Right now, he was in the house with Jewel and her husband. I figured it must be tough on Mr. Pierce—him being in there with the man who took his girl away from him so many years ago.

I made up my mind right then and there I was going to win this girl's heart, and no one was ever going to take her away from me.

On the way back to the farm, Mr. Pierce and I shared our thoughts on the Rudy ranch, and he explained how the business part of the evening had gone. He told me he and Mr. Rudy signed an agreement and that Mr. Rudy gave him a check right on the spot. He was to deposit it right in the bank tomorrow. I listened, but I didn't hear much more than a word or two because I could only think about Carol and how wonderful the night had been. As we drove up the hill to his house, Mr. Pierce slapped me on the shoulder.

"Well, son," he said. "I guess you've gone and fell off your John Deere tractor right into a field of love."

"It's something like . . ." Before I could finish my sentence, Mr. Pierce put the brakes on and brought the truck to a sudden stop.

"What's wrong?" I asked.

"Look," he said. "Think I saw someone run into the barn just then."

Mr. Pierce reached behind the seat, grabbed his rifle, checked the old gun, and made certain it was loaded. He turned toward me, and the moonlight lit his worried face.

"I don't see a car or truck anywhere, but I know I saw someone. Matt, you stay out here, son. I'll go round the back and try to catch whoever it is. Now you stay right here, understand?"

"Yes, sir," I said, as he moved out of the truck toward the barn.

In the bright moonlight, I watched Mr. Pierce walk to the far end of the barn, then disappear into the shadows. From that moment on, I lost all track of time.

I don't know if it was five minutes or thirty minutes before I heard it. I'm not sure. But when that shot rang out through the night, the fear within me gripped my insides so tightly that my legs seemed frozen stiff. My heart was beating so loudly I'm sure they heard it over at Bronson's Corner.

I kept hoping to see Mr. Pierce walk out the front door of the barn, but I never did. What should I do? He'd told me to stay there, and to tell the truth, that's what I wanted to do. But maybe he was hurt. Maybe he needed my help.

"Please be okay, Mr. Pierce," I whispered to myself.

Finally, I overcame my fears enough to get out of the truck and sneak up to the barn. The moonlit night—so beautiful while I shared it with Carol—was quickly turning ugly. Slowly I opened the creaking wooden door and moved into the vast darkness of the smelly barn. The interior was black, and I realized I would make a perfect target with the moon behind me, so I eased away from the open doorway.

Stepping softly onto the hay-covered floor, I inched my way toward the tack room where a narrow stream of light escaped into the black barn. With each step, I expected someone to rush at me from the shadows. Then a horrible thought crossed my mind. What if there were more than one intruder?

Opening the door of the tack room, I peered in. Mr. Pierce lay on the floor, his shirt soaked with blood. A large dark figure was leaning over him. The tall man turned toward me, and I knew it was Thurman Spencer. Evil, menacing eyes glared at me from across the room.

"See what happens when someone pulls a gun on me?" he growled. I tried to answer, but I couldn't make one sound.

"I only want what's mine," he said. He stuffed a small piece of paper into his shirt pocket.

On the floor beside Thurman Spencer, Mr. Pierce groaned in pain. He was alive. I moved forward to help him only to feel the back of Thurman Spencer's massive hand strike heavily against

202

my face. The unexpected blow caught me off guard. The skin on my face stung, and it felt like my jaw was broken. I tried to move toward Mr. Pierce, but the pain and fear kept me frozen in place like a scared rabbit on a farm road.

"I'm okay, Matt," Mr. Pierce said. I couldn't see him very well, but I knew any wound on a man his age had to be serious. He needed help, and he needed it fast.

Thurman Spencer cocked the rifle and fired a round into the air. Then he repeated the firing twice more. When he was certain the thirty-thirty was empty, he tossed it on the ground. He opened the door and looked back into the tack room with an evil grin. Traces of moonlight surrounded his head and shoulders, while blue smoke from the rifle hung in the air.

"Make any more trouble, and you'll never make it back to Tulsa, kid."

When he slipped out the door, I ran over to Mr. Pierce. He coughed as I held up his head, and the pain in his eyes got worse when he tried to talk. At first it was just a mumble, then I heard him more clearly.

"He's got the check. He ga … got … the check, Matt."

Not sure of what to do, I grabbed a blanket and put it over Mr. Pierce's chest. Hopefully, it would make him more comfortable. Should I go get a doctor? Or go get the check? I felt fear and anger all mixed together, and the outcome was sheer panic. I ran out the door of the tack room into the barn and then sprinted out the rear door.

Once outside, I saw Thurman Spencer running through the corral and down the hill toward the creek. I figured he must have parked his car in a field down there. I hurried toward the corral, wishing I was longer-legged, and then noticed June standing there. She must have heard all the shooting because she looked frightened and upset. The old horse's breathing was fast, and her ears were pinned back, and I knew she was disturbed. There wasn't enough time to settle her down or to get the saddle, so I decided to ride bareback.

I ran up to the frightened horse, grabbed a handful of mane, and then threw my leg up and over her back. While nudging her with my heels, I pulled her mane to the left, and instinctively she raced toward the creek as if she knew exactly where to go.

My eyes adjusted quickly to the moonlight, and as we rounded the corner, I ducked just in time to miss a branch, then raised my head and glimpsed Thurman Spencer. The man was running hard along the sandy edge of the creek.

June was running flat out, causing me to hold on as tight as possible or wind up on the ground. Before I knew it, we had closed the gap and were a few steps behind Thurman Spencer. Approaching the fleeing thug, I dug my heels into June's sides. June lurched forward. I quickly stuck my foot out and landed a solid kick right against Thurman Spencer's upper back. The tall man went spiraling across the ground, but he jumped right back up and continued running along the creek. I took a deep breath and brought June around for another try.

This time, as we got right behind him, the huge, agile man spun around and faced me. I kicked at him, but he dodged my boot and thrust a large knife at me. Light glinted off the silver blade as the knife was thrust upward, barely missing my leg. Instead of striking me, the knife struck June solidly in her barrel-like rib cage. Whinnying loudly from the wound, June reared up. Valiantly she trotted a few more steps, lost her balance, and fell into the creek.

Frightened, soaking wet, and lying on my back in the mud, I wiped the grime off my face, but there was no time to rest or catch my breath. The silhouette of Thurman Spencer towered above me. His breath came in hard, labored snatches. The knife in his hand seemed larger now as the blood from June's rib cage oozed off of it and dripped into the creek.

Thurman Spencer leaned down, grabbed my shirt, and pulled me up to him. I felt helpless, frozen in fear as he held me in the air with his left hand. A sinister grin crossed his sweaty face as he held the knife back with his right hand, a foot from my stomach, ready to strike. It was quiet for a split second. My heartbeat, June's whinnying, and the slight rustle of creek water were the only sounds. My mind raced to think of a way out of this.

Grinning at me, Thurman Spencer spoke in his deep, flat voice, "Good-bye, kid."

Suddenly, something behind him caught his attention. He let go of my shirt, twisted slightly to his right, and took a step backwards. Just as I fell into the mud, a lightning-quick blur streaked in front of me.

Lifting my head off the ground, I looked around, but couldn't see Thurman Spencer. I stood up, shaken and confused. Where was he?

Then I saw him—or what remained of him. Thurman Spencer's crumpled body was 20 feet away, pressed up against the trunk of a tree. He no longer had that mean, sinister expression on his pockmarked face. That meanness was replaced by a pitiful, almost pleading expression.

He no longer held the knife in his right hand because both his arms appeared to be broken, along with, I figured, a lot of other bones. Thurman Spencer's glassy eyes stared blankly across the creek as if he were still trying to figure out what kind of train had hit him. A noise coming from across the creek caught my ears, and I immediately recognized the backside of the orneriest bull in Oklahoma.

Pluto must have been running flat out when he lifted Thurman Spencer off the ground, hurled him through the air like a rag doll, and slammed him against the trunk of a blackjack tree.

I watched that cranky bull as he snorted and disappeared into a thicket. Thurman Spencer slumped further down the tree trunk and onto the ground. His eyes finally fell closed.

Relief washed over me in waves. It was finally over because Thurman Spencer had been outbullied. He could never hurt Mr. Pierce or me again.

It was quiet again, very quiet. My thoughts immediately shifted to the other problem I faced. Our beautiful horse lay in the creek with a slit in her side large enough to put my foot in. The water all around her had turned dark red from the blood pouring from her worn, wounded body. She tried to pull herself up, but could only manage to move her head a little bit. She whinnied, then fell back into the creek.

I knelt beside the dying animal, stroking her long, black hair, and attempted to comfort her as best I could. Her eyes told me of the pain she felt. I wanted so badly to do something, anything, to help her. I just couldn't. Tears fell from my face as I watched the pitiful animal draw closer and closer to her inevitable end. She looked up at me for the last time, let out a final gasp of air, and closed her eyes.

Wiping my eyes with one hand and stroking her with the other, I knew I shouldn't stay there any longer. Mr. Pierce was hurt, and I had to help him. Up and running as fast as I could, I was almost back to the barn when I realized I'd forgotten about the check. But there was no time to go back; it would just have to wait.

I pushed back the large barn doors and drove the pickup right into the barn a few feet away from the tack room. It wasn't easy loading Mr. Pierce into the truck, but somehow I managed it. Soon we were on our way to Alva.

The darkness hid the wheat fields and farms along the highway, but I'm sure I wouldn't have seen them even in the daylight. I just kept looking over at Mr. Pierce to make sure he was still breathing.

The wounded farmer drifted in and out of consciousness during our short trip. I closed my eyes for a few seconds at a time—not for rest but strength. I knew I could only find that kind of strength through prayer.

17   EVEN BIGGER NEWS

F riday evening, the night before the newspaper reporter from Oklahoma City was to visit Camp Alva, Corporal Henry Pierce had a special date planned with Jewel. It was the "quiet meal" he had promised her. In preparation, Jewel took more time with her hair and makeup than usual and put on her navy silk polka-dot dress. She knew how much Henry loved the neckline, but what she loved was the way the bodice showed off her attractive waistline. Before Jewel left her house to walk into town, she took a final look in the mirror. A special dress for a special night.

When Jewel entered the restaurant, she smiled at the manager. Behind him, there was a commotion going on at one of the booths.

The restaurant owner recognized Jewel, walked up to her and said, "Corporal Pierce is right over there with some of his buddies." He raised his eyebrows and said, "They're getting loud."

"I'm sorry, Ben," Jewel said. "I'll talk to Henry, and I'm sure it will be okay."

The manager went back to the cash register and watched as Jewel approached the table where Henry and two of his buddies were carrying on. The three soldiers were loud, all right, and even a bit obnoxious. And they weren't alone, either. Two girls sat with the soldiers, girls Jewel did not recognize. And from the looks of it, they were girls Jewel didn't care to know.

"Here she is, everyone!" Henry hollered. "Jewel, come and have a beer with us." To his Army pals, he said, "Drink up, boys!

If this were a firing range, you would be off target and out of ammunition."

The people at the table laughed at Henry's Army humor, and one of his buddies, Private Spencer, slammed his fist on the table as he laughed. Private Spencer pushed one of the other men out of his chair and offered the empty seat to Jewel. She hesitated.

"Come on, Jewel," Private Spencer said. "Sit down and meet these other gals here." Spencer introduced the other two girls and made a show of hugging each of them as he called her name. When he introduced Jewel, he gave her a hug and a little kiss on the cheek. Henry didn't seem to notice, or maybe he just didn't care.

Jewel smiled and said a polite hello to the other girls, but she moved her chair away from Private Spencer, whose behavior was rude, bordering on abrasive. She had never liked the man and had noticed how he had gotten closer to Henry since the tunnel discovery. Once she had mentioned to Henry that she considered Spencer a leech, but he laughed it off.

"Jewel works at the hospital," Private Spencer said as if it was his place to keep the conversation going. "She's a phone operator and takes calls from all the big brass."

"Is that right?" one of the girls said, unimpressed. The young woman looked as though she had been drinking most of the afternoon and seemed uninterested in Jewel. The girl leaned forward in her chair as if she were breathing in every word the soldiers had to say. She wore a nice print dress, low cut in the front, and she was obviously not concerned about her bust being on full display. The soldiers, including Henry, couldn't keep their eyes off her revealing outfit. Very quickly, it became too much for Jewel to sit and watch.

"Henry," Jewel said. "I won't be able to stay long. I only came by to tell you I have to fill in for one of the girls at the hospital tonight." Jewel stood up to leave, fully expecting Henry to walk her to the door, but Henry remained sitting. He glanced up at her without any effort to move in her direction.

"Sorry, doll face," Henry said nonchalantly. "Want me to have someone walk you to the camp?"

"No," Jewel said.

If Henry had paid attention to Jewel, instead of staring at the woman across the table, he would have known how much Jewel was hurting.

"I'll be all right," Jewel said. She put on her coat and walked to the door without saying another word to Henry. Outside, Jewel started walking along the sidewalk. Hearing footsteps behind her, she turned with a hopeful expression on her face, expecting to see Henry. Instead, she saw the solemn face of Private Spencer. Jewel looked down at the sidewalk, disappointed.

"Henry told me to walk you back to camp," Spencer said. He looked into her eyes, and his stare was a cold, penetrating leer. Jewel had to suppress a shiver. The man's intimidating face was evil, his eyes threatening. She didn't want to be around him, let alone walk a mile with him.

"I'm fine," she said. "Thanks for the offer. You're very nice. But I like to walk alone sometimes, and it's a nice night." She turned on the sidewalk and walked away from him.

"Wait a minute, Jewel," Private Spencer said. He grabbed her arm and spun her around. "Think you're too good for me or something?"

She tried to pull away, but he was strong, much too strong for her. They were at the corner, and he shoved her around to the other side of the building. She resisted, but he laughed out loud. A young couple walking by glanced at Spencer and Jewel, but mistook their struggle for horseplay. Spencer wasn't playing at all. He was serious. He shoved her a little farther along the sidewalk and into a narrow doorway. They were practically hidden from view.

Private Spencer pushed Jewel against the door and held her hands behind her back. She tried to look around him as if she expected to see Henry appear at any moment. He pulled her arms down as she turned her head away from him. He kissed her beautiful neck, and when she turned to yell, he put his mouth over hers and kissed her so hard it bruised her. He held both her hands behind her back with his huge left hand, and with his right, he grabbed her chin to keep her still.

Even in the dark, with the snow obscuring some of the streetlights, Jewel could see his rugged face and ominous eyes. She knew now that Henry was not coming for her.

For a split second, Jewel stopped pulling against her attacker. She seemed to relax. When she smiled and relaxed, it surprised him. Although he never let go of her hands, he seemed to relax too. But that was all the relaxing Private Thurman Spencer would do this night. The second he let up, Jewel bit him on the cheek, jerked her hands free, and kicked him smack-dab in the place she knew it would hurt him the most, right below the belt.

"You bitch," Private Spencer growled as he fell backward.

It had been a solid thrust that wouldn't have caused much damage if she had been wearing peep toes or platform wedges like the other young ladies. But Jewel wasn't wearing dainty, stylish shoes. Jewel was wearing men's work boots, the ones she always wore throughout the winter. The same ugly brown ones Henry had often joked about, and the boots Private Thurman Spencer would never forget. When Jewel hurried away, Private Spencer was lying in the snow moaning.

The next day she related the incident to her father and told him that the sight of Private Spencer lying there was the most beautiful sight she had ever seen. Her father told her to report the incident to the camp commander, but she didn't want to make any trouble. Besides, it was a problem Henry should take care of if he loved her. But when she told Henry about the incident, he didn't believe her. Even after she repeated the story, Henry was almost cold in his response. She was shocked by what he said and crushed that he didn't come down hard on Thurman Spencer.

"Calm down, Jewel," Henry said. "It sounds to me like you're just exaggerating, and you know how much I hate it when people exaggerate."

#

Saturday morning arrived, and Brian Edwards, the newspaper reporter from *The Oklahoman,* entered the gate at Camp Alva right on time. First, he was to interview the camp commander, Lt. Colonel Richardson. Afterwards, he would accompany the colonel to a few preapproved locations for photographs of the camp. Finally, he was to interview the new Corporal Henry Pierce at the Alva train depot. That would be his magnum opus.

Brian Edwards was tall, thin, and one of those dark-faced men who always needs to shave. He had been a reporter for almost 25 years and had covered stories all over Oklahoma and parts of Texas. He had witnessed the Depression and had written numerous accounts of the drastic changes in Oklahoma after the nation's financial collapse in 1929. His coverage of the Dust Bowl years and the erosion during the "Dirty Thirties" brought the young reporter critical acclaim, as well as a staff position with Oklahoma's most widely read newspaper. Brian was a reporter at heart, and people often said Brian Edwards could smell a story like a lion could smell a lamb.

Now an aging newspaperman, Brian was famous across Oklahoma and parts of Texas. Once he was interviewed on the radio, and during that interview the radio announcer, searching for a good question, asked Brian if considered his job as a reporter "*interesting*."

Brian, obviously put off by the stupid question, took a deep breath, leaned into the microphone and said, "Son, during my twenty-five years with this newspaper I have interviewed mayors, majors, managers, and mechanics. I used pens, pencils, pocketbooks, and posthole diggers. Getting a good story, I have had to sleep in cars, on cots, carpets, cowboy boots, and canvas chairs. Getting to the story, I have traveled in bikes, Buicks, buckboards, borrowed cars, and buttoned-down shoes. Now, son, the truth is, I can't spell worth a damn, but once I climbed all the way across a new dam and did a feature story when the government put it into service. I'm not afraid of animals, the IRS, or even Republicans, but old ladies scare the hell out of me. I've covered stories on boxing, baseball, bad bankers, barnstorming, and brass knuckles." And then the old reporter's voice grew more gentle as he said, "Son, I guess I would say yes, my job as a reporter has been interesting, but your questions have not."

#

Brian Edwards had certainly been around, but he had never seen a Nazi prisoner of war camp. So that exciting morning when the old reporter was introduced to Colonel Richardson and was shown around Camp Alva, he was a happy man. With Colonel Richardson as his guide, the reporter was allowed into sections of the camp that were normally off limits to civilians. He took full advantage of his privileged status and spent two full hours interviewing the camp commander and looking at the carefully selected sites.

When they finished that portion of the visit, the camp commander had coffee brought into his office along with a few baked goods from the mess hall. So far, the reporter seemed to be pleased with everything he had been shown, and that made the colonel happy. While Colonel Richardson smoked a cigarette, the reporter drank coffee and lit what was left of his daily cigar. Colonel Richardson watched his guest carefully, and it appeared the reporter was anxious to move on.

"When do we get to talk to Corporal Pierce?" the reporter asked.

#

That morning while the newspaperman was given the grand tour of Camp Alva, Corporal Pierce was on duty near the train station, where 30 German POWs in groups of 10 were busy unloading coal from railway cars. As part of his new responsibilities, Corporal Pierce was in charge of group two. Three MPs were assigned to Corporal Pierce as guards, and one of them was his buddy, Private Thurman Spencer. Corporal Pierce had enjoyed his new assignment, mostly because he loved working outside, but also because the prisoners behaved better when they were away from the prison. They were happier and less troublesome when they were working.

So that morning, even with a hangover, Corporal Pierce was upbeat and his three MPs were in good spirits. Even the POWs seemed to enjoy their work.

Corporal Pierce looked at the men around him, then gazed toward the train station less than a block away. The air was crisp, and there was a light wind from the south and the delightful aroma of civilian food drifted toward the men from a nearby restaurant. As the prisoners shoveled coal into an Army truck, they talked amongst themselves and occasionally sang a few German songs. The men needed another two hours of shoveling to fill the truck.

What Corporal Pierce needed was to go to the toilet. He figured it was a good time to get that done, so he ambled over to Private Spencer and said, "Walking over to the train station a minute."

"Going to the head again?" Spencer said, grinning. "That's the third time this morning, corporal. If you drink whiskey instead of beer, you don't have to pee as often."

"Keep your eye on your work, private," the corporal said. Then he winked and walked toward the station as the eleven o'clock train pulled into Alva.

When Corporal Pierce came out of the toilet, he crossed the wood-planked deck of the train station on his way back to the work detail. He heard the train porter yell, "All aboard!" Several passengers waved at departing family and friends, and the massive train began to move slowly, struggling to gain speed.

Corporal Pierce had just washed in the sink and had let the cold water run down his face to fight his lingering hangover. He noticed the last few passengers running to catch the departing train and recognized a man in civilian clothing. The man's back was to Corporal Pierce, but from his wide shoulders and thick neck, he knew it was Sergeant Swim. Corporal Pierce wasn't aware that Sergeant Swim had finagled a weekend pass, but he knew his boss needed one.

Corporal Pierce hurried toward the moving train as the last few passengers jumped on. Gray smoke from the locomotive ran horizontally along the top of the train and spilled downward into Pierce's eyes.

"Sergeant Swim!" he yelled, coughing a bit. "Sergeant Swim, have a good time!" But Swim never turned around.

As the corporal walked back to his group of POWs, a smile crossed his face as he thought of how well the big sergeant had been able to keep his secret of getting a three-day pass. Passes like that were as rare as hen's teeth. Most likely, the old fox had a girlfriend lined up.

As he arrived near the work detail, Corporal Pierce glanced at his MPs, then at the German prisoners who were working steadily. He heard the whistle blow as the train, now a mile away, made its way east. As the whistle blew, he noticed almost all of the prisoners glanced in the direction of the train for a second, but then their eyes went right back to their hill of black coal.

"Here comes your reporter," Private Spencer said. The private pointed to a shiny black sedan with a small United States flag fixed to the front bumper. The car was headed right toward them, and everyone, including the prisoners, knew it was the camp commander's car.

"Look sharp, men," Corporal Pierce said. He turned toward the approaching sedan. When it stopped in front of him, he called out, "Attention!"

Colonel Richardson stepped out of the shiny sedan and saluted.

"At ease, men," he said.

The tall, cigar-smoking reporter stepped out of the car and stood by Colonel Richardson. He looked closely at the "camp hero," then he glanced behind the corporal at the prisoners, who continued to shovel coal energetically.

"Mr. Edwards," the colonel said. "I would like to introduce Corporal Henry Pierce."

"Glad to meet you, young man," Mr. Edwards said, extending his hand.

Then to Colonel Richardson, he said, "Would it be possible to get a couple of photos right here at the train station? First, I'd like a photo with you and Corporal Pierce, and then I'd like another one with all three of you: the colonel, the staff sergeant, and the corporal. Sort of a chain-of-command shot."

"Certainly, Mr. Edwards," the colonel said. He moved closer to Corporal Pierce and adjusted his hat.

"But, sir," Corporal Pierce said. "Sergeant Swim can't be in the photo."

"What?" the colonel said. He grinned at Corporal Pierce as if it had been a joke. "Of course he can."

"But, sir," Corporal Pierce said. "He's gone."

"Who's gone?" Sergeant Swim bellowed as he walked around the front of the car, looking fit as a fiddle in his spit-shined boots, starched uniform, and Army green winter coat.

Corporal Pierce looked at the sergeant, pointed toward the train station, and tried to form his words. "But-but," he said. As he tried to speak, a loud siren was heard in the proximity of Camp Alva, which was about a mile away.

So with the corporal's mouth wide open, the siren blaring, the staff sergeant looking at something in the distance, and the camp commander's eyes looking like a deer caught in headlights, Brian Edwards shot his photograph. The flashbulb fizzled and lit his prizewinning photo, the one that would be on the front page of *The Oklahoman*, just below the headline that read

"Nazi Sergeant Escapes Camp Alva by Train"

POW BULLETIN BOARD

Left on the bunk of an escaped POW
Posted without permission

*Good-bye, big country, rich country, after 1,000 days
I'm leaving you forever. Goodbye you level farm land,
you wheat-raising state, you proudest soil under the
sun.*

"My Oklahoma."

*Goodbye especially to you, Fortress Swift, Camp Alva
with your barracks and training grounds. You took it
from me, finally, this consciousness of mine to belong
to mankind. Goodbye busy office at the post. Goodbye
dear desks and typewriters. Goodbye folks, all you
clerk-typists and lovely stenographers, with silk
stockings, powdered faces and rouged lips. I was
amazed seeing you sitting leisurely at hard work with
cold bottles of Coke at hand.*

*Goodbye America. If you catch me, then you'll be
sending me to England as a young slave and then to
Russia as an old one.*

Goodbye - You swell life.

18   SPECIAL LETTERS

Alva only had one hospital, and the waiting room that night became very crowded as several people asked me more questions than I could ever answer. It seemed like the whole town had heard about Thurman Spencer, and several of them had stopped by to find out firsthand. I had told the full story to the doctor and the Indian deputy, but I didn't want to tell anyone else. I was too tired.

I sat there through the night and dozed off from time to time. As I slept, I had a strange and eerie dream. In my dream, I saw Corporal Pierce; he was a handsome young soldier standing at the train station in his Army uniform. The train in front of him was loaded with passengers, and it was starting to leave the station. Sergeant Schmitt was boarding the train in his civilian clothes, but I could only see the sergeant from the back. Onboard the crowded train, the passengers were staring out the windows at Corporal Pierce. But they weren't civilian passengers; they were Nazis in full uniform. Major Wolf was there, and the German prisoner who had the red mud on his boot was there, too. Several of the POWs from Major Wolf's barracks were on board. But the strangest thing of all was seeing Thurman Spencer on board, standing with the Nazis, in full Nazi uniform. As the hideous enemy soldiers stared out the windows at Corporal Pierce, they laughed and taunted him. It was repugnant, uncontrolled laughter. Corporal Pierce stood watching helplessly as the train moved slowly away from the station. He tried to move, but he couldn't. He tried to scream for help, but he couldn't utter a sound. He was helpless.

When I woke up, it was after sunup. The doctor came in to give us an update on Mr. Pierce's situation. The spry old doc frowned as he peered over his glasses at all the people in the room. You could tell he didn't like the crowded atmosphere.

"The bullet hit Henry in the shoulder," he said. He pointed at his arm. "But it didn't break any bones, fortunately. He lost a lot of blood from the bullet wound, and it looks like he was struck in the face several times before he got shot. So, he'll need plenty of rest. I want him to stay here in the hospital for a while."

"But he's okay, right, doctor?" I said.

He smiled and said, "Yes, he's okay, but Henry is a little up in his years and hasn't taken care of his body. So, it will take him longer to heal than it would a younger man. I'd venture to guess he'll be here for two or three weeks."

"Can I see him?" I asked.

"Son, he's in pretty bad shape right now," the doctor said. He scratched his head. "Why don't you go and get some rest right now? Come back this afternoon, and if he's up to it, you boys can have a good visit. How does that sound?"

"Sure," I said. "But if he comes to, please tell him I'll be back later."

"I'll tell him."

About the time the doctor walked out of the waiting room, the deputy sheriff walked in. He'd come in and talked to me when I first got to the hospital, then he left to drive out to the farm. I was glad it was the Indian deputy instead of the sheriff. He seemed like he was more Indian than policeman. He was always watching a person's eyes in case there was something he might learn from them. I was worried he might say something about the time he had brought me into the station for fighting, but he didn't.

The deputy walked into the waiting room and gave the nurse a package of clothing.

"This is for Henry Pierce," he said. "It's just some clothes and stuff he might need."

"I forgot about him needing his clothes when he gets ready to leave here," I admitted.

"Never mind," the deputy said. He pointed toward the double doors the doctor had left through. "I saw the doctor as I came in. What did he have to say?"

"He told me Mr. Pierce was pretty beat up. The shot went into his shoulder, but it wasn't too serious. He should heal after a few weeks. The doctor wants him to stay here for a while."

"That's wonderful," the deputy said. "Say, you hungry? Why don't we go and get some breakfast? I'll bet Lana's is open by now."

"Yes, sir. That sounds pretty good."

#

After a large stack of hot pancakes covered with plenty of maple syrup, I had to tell Lana I couldn't eat another bite. She wasn't easily turned down, but she seemed to understand when the deputy gave her a hard look. Of course, Alva is a small town, and I'm sure she knew all about the shooting. But she never mentioned it.

The deputy asked me more questions about the whole episode, but I couldn't say much because I hadn't seen the actual shooting or beating. His questions were subtle and well timed, so I never felt I was under any pressure to answer or explain.

He told me Thurman Spencer had suffered a broken back and several other injuries when he hit the tree trunk. Then the deputy took something out of his pocket.

"I took this off the body before we moved it over to Springer's Funeral Home."

"Is that the check?" I said.

"Yup," he said. "Guess I'll put it in the safe over at the sheriff's office. We can hold it until Henry is well enough to deposit it in the bank. I made a list of all the items on the body, and this is one of them, of course. So it'll be part of the evidence in the investigation. Of course, Mr. Pierce will be able to have it back whenever he wants it. I just wanted you to see it because you almost got yourself killed trying to get it back."

He handed me the check, and I looked at it. I'd never seen so many zeros—$15,000.

"Man, that's a lot of money," I said.

"Yup," he said, "My guess is that's just what Thurman Spencer said too."

I handed the check back to the deputy and looked out the window. People were walking around, and a few cars and trucks moved slowly along the street in front of the café. I hadn't noticed before, but I was starting to get tired. The deputy paid Lana, and we walked out to the sidewalk.

I felt like I had just gone through the longest night of my life. It had been the longest, the most frightening, and the most wonderful night of my whole life. It was hard to believe it all happened on the same night.

"If you come over to the sheriff's office, I'll let you use the phone and call Tulsa," the deputy said. "You need to call home and let your parents know about all this, especially since Mr. Pierce won't be back home for a while."

"I hadn't thought about that," I lied. The truth is, I didn't want to call them because they would make me come home. I looked into the deputy's dark eyes, and I could tell he knew what I was thinking.

"Yeah. You really need to call them, son."

"Yes, sir," I shrugged halfheartedly.

#

In the deputy's office, I called home, and after I talked to my mom and dad, the deputy got on the phone and explained what had happened. He told my parents that I was okay and that their son had been a real hero. I'm sure they found that hard to believe. I know I did.

After the deputy was finished, I talked to them again, and after begging them to let me stay, I promised to catch the bus home at the end of the week. At first, they had wanted me to come home immediately, but the deputy convinced them I would be a lot of help to Mr. Pierce for the next few days while he was in the hospital. He also assured them he thought I could handle it just fine. When I finished the call, I thanked the deputy for all his help and especially his help with my parents. He grinned and told me not to think twice about it.

I drove back to the farm and spent the rest of the day sleeping in the attic. I must have been tired because I didn't wake up until suppertime. When I went downstairs, the house was quiet without anyone else around, but I felt so hungry I didn't think much about being alone.

After eating some reheated beans, I drove into Alva to visit Mr. Pierce. The hospital's waiting area was almost empty when I walked through it. Then I stepped carefully along a dimly lit hallway past the patients' rooms. The strong smell of urine, medicine, and sweating bodies seeped out of the rooms and into the hall. My stomach felt squeamish and perspiration formed on my back. Finally, I made it to Mr. Pierce's room.

There were four beds in his crowded little room, but three of them were empty, leaving Mr. Pierce to have the room to himself. His hospital bed had a high mattress, a large tubular-steel headboard and footboard, and was located near a small open window. Beside his bed, there was an ugly steel end table with an assortment of ointments and medical equipment. Mr. Pierce lay on his back, propped up by a collection of pillows that appeared to be taken from the three empty beds. He wore a kind of one-piece cotton pajama which started at his neck and went almost to his feet. I'd never seen pajamas like that before, and to tell the truth, it looked a bit like a dress. I made a mental note to be sure and not say anything to him about it.

The poor man's right arm and shoulder were wrapped in thick bandages, and his face was bruised and cut. His long body was several inches too long for the short hospital bed, and his feet stuck out of his pajamas and through the footboard rails. But in spite of the hot room, his cuts, bruises, and gunshot wound, the minute the old farmer saw me, his face lit up like he'd just struck it rich.

His eyes showed the strain of the ordeal he had gone through, but as he reached for my hand, his grip was firm. He was still a pretty tough old guy.

"Are you ready to go home yet?" I asked.

"Sure," he said with a weak smile. "I'd go right now if I could take one of these pretty nurses with me."

It seemed to be a real strain on him to talk, so I knew I shouldn't stay long. I explained how the deputy found the check and put it in the safe for him. Then I told him about the call to my parents. He wasn't surprised that they wanted me to come home.

"Dale came in today," he said. "He's going to help out over at my place until I get back on my feet."

"That's great," I said.

"Son, do you want to stay with Dale tonight?"

"No, sir," I said. "I'll be going back to Tulsa in a few days, so if it's okay with you, I'd like to stay at your house until I go."

He looked at me closely and said. "You sure you're okay?"

"Yes, sir."

"Then it's fine with me," he said.

A nurse came into the room. She was a bit older than the other nurses I'd already seen. She looked at some of the equipment near Mr. Pierce's bed, then turned toward me.

"He needs his rest now," she said. "Why don't you come back tomorrow?"

"Hanna, give us five more minutes," Mr. Pierce pleaded.

"All right," Hanna said. She looked at Mr. Pierce, and they exchanged a friendly smile. Then she turned to me. "But you need to be out in exactly five minutes."

When the nurse was out of the room, Mr. Pierce motioned for me to come closer to his bed. I felt a little uncomfortable with all the medical equipment, but I moved in closer. Once again, the strong smell of medicine filled the room. He placed his hand on my wrist and looked at me with his glimmering eyes.

"Matt," he said. "You know you saved my life, don't you?"

"Mr. Pierce," I said. "I don't think so, to be real honest."

"I'm not just talking about last night," he said. "I'm talking about this summer. Everyone else thought I was just a drunk

223

farmer, but you believed in me and showed me things don't have to stay the same forever."

I could tell that if he kept on, I was going to cry, so I interrupted him.

"Thank you, Mr. Pierce," I said, "but you taught me a lot, too. I've never been on a farm before, and you taught me about wheat, how to drive a tractor and a pickup truck. And something else; you told me all those stories of your days in Camp Alva and all the exciting things that happened there. I got a real history lesson from someone who lived it."

"Oh," he said. "That wasn't so much."

"Sure it was," I said. "By the way, before that nurse comes back to flirt with you, I need to know something. You never told me what happened after the German sergeant escaped. Where did they catch him? Mexico?"

Mr. Pierce grinned and said, "No, they didn't catch him there." Then he gazed over toward the window, remembering some of the details. He shook his head and said, "There were other escapees, and most of them were caught pretty quickly, but some weren't caught at all. Sometimes they made it out through Mexico, and sometimes they took other ways. But they didn't ever catch Sergeant Schmitt; that guy was a son of a gun."

Mr. Pierce smiled and shook his head again. "You see, Sergeant Schmitt had helped us find the tunnel, and we trusted him. So, when he requested to work outside the camp and shovel coal with the enlisted men, they gave him permission. Some of us figured he would be a good influence on the enlisted men and maybe keep an eye on things."

"What happened?" I asked.

"He kept an eye on things, all right. He figured out how to steal a complete set of civilian clothes and hide them in a suitcase near the train station. He got the other prisoners to watch out for him while they were shoveling coal. Then he bought a ticket and boarded the train right under my nose."

"Did you get in trouble?" I said.

"Not really," Mr. Pierce said. "He wasn't in my work crew, so I didn't get the blame. But I always felt guilty for not stopping him when I had the chance. For months, I worried that he might hurt someone while trying to leave the United States, but no one ever heard another word about him. I don't know what happened to him."

"Wow," I said. "Oh, there's one other thing . . . something else you never told me."

"What's that?" he said.

"Well, how did you and Jewel split up?" I said. "Unless you don't want to talk about it."

"No, you ought to know," he said. "You know everything there is to know about me."

Mr. Pierce tried to turn my way a little more, but grimaced, then lay back on his collection of pillows.

"Son," he said. "You already know that after the tunnel discovery, they made me out to be the big hero, and I was stupid enough to believe it. All my drinking and playing around got to be too much for Jewel, and one day I just lost her. That's all. It was all my fault. So, after the war was over, I bought my little farm here and eventually realized what an idiot I had become. By that point, all I had left was the whiskey and a wheat farm. I had completely let the whiskey ruin my life. Jewel met Bill Rudy, and they have made a good life with each other."

I started to say something, but I noticed the nurse was standing at the door. The expression on her face wasn't what I expected at all. She didn't look angry at me for staying over the five minutes. She seemed to be listening carefully to Mr. Pierce's story.

"Now, Hanna," Mr. Pierce said, noticing her there. "This young man has been through quite a bit the last few months, and I'm about to lose him to the big city."

"Yes, I know," she said. When she spoke to Mr. Pierce, it seemed more personal than a nurse taking care of a patient—more like they were starting to be friends. "But Henry," she said. "You need to rest in just a few minutes."

"You're very sweet, Hanna," Mr. Pierce said, his Southern charm resurfacing, even in a hospital bed.

"By the way, Matt," Mr. Pierce said. "Hanna just moved to Alva. I'll bet you can't guess where she's from."

I looked at her and just threw out a wild guess.

"Enid," I said.

"Now, how in the world did you know that?" Mr. Pierce said.

"OK, you two," Hanna said. "Let's wrap it up." She smiled at her patient, turned and walked down the hall.

"Mr. Pierce," I said. "Looks like you might have a new girlfriend."

"Never you mind," he said with a slight grin.

"Before I go," I said, "guess you better give me my work orders. Want me to plow the south pasture tomorrow?"

"Sure, and see to it that you grease the equipment one last time. And one more thing," he grinned and said, "you need to clean up the kitchen, too. You know I'd help with that if I could."

His expression turned more serious again, just like it had been a little earlier. "You know, Matt, there have been a lot of sunrises, stars in the sky and good things I missed because I was too blind and too foolish to enjoy them, but you opened my eyes, son. I want to thank you."

"Yes, sir," I said, as I fought back the tears. "You opened my eyes to a lot of things, too. I took a lot for granted before I came here. Every night when we sat and talked, you opened up a new world for me—a world that's hard for a city boy to see. We helped each other, didn't we?"

I reached for his hand again and shook it gently. Neither of us said anything, but we both knew what the other person was thinking. We just knew.

#

During the remainder of the week, I worked hard to finish all the more important chores, and in the afternoons, I drove the pickup into town for my daily visits with Mr. Pierce. One night I drove out to the Rudy ranch and sat on the front porch with Carol. We were both melancholy about my leaving, and it seemed like I had no sooner sat down beside her than it was time to go. But I didn't leave my visit without a kiss.

That night, when I got back to the farm, I wrote my grandmother a letter. It wasn't long and it left out a few details here and there, but the main thing is that I let her know I was okay and I was thinking about her.

> *Dear Grandma,*
> *Mom tells me that you are feeling good these*
> *days and walking to the store in Pitcher*
> *once a week. I'm glad you are OK,*
> *Grandma. I'm OK too. I've been working*
> *for a real nice farmer named Mr. Pierce. He*
> *taught me how to drive a tractor. We*
> *harvested his wheat and plowed the fields,*
> *and he even owned a horse which I was able*
> *to ride anytime. Oh, and something else,*
> *Grandma; I met a pretty girl named Carol.*
> *I'll tell you all about her when I see you next*
> *time. Wish you were here to cook for Mr.*
> *Pierce and me, but I did the best I could.*
> *Grandma, I learned a lot this summer and*
> *thought about you and some of the things*
> *you've taught me.*
> *I love you, Matt*

#

Sooner than I could believe, it was Friday morning. I was to take the ten o'clock bus from the station in Alva. But first, I drove to the hospital to say a final good-bye to Mr. Pierce. He paid me my summer wages as well as a healthy bonus. But there were too many of his friends in the room for us to talk at length. I think we were both happy we'd had the opportunity to tell each other how we felt that first night in the hospital. Mr. Pierce was opening yet another get-well card when I put the truck keys on the table beside his bed and quietly slipped out of the room.

Because I had left the truck at the hospital for Mr. Pierce, the easiest way to catch the bus was to walk the few blocks to the drugstore. After purchasing a bus ticket in the old-fashioned drugstore, I walked outside and stood on the sidewalk. I felt kind of emotional as I placed my suitcase on the sidewalk. Then I sat on it awhile and watched life go on in the little town that had grown to mean so much to me in such a short time.

The usual farmers and their families were going in and out of Lana's Café. Over at the city square, a group of older men sat on a park bench swapping stories and enjoying the morning.

A couple of cute girls walked along the sidewalk past me. Behind them were two tall, shy-looking farm boys who looked embarrassed about tagging along so close to the girls. The small-town ways were such a contrast to what had been my city life back in Tulsa. It's funny, but when I first came to Alva, I thought all the farmers and cowboys were ignorant. I kind of felt sorry for them. But after three months here, I realized they were the lucky ones, and the smart ones. They lived a life surrounded by nature and they understood the pleasures of hard work. And they appreciated the blessing of good friends.

But that morning, they weren't the only lucky ones. I noticed a sweet fragrance in the air, and I turned to see Carol Rudy standing just a few feet from me. She wore a white summer dress that showed off her bronze, well-tanned skin. Her light brown hair shined in the sunlight, looking like she might have spent all morning brushing it.

"Well, well," I said. "*Seventeen* magazine could never find a more beautiful face for their cover."

"Thank you," she smiled, and a blush crept up her cheeks. "I came because I wanted to ask you something before you left."

"I can tell you right now, the answer is yes."

"You haven't heard the question yet, silly," she said. "I want to know if you will write me."

"I guess so," I said. "I mean, yes, of course I will. Hey, maybe you could write me and let me know how Mr. Pierce is doing, and if your uncle finds oil on the Pierce farm."

"Of course," she said. "Oh, and one more question, and I
hope that the answer is yes too."

"Yes," I said, smiling broadly. "Okay, what's the second
question?"

"Will you come back next summer?"

About that time, I heard a loud noise, and I saw the big
Greyhound bus lumber into place behind Carol. The bus's brakes
screeched as the huge vehicle came to a halt. Carol turned toward
the bus and back to me. The man at the ticket counter had
mentioned the bus was running behind schedule. I grabbed my
suitcase and quickly looked into Carol's incredibly blue eyes. I
was excited about going home, but I was really sad about leaving
her and Mr. Pierce. I was suddenly tongue-tied.

It was just like the day when I left Mom at the bus station
in Tulsa. Carol stared at me with such a shy smile.

"Enid, Stillwater, and Tulsa!" the driver shouted, standing
in the open doorway. "All aboard!"

"I've got to go," I said. "You know I'll come back if I can,
and you know how I feel about you, don't you, Carol?"

"I'll miss you, Matt," she said.

"I'll miss you too, Carol."

She stuffed an envelope into my hip pocket and said,
"Here's my address; write me and tell me your address too. I
promise I'll write back!"

I walked to the bus's open doorway and handed the driver
my ticket and suitcase. While he loaded my case in the lower
compartment of the bus, I stood close to Carol for one more
precious moment. Looking up, I noticed the bus was crowded, and
it seemed to me that everyone on it was watching us. The driver
walked past me and started up the steps. It was the same big guy
who had driven the bus three months before when I got off at
Bronson's Corner.

"Well, kiss her, son!" the driver hollered with a grin, "so
we can get outta here."

Gently, I put my right hand on Carol's shoulder and pulled
her toward me. As I kissed her, I could feel her heart beating
against my chest. It wasn't a long kiss compared to a few we'd had

on the front porch those other nights, but it was the one that will live on in my mind forever. Behind us, the amused passengers on the bus began to applaud. I guess we'd given them quite a show.

Turning to walk up the steps, I sighed and tried to ignore the cheering. My face must have been beet-red as I walked through the crowded bus to the very back row. Finding an empty window seat on the curbside, I sat down quickly so I could watch Carol. A moment later the bus pulled away from the curb, leaving her just standing there, waving enthusiastically back at me.

Carol stood there on that Alva sidewalk, her brown hair gracefully blowing in the breeze. I watched her until we turned onto the main highway and headed toward Enid. Remembering the envelope she gave me, I pulled it out of my hip pocket. Just as I was about to open it, someone next to me spoke.

"I heard what happened to Thurman Spencer." I turned, and there on the same long row sat my buddy Sam, the dishwasher from Lana's Café. He had a shy look on his face as if I might not recognize him. Or maybe he was worried I might not speak to him around the white passengers. He visibly relaxed when I grinned and spoke to him.

"Hi, Sam," I said. "You heard about the red bull doing Alva a favor?"

"Yes, I did," Sam said.

"Sam, you're the last person I expected to see on this bus. Where in the world are you going?"

His friendly smile disappeared, replaced by a worrisome frown. Because we were the only ones back there, he scooted across the long bus seat to sit right next to me. He spoke under his breath.

"My daddy's in a hospital in South Carolina. He and my uncle got beat up when a group stopped their freedom rider bus in Rock Hill."

"I heard about that on the radio," I said. "Firebombs and everything, they said. Will they be all right?"

"Mom said he's going to be okay."

"That's good," I said, but I had my doubts.

"But late at night, Mom's been crying a lot, so I think it's worse than she's telling us kids. I told big Lana I figure my daddy might be dying. Know what Miss Lana did? She opened up the cash register and took fifty dollars out. She handed it right to me and said she'd trust me to pay it back someday."

"I knew Lana was nice," I said, "but not that nice."

"She's an angel," he said.

"But aren't you afraid? Going all that way by yourself?"

"I have never been away like this, but I'm going," he said. "It's my daddy. I just got to."

Sam looked away. I could tell he was about to cry. Almost every day, the news was filled with stories about the freedom riders. They seemed to be a mixture of brave white and black people who rode together on buses from Washington, DC, down into the Deep South. I knew they were attempting to get more rights for the Negroes somehow, but that's about all I knew. Sam seemed fully aware he was headed to a dangerous place. Several minutes went by before either of us spoke again.

"Sam, will you be stopping in Tulsa?"

"No, I get off in Enid, then I transfer to Oklahoma City."

"At least we can ride that far together," I said.

He smiled, nodded his head, and then he slid back across the seat to the other side of the bus. It looked as though he needed a little time to think. I decided I should learn more about the freedom riders now that I had a friend involved.

Glancing down, I noticed Carol's note still lay on my lap. Opening the light blue envelope, I took the letter out. The thin paper smelled just like her—fresh and lovely. I expected Carol to say some nice things and maybe some funny things in her letter, but I was surprised as I read it.

> *Dear Matt,*
> *Meeting you this summer was the best thing*
> *that ever happened to me. You call yourself a*
> *city boy, but you're really no different from a*
> *good ole country boy. You and I did have some*
> *good times this summer, and my favorite one of*

*all was the first time you kissed me out on Aunt
Jewel's front porch swing. You are a swell guy,
Matt. I will never forget all the fun times we
had with each other.*

*I do hope you understand that even
though I have written a couple of notes to boys
in school, I have never written a letter like this
one. I never wanted to before now. So don't
laugh at me, please don't laugh . . .*

*Summer is over, the wheat is harvested,
the farmland is plowed, and now you have to go
back to your big city life, to the drive-in movies
and skating rinks and all those fun places to go
on a Friday night. But Matt, please don't forget
about Alva, and please don't forget about me. If
you do, I'll send that mean bull Pluto to your
house and let him rough you up. Ha ha! I'm just
teasing.*

*But now I'm going to be dead serious
with you, Matt, . . . I mean about this next part
I'm going to tell you. I read a poem in school
last year, and I never knew just what it meant
until now. I want you to read it carefully, so
here goes:*

The mind has a thousand eyes, and the heart but one;
Yet the light of a whole life dies, when love is done. [1]

*Matt, this poem describes my feelings a lot better than I
ever could. I really hope you understand how I feel, Matt.
Good-bye, Matt. Please don't forget to write to me.
Love, Carol*

I held the letter tightly in my hand and read it again. I
couldn't imagine someone as sweet as Carol could feel that way
about me. I made myself a promise right then and there to write her

a nice letter as soon as I got to Tulsa. No matter what else happened, I would write that letter.

I glanced out the window as my mind and my heart spun out of control. Things were happening so fast. Outside the window, I could see the brown, plowed-over farmland thirsting for moisture and waiting for next year's wheat crop to be planted. I thought about the tender words of Carol's letter and knew they were planted in my heart forever.

The crowded bus bumped along the highway, taking me back to city life in Tulsa, which would be just like before.

Everything would be the same as it was before I went to work on Mr. Pierce's farm. The same as it was before I watched a man die, or before I learned to respect a person even though his skin was a different color. It would all be the same even though I had fallen in love.

Yes, it would all be the same, and nothing I could do would ever change it. But I would never be the same. Never again, not after Alva.

The End

Author's Notes

Since most readers like to know what part of historical fiction is based on fact, I thought I should enlighten the reader on a few things.

Matt Turner. A fictitious character based loosely on one of my childhood experiences. In 1960 I was sent to work on a farm west of Alva, Oklahoma. It was the summer before I started high school in Tulsa. The farmer I worked for was not named Mr. Pierce, but he was a kind old man, living alone on a run-down wheat farm. He was quiet, patient, and he taught me how to drive a tractor and do farm chores. Many things in the story happened; we slept in the attic, bathed in the water trough, and I did the cooking and kitchen work. His kitchen table had everything imaginable piled on it, but somehow we got along just fine. Of course, there was no Thurman Spencer, and the farmer I worked for did not work at Camp Alva.

Mr. Pierce. I used the name Henry Pierce because of an actual farmer in Anthony, Kansas, named Henry Pierce. I'll always remember him because he loved wheat farming and had a beautiful granddaughter named Barbara.

Sam. Sometimes on the weekend, I roamed the streets of Alva. That's when I met a few African American boys. There was a deep chasm between white and black teenagers in those days, but left alone, we enjoyed each other's company. I used the terms "colored" or "Negro" in the story because that's what we called African Americans in those days.

Camp Alva. During World War II there were a number of POW camps in the United States. These camps were located near small towns and major cities and held German, Italian, and other prisoners of war. Camp Alva was real. It was the home for almost 5,000 of those who were considered the "worst of the worst." Troublemakers from other camps were sent to Camp Alva, and it became known as "Little Alcatraz."

Escape Tunnel. There was a tunnel built under Camp Alva, but it wasn't a long one as in this story. There were several escape attempts at Camp Alva. Some of them ended in the escapees getting shot and a few ended with the prisoners getting away, only to be recaptured. I got the idea of the large escape tunnel in *West of Alva* from the famous Papago Park tunnel built by 25 German prisoners in 1944. In that escape, the Germans successfully escaped from their POW camp near Phoenix, Arizona.

Camp Alva People

> **Lt. Colonel Richardson** was the real camp commander, and there are military records available that indicate that he did an outstanding job.

> **Chaplain Verner Jordahl**, an American chaplain, who was a highly respected religious leader. One official report

stated, "Contributing to the good morale of the whole camp is the American Chaplain, Chaplain Jordahl, who never let political considerations destroy the value of his work, and who serves Americans and Germans with tact, discretion, and realism." There have been several excellent articles written on Verner Jordahl.

Sergeant Swim. To my knowledge, there was never a Sergeant Swim at Camp Alva. I used that name because I served under a Sergeant Swim in Fort Gordon, Georgia, and he was every bit as tough as the character in this book. After Fort Gordon, I attended helicopter flight school, then flew helicopters in Vietnam. Sergeant Swim had trained me well.

"Ya'll Git." A true story. Three German POWs escaped from Crossville, Tennessee, and then fled into the mountains, where they came upon a cabin. There, they startled an old hillbilly granny with a gun. She shot one of the POWs, and he died instantly.

Der Ruf, the American-published German newspaper *The Call.* This was one of the American government's many attempts to reeducate the German prisoners. But most of the German prisoners hated the publication and it was the subject of constant debate among the prison population.

Major Fritz Wolf, an actual German POW at Camp Alva. Fritz Wolf escaped twice and was well known to the Americans. His second escape was successful, and it appears that he made his way back to Germany, where he rejoined the post-war German military.

Camp Notices. The camp bulletin board notices were written by the camp commander, Lt. Colonel Richardson. Those listed in this book are almost word-for-word documents posted on the Nazi bulletin boards. They were sarcastic and often crude, but keep in mind there was a war going on and it is difficult to fully understand how the camp commander must have felt with such tremendous responsibility on his shoulders.

Sources

Discography

(Till) I Kissed You: Don Everly, Cadence Records, 1959 #1369, Single 45 RPM 7-inch Vinyl

Great Balls of Fire: Jerry Lee Lewis, Sun Record Company, 1957 #281, Jerry Lee Lewis And His Pumping Piano. Single, 45 RPM, Vinyl, 7-inch Hammer/Blackwell.

Loving You: Elvis Presley, Loving You LP, Mono July 1957, RCA Victor LPM 1515, Leiber-Stoller.

For the portion of this book that pertains to Camp Alva and German POW camps during WW II, I used the following sources;

US National Archives and Records Administration
Information related to Camp Alva, Army Service Forces, Headquarters Prisoner of War Camp. Headquarters Army Service Forces Office of the Provost Marshal General Prisoner of War Special Projects Division, Field Service Branch. Subject Files, Folder: Alva, Oklahoma, Box 2505 SL: 290/34/25/2, ARC 899479, Memo postings: Col Ralph Hall Infantry.

Articles

Jeff Roberts, "POW Camps in World War Il," *Tennessee Encyclopedia of History and Culture*, 2013, last updated March 1, 2018, http://www.tennesseeencyclopedia.net/entry.php?rec=1076.

John Hammond Moore, "Hitler's Wehrmacht in Virginia, 1943–1946," *The Virginia Magazine of History and Biography*, Vol. 85, No. 3 (July 1977).

Books

John Hammond Moore, *The Faustball Tunnel*, reprint (1978; Annapolis: Bluejacket Books, 2006), 125, 133, 134, 175.

Poetry

Francis William Bourdillon (1852–1921), *The Night Has a Thousand Eyes*.

ABOUT THE AUTHOR

Dave Eagleston grew up in Tulsa, Oklahoma, and graduated from Will Rogers High School and Oklahoma State University. He worked for a few years as a cameraman and vocalist at KTUL-TV in Tulsa before joining the Army. After a tour as a combat helicopter pilot in Vietnam, Dave traveled the world as a commercial pilot and aviation advisor. He has had the privilege of living in exciting locations such as Burma, Russia, Kazakhstan, Thailand, the Philippines, Turkey, three provinces in Canada, as well as several beautiful cities in the United States. He has flown prime ministers, premiers, ambassadors, the United States secretary of state, firefighters, roughnecks, game wardens, poachers, prisoners, movie stars, and a few thousand ordinary people. As a combat pilot, he was awarded two Purple Hearts, twenty-two Air Medals, and the Silver Star. As a commercial helicopter pilot, he received the Helicopter Association International (HAI) Safe Pilot Award. Dave lives in McKinney, Texas, with his wife Janie. Dave sings and plays the guitar professionally in the Dallas area and can be seen in plays and musicals as well as on television and the occasional low-budget short movie. You can watch his music videos on YouTube by simply searching for his name. Dave's second book, *A Private Heaven*, will be available soon on Amazon.

For more about Dave, visit www.eagleston.com or email him at dave@eagleston.com or *follow* him on Facebook: www.facebook.com/eagleston-books

Made in the USA
Monee, IL
24 July 2021